Enthusiastic reviews for Lior Samson's novels –

Distant Sons

" [A] book that will stay with me, probably for the rest of my life, and that I know I'll read again. ... It enlarged my experience of being human."
— *M. Thornberg, author*

The Rosen Singularity

" The plotting is ingenious and the characters come through strongly."
— *Rebecca Goldstein, MacArthur Fellow, author*

The Millicent Factor

" A solid page turner. The author keeps the pace just right with action and chases ... and backroom dealings." — *RJ Beam, author*

The Intaglio Imprint

" Super-realism and compelling rationale, ... an intricate and incisive creation,"
— *George Church, geneticist*

Bashert (The Homeland Connection)

" Samson writes with a crisp elegance, like John Le Carré, and weaves his plot magically,"
— *James A. Anderson, author*

The Dome (The Homeland Connection)

" An excellent read, and very highly recommended."
— *Midwest Book Review*

Web Games (The Homeland Connection)

" This extraordinary author has the ability to anticipate events. ... You will not put it down."
— *Alan Caruba, critic, BookViews*

Chipset (The Homeland Connection)

" [A] multi-dimensional thriller ... populated by flesh-and-blood characters."
— *Avraham Azrieli, author*

Gasline (The Homeland Connection)

" [A] great novel . . . high concept, flesh-and-blood protagonist, and realistic action. ... [It] will raise your blood pressure and make you think."
— *Columbia Review of Books and Film*

Flight Track (The Homeland Connection)

" Stunning, compelling, thought-provoking. To the book's broad scope and expert pacing, add three-dimensional, engaging characters."
— *M. Thornburg, author*

The Four-Color Puzzle

" [A]n authentic thinking person's ideal mystery; an eloquent feast of words and an excellent story."
— *Jeanie B. Clemmons, author*

DEATH
REHEARSALS

DEATH
REHEARSALS

Stories of Endings Dark and Bright

by Lior Samson

GESHER PRESS

Gesher Press
Rowley, Massachusetts

Gesher Press and the bridge logo are trademarks of Gesher Press.

5 4 3 2 1

ISBN 978-1-7326091-2-9

Cover and book design: Larry Constantine
Cover photo: Atatürk Cultural Center, Istanbul (Wikimedia)
Set in Rufina, titles in Perpetua

To Richard Horobin

We are already dying. – Sheldon Kopp

Contents

Author's Preface

Everyone dies. Not everyone reads a preface, foreword, or introduction, but at least now I have your attention. We can be more general. Nothing lasts. Psychologist Sheldon Kopp included that pithy platitude in his famously incomplete collection of so-called eternal truths.

This is a book about that one eternal truth, about endings in general and about death in particular. Even those enthralled by invitations to immortality or fantasies of power over Death, even most believers in an afterlife in a heaven, generally acknowledge that they must die to get there. Death is the universal experience, the common fate that ultimately unites us all.

Of late, death has been nearer the front of my mind. I am keenly attuned to its salience in human experience. I have even written four novels, The Immortality Quartet, centered on the contemporary and quixotic quest for immortality, a fear-driven flight from finitude through technological and scientific salvation. The first book of the quartet, *The Rosen Singularity* (Gesher Press, 2011), quotes Steve Jobs, who famously said, as he faced with no small courage his own impending end, that Death was Life's greatest invention, making way for the new by clearing the way, shedding the old and obsolete. I sympathize. Death, even mine, is not all tragedy. But then, I haven't been there. Yet.

I am reminded also of Thomas Kuhn, he of the structure of scientific revolution, who famously argued that the old paradigms, the outmoded models and perspectives in the evolution of science, the worn-out modes of thought and inadequate theories, are not ultimately superseded by the new because of superior reasoning or better evidence, but finally because the defendants of the old paradigms die off. Death is the midwife of meaningful progress and an antidote to stagnation. Death is, ironically, a mentor of the young and the to-be-born. Imagine a world in which the old-guard white males who have consolidated so much wealth and power and have steered the ships of state to the edge of planetary disaster, imagine if these very same handful of men were to hang on for centuries more. Enough said.

Still, I am not myself ready to die, and most of us probably say much the same nearly to the very end. Dying as a construct is one thing, dying as personal experience is quite another. We can see death as serving a biological and eco-systemic purpose but still hesitate when it comes to applying such fundamental principles to ourselves. Understandable.

We all will die, but we do not all die the same. For most, but not all, Death comes knocking too soon. Some of us have some say in the matter. We can live right, be prudent in our actions, and maybe, just maybe, postpone the inevitable. Some of us get the luxury—or burden—of choosing the time or the manner; many of us have no such choice, and some never see it coming.

As with most speculative fiction, this book, even when it is written in the declarative, is an interrogative, a book of questions, questions about death and its meaning, about life and the meaning we might give it in our dying, about tragedy and, yes, even triumph in death. It asks about mattering in the world, and about agency, the limits of what we can do in our lives, even at the end.

It has no answers because I have none. I am a man of faith, but not a faith that denies death or defies dying or that promises a path to an emergency exit, a way out of the inexorable march decreed to us by the laws of entropy. My faith is one of ethics and choice, a belief that even no choice is a choice, that it is possible to live a life of meaning and to die a death of meaning. Mine is a deeply held belief in the value of questions and quandary, requisite elements in the pursuit of meaning.

Throughout history, people have died for reasons. Young men and women—and it is almost always the young—have put themselves in harm's way in defense of country and home. Just as often they have been put there by their elders, who command from the rear or stay home and debate.

There are things I would die for. I would—as I imagine most people would—die to save my family. I might even die to save strangers, but I would have to be there, in the moment, to know for sure. I doubt that I would die for my faith, but there are principles for which I might be prepared to give my life. If they came to shutter the presses, burn the broadcast stations, and silence the journalists, you would find me on the barricades, prepared, if needed, to make the ultimate sacrifice in defense of information, the principle of a free and independent press. Or so I have always told myself.

I am propelled to complete this book at this time by a certain sense of urgency, of personal relevance. I am not yet myself at the very edge of death—at least not to my knowledge—but I long ago passed my personal use-by date, having outlived my parents and all my siblings and too many of my friends. I am not yet where I can hear the swish of the Reaper's scythe through the fields at sunset, nor am I counting the days, but I acknowledge that I am already well along into the countdown.

Behind each of the stories here is a story, but to keep from spoiling the experience, I have saved the backstories to the end. If you are interested, you'll find them in the Afterword.

The book title and that of the titular story come from a dear friend, who told me the idea originated with the Greek philosophers. Indeed, Plato, in his writings, has Socrates arguing that philosophy is itself a kind of dress rehearsal for death. If rehearsal is a means to improve performance, then death rehearsal and its confrontation with meaning and the philosophy of life, is a way to better approach and manage our own dying. To that end, I hope readers find something of use in what follows.

DEATH
REHEARSALS

A Concentrated Mind

"Crap!" Gabriel looked heavenward before slashing in anger. "Utter crap!" he said, striking out the entire last page of the paper with a stroke of his roller-ball pen. Before closing the work, he scribbled in the margin: "RRE." It was one of his standard editorial annotations: Rewrite in Real English. He had no patience with the international students who studied in Boston but who, to him, could manage only a stumbling Pidgin-English in writing and a halting, undecipherable babble in speech.

"There," he said, addressing his visitor. "That's done. Please forgive me. Now, where were we?" It was the art of control through multi-tasking, learned over many decades of arranged interviews. "You know, I taught myself English. And I spoke and wrote it better than these graduate students who now come here with aspirations of becoming American-educated researchers on an international stage." His accent still betrayed hints of his years at Oxford but none of his childhood in Curitiba. The reporter from *The Globe Magazine* smiled and nodded as if she did not already know this.

"When exactly did you leave Brazil for England?" she asked.

It was a trick question that earned a dismissive wave of

3

his hand. "Ask me something for which you don't already have the answer. That stuff," another flick of the hand, "is in the standard biography." He drummed his index finger on the green blotter that topped the old-fashioned walnut desk. "Google it," he said.

"But, Professor Costa, there is more than one version of the 'standard' bio. Even your date of birth is murky. I was hoping you could set the record straight." Her unlined face was a study in self-control as she strove to turn a meaningless assignment into a genuine story. She was clearly unprepared for a faceoff with Gabriel Costa, the phenomenon, the oldest full-time academic in North America.

"The record is straight," he said. "The recorders are not. If you have run out of questions, I have"—he tapped the stack of still untouched papers on his desk—"more crap to review in the hopes that it can be made less crappy before it appears in print with my name as one of the co-authors."

"About those papers, Professor? How is it that you are one of the most productive writers in the history of biology? How do you manage at—"

"One-hundred-and-five. At least that's what it says in the bio on the University website. And at 105, I manage quite the same way as I did at 65. I exploit grad students and post docs. They do the work, I correct it, and I append my name to their papers. It's the American Way, the Academic Way. That has not changed in the 75 years I have been at this university. And, yes, you may quote me on that. The University employs a whole platoon of professional protestors who stand ready to write letters to the *Globe* setting the record straight, saving face for the University, and allowing your employer to stretch a boring non-story out over extra issues."

"I would hardly consider your life story boring, Professor Costa."

"Now, you are being polite. Or manipulative. Yes, more likely the latter. You're here to interview a stubborn old man on the occasion of his jubilee celebration at the University. Boring. You got this empty task because you have been writing for the magazine for—what?—all of two weeks?"

"Two years. I—"

"Pity. You should have graduated to better assignments by now. You were bright enough to ask some good opening questions, and you are pretty enough to charm your interviewees, at least the dirty old men and the young lesbians. And yes, I can say that, because a 105-year-old can get by with saying almost anything that others must bite their tongues over."

Had she been taking notes, Samantha Roth would have been scribbling madly on her reporter's pad, but instead, she thrust her digital pen recorder a few millimeters closer to him in a pointless gesture that had somehow survived since the early days of television remotes. Her grin broadened and the nods deepened.

"Ah, she is saying to herself, now we are getting into some meat." He glanced at his watch, the Rolex given to him on the occasion of his fiftieth year with the University, an overly generous token intended to help induce him into retirement. "And now, I regret to say, we are nearly out of time."

"Just a few more quick questions, Dr. Costa. You are very well connected in the academic world, not merely in biology, but in other fields as well. Your Erdös Number is 3, owing to a paper in genomics you co-authored with,"—she glanced down at her notes—"Eric Lander of MIT."

"Yes, and my Bacon Number is also 3, because I appeared with Alan Alda on a television special about the so-called New Biology on 'Scientific American Frontiers.' You did your homework. Or you collect trivia."

"Both. Habits of a journalist. My question is whether you think it is in the best interest of science for influence—power—to remain concentrated in the hands, or the pens, of so few?"

"The real power is certainly concentrated, but not with academics. Even the best connected of us are mere instruments of wealth and industry. That wealth, as your own mag's recent series attested, has become ever more concentrated. We study what the foundations and big pharma and other funders want, and we skip over what they want us to ignore. Any pretense of a public agenda in science was long ago lost. Government funding of science, save for defense, has become inconsequential, pocket change.

"No, even with legions of grad students and researchers, I am merely a follower, a follower of funds, not a leader."

"One last question: are you excited about tonight?"

Gabriel laughed, a deep hacking laugh. "Excited? It's a rubber-chicken banquet, a night of bland champagne and platitudinous speeches. And at the end, a diamond-studded pen-and-pencil set for the left side of my desk to balance the one on the right, the one given to me on the occasion of my sixtieth." He gestured like a priest saying a blessing over the expanse of his desk. "And, of course, there will also be the mumbled prayers of my colleagues petitioning a higher power for my long-awaited retirement. That will, no doubt, be followed by tedious dialogue spiced with speculation over why the University does not simply use its legal forces to break my contract."

"And why is it they do not?"

"Obviously, it goes back to what we were saying about funding. I am a biologist, but I have done very little science for a very long time. What I do is bring in money. If . . . no, when . . . when I go, those connections go with me. And those are the connections that matter, not my ancient collaboration with Eric Lander, or my Hollywood link with the duly lauded Alan Alda. My connections mean money. As long as I can keep getting grants, my tenure is secure."

"You never think about retiring?"

"I think often about retiring and always conclude that it is not the time. However, it is time for you, Ms. Roth, to retire to your little desk or corner stool and write up the notes on your encounter with a very old and very annoying academic. Just what your readers will devour with enthusiasm, I am sure."

He ushered her out of the office quickly, stealing a glance down her blouse as she gathered her purse and paraphernalia. What goes round comes round, he thought. Live long enough and eventually even the bra-less look returns. Lechery had become little more than harmless habit with him. It had been some years since he had succumbed to the advances of a young research-er with fantasies of becoming the fifth Mrs. Costa. In fact it was the fourth, the 28-year-old Dr. Mi-Kyong Rhee, who had seduced a nonagenarian Visiting Professor on sabbatical at the Korean Advanced Institute of Science and Technology, thereby securing herself a plane ticket to Boston. From KAIST she had moved to MIT and eventually a top post in physics. In the process, she had married and reined in her elderly escort.

Except elderly was hardly the word for a man with a full head of hair—still a natural brown-black—and a flat stomach and 20-40 vision, a man who looked to be in his mid-fifties and whose calendar and biological clock were massively misaligned. He had been asked repeatedly to join one of the Centenarian Study Panels researched by the Medical School, but he knew that was impossible. It would take them no time at all to learn that he was no longer the Gabriel José Maria Abreu e Costa, son of Ana Abreu and Manuel Costa, who had left Brazil for England at sixteen in the first decade of the previous century. He was, in truth, a chimeric specimen in an ongoing experiment, a genetic mosaic with, by now, hundreds of cell lines co-existing in a dynamic dance at the very edge of cellular chaos. Only the treatments kept his body, his patchwork physical self, from plunging over that edge.

The calendar on his iPad XV kept track of his appointments in London. The bi-monthly treatments had now become quarterly, owing to advances that his own researchers had helped shape. That was the unpublished research, the vital investigations shunted quietly aside at the behest of the Foundation. He was, in his native Portuguese, a *figura da proa*, front-man for the Foundation. But their scientific agenda had changed, and more and more of the real research had been moved in-house, to Biontolics, their sham company on Boston's North Shore, or to one of their other, less visible venues scattered around the globe.

Costa was an anomaly among the anomalous. He was not one of the Underwriters, whose obscene wealth had funded the original research and development on longevity from which they all benefited. He was a hitchhiker, who had stumbled on early research papers while they were still unpublished and who had then filled in the blanks. His deal with the devil had been simple. He would keep quiet about their results and would, in return for silence, get to outlive all of his competitors. It had been early days for the Foundation, before their long-lived and well-placed Underwriters had insinuated themselves into so many institutions, before their global reach and resources allowed them so easily to rid themselves of annoying personnel problems. Like Gabriel.

Gabriel had been useful to them. Now he was becoming less so and more visible in the decrepitude that never quite materialized. His official bio could only be edited so far or so many times before he would have to become someone else, as others had before him, or finally have the long overdue infarction that had felled others who had outgrown their usefulness to the Foundation, the deathless enterprise of undeath.

He was interrupted by a nervous student being ushered in by his assistant. Lia Hwong had her deep-apologies expression painted over her face, and the student, who towered over her, seemed to be caught in the act of trying to melt into the door jamb like some wicked witch of the West Campus.

Lia crossed over to Gabriel's desk with his *cafezinho*, the Brazilian-style espresso that subdivided his afternoon routine. "You said you would have five minutes for Dennis," Lia said, using her generation's up-speaking vocal habits that turned every assertion into an inquiry.

"I did?"

The Dennis, shrinking still further, replied, "It's about the paper I sent you. On methylation."

"Paper you sent me? And you are?"

"Dennis McGuire. I emailed the paper—"

"Mistake one. I don't open email attachments, and I don't read papers that are not on paper. Print it out, put it in one of the standard interdepartmental envelopes, and send it to me."

"I have a copy right here." He stepped forward, a thick, stapled stack extended, and Lia stepped back, closing the door behind her.

Gabriel took the paper, read the title, and tossed it into the wire wastebasket at the side of his desk. "We don't do genetic voodoo here, Mr. McGuire. The whole epigenetics paradigm—it's just Lamarkian inheritance reinvented. Even the poor Russians long ago took leave of Lysenko."

"It's D-d-doctor McGuire, Professor," he stammered. "And I'm . . . I'm doing physical chemistry. Using picosecond laser pulses to study the bond formation. It's—"

"High-tech voodoo, then, but still voodoo. So, that excuses it? Why, I ask, why are you even wasting your time on this?"

"B-b-because no one has ever done it. We know almost nothing about the dynamics—"

"No one has ever tried to jump from the roof of the

Mugar Library, either." He gave a stir to his cafezinho. "And we know almost nothing about the dynamics of dissolution of sugar in espresso. Why not study those?"

"But this could . . . could have application in medicine. We might—"

"Spare me, please, the final refuge of researchers in obscure biology, that their work might—just might— lead to a cure for cancer or a treatment for obesity or . . ." He held his head in his hands. "No. Stop. I'll read your paper, your Lamarkian, laser-pulse paper. Just send it to me—in hard copy."

"It's . . ." McGuire pointed toward the wastebasket.

"Right. Okay. But I can tell you already that I won't like it. It's obviously trash." McGuire blinked, unsmiling, and Gabriel dismissed him with another hand wave and a sigh.

He was retrieving the paper from the wastebasket when there was a triple tap on the door. Mi-Kyong peeked in. "Time to wrap it up, Gabe. Big night ahead." She was beautiful, still, with the sweet face of perpetual neoteny that drew so many Western men to marry Asian women. Gabriel had always wondered what she saw in him, in his dark, middle-aged face and severe features. She always told him she had fallen in love with a man, not a face, and that man happened to be him.

He sent her a quick smile followed by a flash of a frown. "I have a few more boring papers to go through, then I'll come back to the apartment and change for the big night, the boring big night."

"Boring papers, boring night. Everything is boring with you."

It was true. Out of every hundred or so papers he read,

one or two might have something interesting to say or might say it in other than the standard, boring way. But it was to him all just more of the same academic bullshit that drove normal science. Even the so-called paradigm shifts, announced every decade or so by over-enthusiastic young researchers chasing grants or tenure, were just another part of the same pattern viewed one step further removed. He had lived through paradigm shifts, most of which had fizzled, lost again in the blur of boring bullshit.

There are only so many ways to write an Introduction, Background, Plan, Results, and Discussion, just as there are only so many positions for sex. And among those positions open to the physically ordinary without fetishistic inclinations, the experience was not all that varied. It helped having a young, attractive, and enthusiastic partner, but even that, on the tenth or twentieth affair, eventually began to feel too familiar, too scripted, too old. After a hundred-and-twenty years or so, everything began to be boring.

Mi-Kyong liked to tell herself that she had finally been the one to tame him, to keep him satisfied at home, but the truth that Gabriel knew was different. There was simply nothing out there that he had not been through many times. An orgasm was an orgasm, still nice, but then, so was a hot bath.

Only wine and food had continued to excite him after well over a century. Every vintage and every *terroir* was different, and once the last bottle of a given year from a particular place was finished, the experience was gone, never to be repeated. There was also no end to recipes, and new tastes awaited only the arrival of another young chef or a trip to a new restaurant.

Gabriel was saved from obesity only by his genetically-engineered gut bacteria and protected from cirrhosis of the liver only by the lightning speed by which his every organ and tissue repaired itself. Tonight, though, would be just food and drink, neither special nor memorable. It was merely another dinner to be gotten through aided by a little too much alcohol.

Gabriel, bored with red-penciling the research papers, stood and paced. The pain in his right leg sharpened. He was not used to pain. The treatments not only repaired everything quickly, they all but eliminated anything more than a passing ache. If he burned his hand on a hot pan, it hurt, but by nightfall the pain would be gone, and by the next morning the burn would be healed. This pain, a localized searing on his inner thigh, had persisted since its arrival in the morning.

He slipped into the en-suite bathroom and lowered his trousers. There was a white and purple patch on his right thigh, a small open lesion at its center. This was impossible. He was current on his treatments. He had last flown to London at the beginning of the previous month. He had at least another month before he was due back. There must be something askew with the treatments; maybe they were tweaking the regimen.

He glanced at his watch. It was coming up on midnight in London. There would be somebody at the switchboard, but he needed to talk with Doctor Ferguson himself or the new guy, Lyon, Bertrand Lyon. Both would be long gone from the Treatment Center if they were even in the country. The call, however important, would have to wait until morning.

What if the treatments were failing? How long would he have? He had personal knowledge of only a couple of previous cases, precedents that might be valid unless the treatments had changed radically in recent years. He did some quick mental calculations.

What would he do if, instead of the indefinite decades, he knew he had less than a year to live? How would he spend his last few months? Family and friends? He was close to no one, not even Mi-Kyong. A Caribbean island? Boring days on the beach followed by boring evenings with overpriced, underwhelming food? Not. Perhaps he could set off on a world tour, take in a string of the best restaurants the planet had to offer. Yes, that just might be a good way to go. If Mi-Kyong could be persuaded to take a sabbatical and come along, at least she would have some pleasant memories to punctuate their years together. How many was it? Fifteen? Nearly twenty?

Time. Was it time? The mind may still be sharp, he thought, but the memory, that is another matter. He could critique a paper for a journal review as well or better than ever. He could still reduce to stammering incoherence a doctoral candidate who was ill-prepared for a dissertation defense. He continued to make meaningful contributions to the papers that listed him as last author. Most of them, anyway.

But he had noticed something as his colleagues had aged. There were those who began to lose the distant past, whose own life was so layered that the real events and experiences of more distant times were no longer accessible. With each recall, with each retelling, the memory traces had been rewritten until nothing of the original remained. These colleagues lived in the present, unimpaired in handling the now, still coping comfortably with the recent past. Then there were those who could still recite pi to 40 decimal places, who could recall the color of the hair ribbon worn by the first girl they had ever kissed, who could repeat, virtually verbatim, the first paper they had delivered, but could not remember the decision made at yesterday's faculty meeting or the name of the student who had just left the office.

It was as if there were only so much space on the cerebral hard-drive. Eventually, data was lost, overwritten, degraded. For some, the memory management was a first-in-first-out discipline, for others, last-in-first-out. FIFO or LIFO. In the end, it seemed to come down to one or the other, and for Gabriel, it was the past that was replaced. His story had been revised so many times that he had lost track of the original draft. What year was he born? Had he finished his doctorate as a wunderkind or was he already middle-aged? When had he met his first wife. She was Graciella Lombardi, he knew, because he had read her name recently, but was she the redhead or the blonde.

Perhaps it was time.

He was interrupted by Lia reminding him that it was time to go to the apartment that he kept near campus. Monumental decisions and deep matters would have to wait. He had a boring dinner to attend. Except. Suddenly it was not so boring; it was fraught with what-ifs. A little pain in the leg, and the day was becoming unique, special. What if. What if this were one of his last? What if there were no more official University events to suffer through.

He left the building by the front door and, instead of hailing a cab, decided to walk the two miles to the apartment.

¤ ¤ ¤

The standard tables-of-eight were already nearly half full as Gabriel entered the banquet hall. President Hanford strode toward him and greeted him with a perfunctory A-frame embrace. "Gabriel Costa, truly you are ageless. And looking sharp tonight."

"I am looking like a penguin tonight, but that is the required costume at these events. Makes as much sense as the academic robes we wear for graduations, except those are far more colorful. I should have insisted on jeans and tee-shirts for the occasion."

"Ha, ha. Jocular as ever. You do know my wife, Wendy, don't you?" He placed his hand on her shoulder as he presented the skinny woman who was the third Mrs. Hanford. She reached out. Gabe took her hand, bowed ceremoniously, and pressed it lightly to his lips. Wendy Hanford, at a loss for what to do next, said, "Oh, my, so continental."

"I am old-school, Mrs. Hanford, as my students and colleagues will all attest."

Carl Hanford semaphored with his index finger. "Now, now, Gabriel, we are not using that word tonight."

"Which word? Old or school?"

"Ha, ha. As I was saying, always the humor. And how is that lovely young wife of yours? Where is she?"

"She is young and lovely, and she had business across the river, one of those meetings that you do not want to postpone. She's being promoted."

"I am delighted. I shall want to hear all about it."

16

"And that you shall," he said, with a rising voice on the last word. "I would imagine we will be seated near you at the head table."

¤ ¤ ¤

Sighting over his champagne flute, Gabriel scanned the room and realized that he could put names to only a fraction of the faces. He had once been good with names, a skill that served him well in his networking role. But there were by now so many names, tumbled on top of each other, and faces that had begun to lose their individuality, that fell into classes and categories. There, at the nearest table, was a Bradley, and over there was another Hermione. That one was a Diana with a smaller nose and next to her, a Willard, but with a receding hairline. Everyone reminded him of someone else who fit the template. No one was unique.

And there, standing just inside the door in the back left corner, was Charles Ferguson, not another Ferguson with the same handsome but readily forgotten face. It was *the* Dr. Charles Henry Ferguson, sui generis, whose name had changed but whose visage was hot-stamped into Gabriel's cortex. He was not in London. He was here. And he was looking at Gabriel, and now he was giving a nod and a finger-to-the-forehead salute.

Ferguson was here, and Gabriel had a lesion on his thigh. His heart raced as he instantly deduced what was going on. His treatments had stopped; they were cutting him loose. The last round, maybe the last two, had probably been shams, placebo treatments. In the calculus of the unseen empire that was the Foundation, he had finally and fully outgrown his utility and was no longer worth the expensive maintenance or the awkward public attention he drew. He was going to die.

If the last trip to London had been the first sham treatment, then he might have six, maybe seven months. If he used some of his own tricks and techniques, he might buy a few extra months, but the end would come quickly after that. The Foundation would not let him suffer, certainly not in any public way, but the last days would still be messy as his many biological selves escalated their struggles into cellular civil war.

There was always the option of choosing the time and the technique. He would have to look into that. There was even some researcher in the Department who had once worked for an Israeli secret lab and who might know of something quick and clean. The handgun in the drawer of Gabriel's bedside night table was just not his style. And what a mess for Mi-Kyong to have to deal with. No. Clean, quiet would be the way to go. The Foundation would be sure to get the right media spin on it in any case. They were good at that.

Gabriel realized he had been staring at his plate. When he looked up again, Ferguson was already gone. Message delivered. Professional courtesy accomplished. The physician had paid one last house call to his patient. Now the good doctor had other business, other patients, an empire to run and a secret to keep. Nothing personal, mind you. There had never been anything personal in it. It was medicine, very advanced medicine, and a deal first struck under duress. Now it was time to move on.

Gabriel finished his chicken cordon bleu without tasting it and sat through the empty remarks from President Hanford and the embarrassing ones from some emeritus professor without hearing either of them. But he was not bored. He was busy rehearsing scenarios and racing through strategies in his mind. He scribbled notes on the small pad he retrieved from his tuxedo until Mi-Kyong gave him her disapproving face with the double lines between her dark brows. He meekly re-pocketed the notes.

He was reluctant to leave his thoughts, but the ceremonies intruded. It was time for The Presentation, and the assembly would expect him to offer some words of appreciation and wisdom.

He stood and feigned surprise when Hanford handed him the small gift box and led the crowd in sustained applause. Gabriel made a show of slowly opening the elaborately wrapped package. Inside, nestled in silver and gold tissue, was a book. He laughed as he held up a battered, paperback copy of Thomas Kuhn's *The Structure of Scientific Revolutions*. A burst of uncertain laughter echoed around the room. Hanford looked embarrassed, and Lia was positively mortified. "This must be somebody's idea of a joke," she said. "That's not what we got you."

"I suspect some of our grad students are having a laugh at my expense," he said. "Or perhaps there's a message in this." He turned to face the audience and stretched toward the microphone. "You all know this book, or should. Some of you may even have read it and can remember what Thomas Kuhn wrote. Scientific paradigms change, he said, not because of better science but because the stubborn old farts defending the established views eventually die off. I imagine you can guess, I'm one of the stubborn old farts." The laughter this time around was less hesitant, more generous.

"So, rather than a gold Mont Blanc, I get something

more valuable: a book to read—or, in this case, to read again. So, I want to thank, most sincerely, the party or parties responsible for this . . . this unique gift." After another round of applause he continued. "I have a gift for all of you in return." He pulled several sheets of a printout from his inside jacket pocket and slowly unfolded them. He held them up. "This is my present to you." He tore the printout in two and tossed it over his shoulder as the room erupted in enthusiastic applause and whistles.

"Science is not speeches," he said, raising a hand for their attention. "Science is not even about publishing papers or presenting at conferences. Science is something you do. You do science, you don't talk science. You walk the walk."

He sat down again amidst more applause and a buzz of conversation bouncing back and forth along the head table. "Well, that was . . . different, dear," Mi-Kyong said.

"I've got something on my mind. I didn't want to waste time adding to the verbal noise of the occasion."

She responded to him, but, even as he looked her in the eye and nodded attentively, Gabriel was already mentally on his way to the lab, his mind concentrated on the details of what he could accomplish in six months using only discretionary funds. There was no time for grant proposals or negotiations with donors.

He knew pretty much what he wanted to do. It was high risk stuff, not incremental science. It was the kind of experimental work that would be either groundbreaking or an utter bust. Exciting. He would get that kid with his picosecond laser and that young Argentine with her semiconductor wells and the one, what was her name, who was so good at culturing the un-culturable. It was doable. It would require focus, dedication, concentration, but it was just possible that he could pull it off. *They* could pull it off.

He just needed to cut himself loose. Time. Time was the friend and the enemy.

Gabriel picked up his fork and began tapping out a *música gaúcha* beat on the rim of his near-empty water glass. As his taps grew in vigor, colleagues at the head table stopped talking, and a tsunami of silence swept over the room. Nearly everyone turned toward the small man who rose, his body bouncing to the syncopation that he now transferred to the podium, a stand-in for the *timbau* he had once played in his youth in southern Brazil. Gabriel smiled as a few of the younger faculty in the middle of the room began drumming counter-rhythms on their tables. Soon, the hall was filled with clapping and finger-snaps, the thud of stomping feet and the clinking of tableware on glasses. Gabriel finished with a sustained drum-roll crescendo and raised his hands in a triumphant gesture.

"Thank you, thank you." He waited for the room to quiet. "Thank you all for making this banquet—my last—so special. I want to finish the proceedings with an announcement. I am stepping down as Head of the Department, effective immediately."

Jaws fell agape and the room was awash with gasps and quick sotto voce exchanges. "Please, there will be plenty of time to celebrate later," he said, raising an arm. As the implications of his words penetrated, a few of the people began to stand, clapping. Soon he was facing a standing ovation. "They're happy to see me go," he said, leaning over toward Hanford.

Hanford, completely nonplussed, shook his head. "I would be the last to question your decision, Gabe, but are you sure? Are you quite in your right mind? And tell me this: what on earth will you do?" His voice was controlled, but just loud enough for Mi-Kyong and a few others to hear. They all looked at him.

"Yes, Carl, to answer your questions in order, I am sure, and my mind is wonderfully concentrated, as it should well be for one facing the noose, if you recognize the literary allusion. As to what I will do? Why, I am going to do something exciting. I'm going to do something I have not done for many decades. I'm going to do some science."

Magnetic Declination

Like magnets with their poles turned, north facing south, they were sucked into each other, locked in sweaty tantric sex within mere hours of meeting. Jayson was Southern California counterculture, and Celia was New Hampshire bed-and-breakfast. At twenty-nine, they were reflections of each other, reversed images in a dark glass: blonde reflected raven-haired, muscular countered by willowy, intellectual and controlled against emotional and impulsive.

"Power and light," she said.

"Like photovoltaics back-feeding into the grid," he responded.

Her hands around his neck tightened as her hips continued their slow anticyclone. "Mock me, little man, and I will teach you something of power. I was speaking of the light that I . . . we . . . need to shine into the dark recesses of the human soul." A sharp intake of breath punctuated each rush of her words. "And the power that we must learn to channel, the power of the human spirit and of the living spirit in all things that the Mother Goddess has given us. The higher power is not out there. It is in here." She lifted her hands from his neck and cupped her breasts. That gesture of simultaneous strength and vulnerability and the sight of her nipples hard between her fingers, was enough to send Jayson tumbling over an orgasmic waterfall for the second time that evening.

"I had no idea," he said between gasps.

Her eyes rolled back and she grimaced and moaned in her own little death, then finally lowered herself, exhausted, to lie, light as a down duvet, stretched out on top of him. "Do you believe me now?"

¤ ¤ ¤

Neither of them could have explained this convergence of flux lines from personal antipodes. Jayson, the only son of commune founders Jay and Vivian Hillcrest-Cahn, was passionate in his born-again atheism, a perpetual rebellion against the incense-fogged, Zen-and-Sufi-infused Judaism of his parents. Celia Wentworth, in contrast, had turned from the leaf-dry intellectualism of her professional-educator parents to embrace a diffuse, Wiccan pantheism. To him, nothing had a soul; to her, the trees in their dying autumn foliage and the lichen-crusted rocks sheltered at their roots were equally alive, equally endowed with spirit.

The annual "Science and Spirit" workshop sponsored by the Gerta and Ruben Friedmann Heal-the-World Foundation had drawn the customary immiscible mélange of engineers and evangelists, medical researchers and herbalists, scientists and massage therapists. Parallel sessions touted chakra alignment next door to a discussion of rare-earth elements in battery chemistries; panels that featured Catholic priests facing corporate presidents were followed by Zen masters in dialogue with geophysicists. "Bridges Across the Chasm" was this year's theme, but the bridges being built, if any, were subject to quantum uncertainty, differing radically depending on the observer. To Jayson and his engineering colleagues, who were beginning to wonder whether they should have come, the spans of the bridges were formed of heated air and mutual misunderstanding from the one shore and word-salad spouted by certified fruitcakes from the other.

Celia had floated into Jayson's peripheral vision on a cloud of global good vibes still reverberating after the inspirational opening keynote about the nascent nexus of science and religion. Whip-thin and ethereal, she sent a transcendental smile of universal love spinning toward him from the other side of the vegetarian buffet table. Jayson, a confirmed carnivore who was not yet clued in to the fact that there would be no "real food" waiting farther down the table, smiled back, a smile of curiosity and low-level lust ignited by the outline of Celia's dark nipples beneath the layers of her raw-silk blouse.

"Let me guess, you are not in photovoltaic technology or wind turbines," he said.

"And let me guess, you are," she countered. He grinned broadly and nodded as her eyes swept over the "Let the sun shine on" motif of his logo tee-shirt. "I'm Celia Wentworth," she said, extending her hand. "I'm a psychotherapist at a women's health center, a vegan, and a neo-pagan." Jayson was already forming the words of a polite kiss-off in his head when her hand closed on his; then it was too late. As he held her hand two seconds too long, he took a dive into her sea-green eyes, holding his breath as he swam back up to the surface. The woman in line behind him grunted in impatience and interrupted the flow of energy, but his palm burned from Celia's touch even after he pulled his hand back and resumed scooping tabbouleh onto his plate.

◻ ◻ ◻

For the two of them, the week-long conference turned into a fugue of dinners, discussion, and bedroom discoveries. Jayson even attended some of the sessions on her side of the chasm, and she acquiesced to a lecture on "The Agnostic Spirit" in the "Science First" track. Whatever workshops or seminars pulled them down different paths during their mostly divergent days, their compasses reliably pointed them back toward each other as the sun set and the sparks began to bounce between them like images trapped between parallel mirrors. And after, always, the reignited passion of a magnetic pull that left them both breathless.

And then it was Thursday, their last night together, and a wordless dinner at a small Italian bistro.

She brushed an errant blue-black lock aside and looked at him, inquiringly. "You seem sad."

"I'm thinking about not being able to see you, about not talking except over the phone, about not being able to make love."

"Sex at a distance. It's possible, you know."

"Sorry, I'm not into sexting. I'm a reality-driven kind of guy."

"It's about power, the right kind. With enough, you can project yourself through space."

"Yeah. Right."

"No, I am quite serious. There was a man, Brian, in my coven, who would not stop hitting on me. I had no interest in him, but he was very aggressive with his attentions. Eventually, he moved to Connecticut, and I thought no more about him. Then one night, about a month after he left for New Haven, I was home alone in my apartment. I had just drifted asleep when I sensed a presence in the room and awoke with the metallic taste of danger in my mouth. I started to sit up, but was pushed back onto the bed. He covered my mouth with his hand as he hovered over me, then lowered his full weight on me. He tried to rape me. I fought back, but he was a big man, muscular, and with a power that seemed to come from someplace deep in the earth, as if he were feeding on magma itself.

"After he left, I cried myself to sleep."

"This guy drove back from . . . wherever . . . and raped you? The bastard. You reported him to the police, right?"

"No, you don't understand, he projected himself. His power and his hunger were so great that he could reach across the miles and rape me."

"Are you serious? You really believe that is what happened?"

"Yes, of course. It's what happened. I called him the next morning and asked if he had tried to visit me, to use his power to get to me, and he admitted it, that he had conjured a powerful spell and reached out to touch me. I told him that if he ever tried anything again, I would get the entire coven to turn on him, to send him spinning into the void. He never bothered me after that."

Jayson stared at his food, then at the Tiffany light fixture dangling above their heads. "I don't know what to say. That is absolutely absurd, totally impossible. And if you believe that . . ." His head swung in disbelief. He did not want to say it. The whole week had been—he was censoring his own thoughts but the word kept bubbling up—magical. As he looked up again, he saw the uncertainty spreading on her face, the clarity in her ocean-hued eyes clouding over. He wanted her. He wanted to keep drawing on that spark, the something in her that permeated her environment, the magnetic force that infused the world around her with an induced current, with energy.

"I wasn't there, of course. How can I know what did or didn't happen?" He was picturing her slender body beneath him, feeling her legs wrapped around him, hearing the breaking waves of her hard breathing. "You are amazing, Celia. I think you are the most powerful woman I have ever known. And you are beginning almost to convince me, the card-carrying skeptic, the hard-nosed engineer. Maybe, just maybe, there is something to all this . . . this spiritual stuff."

Her eyes opened, pupils dilated again, inviting him in. "Maybe?" She reached across the table. "How much does it take, Jayson? How much? Do you need some more convincing?" The wrinkles at the corners of her eyes deepened with the pouting smile she sent his way.

"Yeah. Convince me."

¤ ¤ ¤

She sat on the motel-room bed, hugging her knees as Jayson finished dressing. "Maybe I'll go back with you to San Diego," she said.

"Really?" There was a mix of excitement and anxiety in his voice. What would that mean? What would his friends think? Hell, where would he put her in his busy life?

"Yes, really," she echoed. "I don't even need a ticket. I

can just get on the plane with you."

"What are you talking about? No ticket? You can't fly without a ticket." Comic images of broomsticks bounced onto his mental stage before he chased them off.

"I don't need a ticket if they don't see me get on." She tucked her legs under her and rose to her knees. "I can make myself invisible. It's not easy, but I've done it. I'll just walk right past the agent. They'll never know that I'm onboard."

"That, lady, is crazy."

"Celia, remember? Celia Wentworth, not 'lady'. And it's not crazy. It's just using the power of the Goddess, the power in everyone. In fact, I think that is exactly what I am going to do, fly with you to San Diego."

Panic was spreading like wind-blown smoke through Jayson. "You . . . Celia . . . are certifiable. Invisible? My God, what have I gotten into for another . . . for one more . . ."

"One more what, Jayson? Another what?"

"Look, this was good. We had fun. We had a lot of laughs and a lot of good sex. But, face it, we live in different worlds. You believe in ghosts and mystic powers and psychic rape, and I know better. I live in the real world and you live in . . . in la-la land."

"Now I get it, you made me think you were beginning to see the light, to accept the deeper reality beneath the surface illusion. You let me think that, and all because you wanted one more fuck. You are no better than Brian, who tried to rape me at a distance."

"Wait just one minute. I . . ."

"No more minutes. In your own way, you were mind-fucking me." She jumped out of the bed, knocking over

29

the lamp, shattering the bulb, and plunging the room into semidarkness, with only the light from the bathroom poured across the floor.

She stood, glaring at him, slowing and deepening her breathing. She gradually shaped her hand around air, then lunged toward him. Midflight, in the shadow and light, the blade appeared, a metallic flash in her hand. Jayson turned to the side and raised his leg in defense. The blade sliced along his thigh before she buried it to the hilt in his stomach. For a heartbeat he felt nothing, only the pressure of her hand where it pushed against his abdomen. Then the cutting-torch of pain ignited, slicing through him, a white-hot agony that left him doubled over and breathless as she drew back and stood over him.

"Now do you believe?"

He pressed his hand to his gut and felt the sticky warmth spreading. He stumbled away from her in panic, pushed his way out of the motel room, and managed to drag himself into his rental car parked outside the door. He was not thinking straight. He knew he should have called for an ambulance, but all he wanted was to get away from her. Now he drove one-handed, guessing at his blood loss, calculating the distance to the hospital, and estimating how long he had before he lost consciousness. He pressed harder against the pulsing wet and clenched his jaw against the pain.

The sign with the blue-and-white H was where he remembered it on the highway from the airport. At the hospital, he drove up onto the sidewalk, braking barely in time to keep from hitting a couple exiting the emergency room. He pushed through the doors, staggering, contorted with the pain. "Can . . . can somebody help me. I . . . I've been stabbed."

A nurse and orderly helped him onto the examination table in the first empty bay. "Where are you hurt? Tell us what happened," she said.

"Here." He lifted his hand. With the easing of the pressure, he could feel the blood spurt between his fingers. "I've been stabbed."

The nurse called for a doctor as she rolled down the top of his sweatpants. "Where?"

"Right there." He looked down at the smooth, unbroken skin, where the whitened imprint of his hand was already fading.

¤ ¤ ¤

They did not meet at the airport as they left for their separate coasts. They did not even see each other, even though their flights departed from the same pier within the same hour. The magnets had been turned, now north pole to north and south pole to south, repulsive, propelling them apart, back to their different universes.

At gate A12, Celia, her feet not always making full contact with the slip-proof rubber tile lining the jet-bridge, glided toward the plane that would take her to Boston and on to New Hampshire.

At gate A16, Jayson limped as he thumped his way along with the other passengers boarding the flight to San Diego. He was returning to his engineering job, where he would walk with a limp and learn to cope with chronic pain that did not respond to analgesics but would fade under the influence of alcohol. To him, the winds he rode took the shape of a Boeing 737.

Celia, who would always afterward sleep with a knife

unseen beneath her pillow, was returning to her practice in holistic psychotherapy and spiritual healing. To her, the aluminum and steel tube that roared down the runway transformed itself into a leafless birch tree, a living missile that flew above the clouds on the primal forces of the Goddess.

Walking Suit

In Kenny's dreams, his arms were stovepipes, and his legs the trunks of trees. Oily sweat oozed from his armpits and congealed at his waist, hardening, tightening, like a gelatinous boa, cutting off the feeling in his limbs, constricting, squeezing the blood into his head. Somehow he could see his own face, sandy hair standing on end, forehead bulging to the brink of explosion.

A hoarse voice whispered in the dark from the bunk below him, "Chill. It's only scary between patrols."

Kenny's chest drummed a three-beat before he realized the voice was not part of the dream. It was part of the nightmare: Elach playing his reassuring role as squad leader and Kenny's mentor. "You don't get scared once you're dressed," Elach said. "Remember that. This stuff, this waiting shit, it's gone once you're dressed. Everything's taken care of."

It's gone when you're dressed, Kenny Osmore thought. Then the reality catches up with the dream.

The breath he had been holding fluttered out of him. He willed himself still and prayed for the sleep he feared, but the lights came on when the warbling siren sounded, a false dawn serenaded by electronic birds. Out on the airfield, a dark sky waited for them to dress.

Kenny wanted to lie in the bunk and think about all the reasons why he should not be going out on patrol with the squad. He did not want a three-day tour in the field, lumbering around like a goddamn Goliath. He did not want to die. He was thinking about his assignment from Internal Studies at the Academy and about the anomaly he was charged with explaining. He was no soldier, only a commandeered academic being sent into combat to solve a staffing problem.

"Start now, Osmore," Elach said quietly, "Get the tape right. Check the urine bag. Take your time now. No chance once you're dressed." Elach had befriended him since he arrived on base, taking him under his wing. Elach seemed to instantly recognize Kenny as a misfit, someone who fit the nominal profile of a suit walker, but didn't really belong.

Despite Elach's advice, Kenny hurried his prep anyway, because he knew the dressers, efficient sergeants with a gruff routine, would soon come in to help, slapping on the pads, snapping fittings into arterial shunts, spraying resin on his head for the helmet. They had done this before, Kenny had not. The hurried week in exo training didn't count. It had been a joke, an exercise to justify a checkmark on his personnel record. Sending an untrained operative into combat was against regs, so, pres-to-change-o, with a few strokes of a keyboard, a combat psych instructor becomes a trained suit walker.

"How the shit was I to know I'd actually have to go on patrol?"

"What?" the dresser asked.

Kenny grunted. He was an ethno-psychologist, not a combat soldier, not a suit walker, but he knew he could not say anything about that.

The dressers finished their routine, lifted him onto a scooter, and drove him through a thousand feet of yellow tile toward the hanger. Elach didn't bother with the scooter; he whined along in his motorized wheelchair, zigzagging skillfully around other people hurrying through the tunnel.

Banks of high-pressure sodiums lit the hanger with light the color of bloody urine, glaring down on the long row of suits. Kenny looked across to where his own suit waited, split down the belly like a lobster readied for broiling, spreading its bloated arms to greet him.

Elach gave Kenny a high-sign as he spun his chair into a space between suits. Dressers lifted him out of the chair and began stuffing his limp, shriveled legs into the suit. Kenny lost sight of Elach because his own dressers had lifted him up to lower him into the legs of the suit and had already begun clamping. Was this really his suit? It felt too tight. He checked the code number inside the left arm. No, this was his suit, but everything was going too fast. He was aware of the blur of others being suited up, of portable cranes moving into position, and he was aware of the catheter and felt the bag at his left leg already filling with warm fluid.

He looked toward Elach.

Elach Witt was a sight to strike terror in the beholder. Nine feet of green-and-drab horror, hydraulic muscles pumping inside the Kelvram and carbon-nanofiber skin. The man had said take your time, but there he was, the first suited up, already on the bench, proving out the MEEGs that picked up minute currents in his brain and linked him to the pattern-recognition computers in the suit. In another minute Kenny would be there, too, would look like that in his gas-proof, radiation-resistant, bomb-proof Self-contained Universal Individual Tank, his SUIT.

Kenny called up a comms screen. The first time he tried to think it up, he got a far-infrared view of the room instead. The dressers and techs and the handlers hurried around in false-color blazes of yellow and green. Elach and the three others in his five-man squad were barely visible blue ghosts in their temperature-regulated armor. Kenny tried to flip his helmet up to yell that he couldn't get a comm screen, but he only succeeded in banging a hammy, metal-sheathed fist against his face-plate.

A tech jammed an umbilical into the socket at his waist and a clear, bored voice came through in Kenny's right ear. "Ready for the MEEG check, Corporal. Are you A-for-green on the comms?"

"I can't seem to think up the visor-screen menu for comms selection," Kenny answered. "I thought it was left-blue-circle."

"Just think all black if you get lost—calls up the help screen. The comms menu is left-green-circle; left-blue-circle is—"

"I know, I know: infrared. I found out."

The tech ignored him. He hooked clamps to fittings on Kenny's suit and hoisted him off the ground. "Kick the target, Corporal. Now right arm to three-o'clock. Left arm full back circle." He began taking Kenny through the alignment dance while a computer displayed deviations from the target movements. The superconducting mag-neto-electric pickups read his mind, or at least picked up certain patterns from his motor strip, then fed the signals to the computers controlling his motorized exo-skeleton. Pressure sensors could tell whether the hy-draulics were leading or lagging a bit, but the inten-tion—the starts, stops, and changes in movement—had to come right from the suit-walker's brain. Kenny was told to repeat the chin-up moves several times before the tech was satisfied. The coordination between muscle movement and the exoskeleton had to be critically close or you ended up bruised and tired after only a few hours.

Maybe the skimpy training for his job had been justi-fied. He was picked as the operative because of his heavy equipment experience while working his way through Carnegie-Mellon. It was all probably irrelevant. This was not like operating a back-hoe or a front-loader. You just did what you did. You moved your arm the way you wanted to, and the suit moved with you. Except you could lift 400 kilograms if you were careful about your balance. You could punch a hole through a masonry wall and not bruise a muscle. Ordinary ammunition didn't touch you, and napalm couldn't hurt. On the other hand, a walking suit was a target for everything and everyone.

¤ ¤ ¤

The blades of a big lifter whacked lazily at the morning air as the squad was wheeled aboard for the ride into the hills. Steenberg, the "old grunt" as he called himself, im-mediately blacked his helmet visor and leaned back. Meacham seemed to be talking to himself, but then Kenny noticed that Arty Hamilton was doing the same thing, so he figured they must be on a point-to-point comms channel.

Kenny called up his comms screen, getting it right on the first try this time, and put through a point-to-point for Elach.

"Yo, got any mission poop yet, Lieutenant?"

"Yo, you. It's a long one, that's all I know: hundred and four hours to pick-up."

"Say, is this channel really private? I mean do they ever listen in?"

"Don't know, Osmore. Probably recorded, but who'd ever have the time to listen to all the crap that goes down between squad members. The closed channels only have a few hundred meters range anyway. What's the worry?"

Kenny thought about the worry, but instead he said, "Just wondering. Say, why would a wheelie ever get into this. I mean, you got full disability. Back in civilization you'd have it made. A hero. Never have to work again. Why'd you volunteer for the SUIT Corps?"

"Why did you? And don't tell me you always dreamed of becoming a suit walker?"

"My brother persuaded me," he lied. "Short tour, bigger benefits." He couldn't tell Elach the real reason. Elach was the reason, Elach and the others like Elach.

"Yeah, well, when we touch down, you run for cover and watch me run ahead of you. Then ask me that stupid question again. I did hurdles in college, before they burned my spine. In a SUIT, I can run a hundred meters in seven seconds flat, with full combat gear. How many other paraplegics you know can do that. The brain is what matters in a SUIT. The SUIT supplies the muscles, you supply the brains. If you got them."

Kenny had them or he wouldn't be in Internal Studies,

but he said nothing. Then Elach flicked on the all-squad channel and briefed them.

The squad was an advance patrol for the marines tied down at São António do Verde. J-Com wanted them down river to take the village at Boa Fonte, and an overland route was planned to avoid the wide meanders of the river.

The lifter set them down amid scattered automatic weapons fire, then shot over the hill headed back to Condoro Base. The squad fanned out and hit the deck. A prompt on Kenny's screen reminded him to switch his comms to battle mode. He concentrated on the thought code. The automatic stereo processing suddenly put Arty Hamilton's voice just back of Kenny's left shoulder, Arty's codename appeared in the lower left corner of his heads-up display, and an arrow on a clock face pointed the direction. You always knew who was where in a SUIT squad.

"I'm at the fence," Arty said. "Got Brassies made at two o'clock, by the tractor." An inset popped onto Kenny's visor screen, showing him what Hamilton was seeing. "The IR says they're in the trees, too."

"I've got 'em," Kenny responded. He raised his hand just above the edge of the ditch, switched views to his hand sight, and sprayed the branches with a burst of nine-millimeter fire. As easy as pointing a finger. Other suit walkers took out their targets. In the quiet that followed, the gain on the exterior mikes pumped up to pick up the sound of wind and birds.

"Okay, let's start walking," Elach said.

¤ ¤ ¤

It would have been an exaggeration to call the double

row of buildings a village. Steenberg looked down from his position on point at the top of the rise, and the whole squad saw the tin-roofed sheds.

"Around or through?" he asked.

"Through," Elach said.

Steenberg kept to the left, against the steep side of the hill. Just past a washtub half filled with rain water, he hit an anti-personnel mine. It blew itself free of the sand, then exploded into shrapnel. Smoke drifted over Steenberg's fallen form.

"Well, that was fun," Steenberg said, doing a kip-up over the shallow crater. Small arms fire suddenly pelted Steenberg and the rest of the squad just behind him.

They were pinned down from two sides. Kenny started over the rise and Meacham pulled him back.

Kenny was surprised. "Why don't we just charge right up at 'em? Stuff they're shooting, might as well be throwing pea gravel."

"Don't forget what David did to Goliath. Sure, they ain't gonna kill you with those pea shooters, but that don't mean they might not hit a sensor or jam your ventilator or something. Ever get a pea up your nose, Osmore?"

Meacham lobbed a guided grenade from the launcher on his back and sweetly tumbled it into the shed across the street. Dark smoke blossomed from the windows and doors.

"I hit something. Now, watch this." He rolled what looked like a smoking teargas canister into the doorway just ahead and to the right. It seemed unlikely to Kenny that the Brassies wouldn't have gas masks, but Meacham seemed to know what he was doing. Somewhere a teakettle started to whistle, then scream. As it climbed to a howl, protective circuits squelched the volume inside the suits. Four men, hands over their ears with mouths open in screams of their own, ran into the street and were cut down by Steenberg with just four pops of his arm-rifle.

¤ ¤ ¤

The SUITs were considered part of an armored division, but a squad was at its best against ordinary infantry and the poorly equipped insurgents they were now facing. They were weakest against tanks, because a suit was a damned big target. A camo-clad, flat-footed grunt was three times as hard to hit and, armed with an anti-tank missile, was as good against real armor as a suited walker. Armor or not, a SUIT was just a glorified foot-soldier when a tank started bearing down. The cannon on the tank turret was the real kicker.

Now he and Elach were pinned down in a depression barely bigger than the two SUITs. At the moment, the tank guarding the pass ahead didn't yet know they were there.

Elach's code flashed onto Kenny's screen. "You don't belong here, Osmore," he said.

"Tell me about it! No self-respecting California boy should ever have to crawl around in jungle slime with a basket case for a buddy. I still can't get over seeing you out of a chair. Any chance you knew a para named Greeson or Creedson or something like that?"

"You're really curious about us wheelies, Osmore. What gives?"

"Just heard this guy was a squad leader like you, only he bought it on his last scheduled patrol. And there was another one like him a while back. That wheelie had a perfect record for three successive deployments, and on the last mission of his last re-up, he buys it."

"Guess it happens. Happens to surfer dudes, too, so you better watch me close and swing your suntanned arm like I do and wiggle your sail-boardin' butt like I do and crawl in the slime like I do, because you get to be squad leader by keeping your suit in one piece and your body whole. I got seven more missions left, and I plan to enjoy every minute of every one of them. You're welcome to come along with me, 'cause us wheelies don't hold no prejudices against you surfer types. And get your boot out of my groin, you motor retard. Pay attention to the feedback pressure, or I'll twist your damn boot off with your damn foot still in it."

A yellow-green light at two o'clock winked dimly at Kenny. His bag was full. There was a way to override the venting sequence, but Kenny couldn't remember it. He thought blackness, bringing up a help screen on the visor, and began flipping through a few pages. Suddenly a fog of urine exploded into the air from a point behind his left knee. Kenny switched to the camera on his backpack in time to see the turret of the supertank spinning in his direction. He froze as the gun lowered for point-blank fire on their position.

Elach was out of the hole so fast that he cleared the fence before hitting the ground. He charged at the tank like a lineman on a broken-field run, kicking great clots of sod into the air. The turret turned toward him. He was not three meters from the muzzle when it fired point blank. Kenny saw the flash, leapt up, and rolled down the hill. Behind him, the hole where he had been erupted in flame as the tank fired again. Kenny dove into the scrub brush behind a pile of boulders.

"Witt, godamnit, where are you."

¤ ¤ ¤

Amidst the rumble and vibration, Elach finally answered. "I'm under the tank. Took a hard right too close and fast for the turret to follow. Fuck. Must've made a minor miscalculation." Elach stopped talking while he went through a rapid body check. "I'm leaking: blood and hydraulic fluid. The left tread must've crushed my right leg and hip. Just a minute. Gotta shoot the leg full of quinocaine." Elach, watching his blood pressure began to drop, cranked the cinches that would tourniquet the leg. All this happened as fast as he could think it. It was not enough. "Must be internal bleeding or too much from my hip." He pressurized the suit liner from his waist down. It tightened like an old-fashioned gee-suit, squeezing the blood to his head. His ventilator began to heave against the added load.

He considered his options. Jamming the useless leg into the tank treads would be futile. He could not torch through the uranium-reinforced underbelly of the tank. It would take a small atomic bomb to get the tank from underneath. On the other hand, all he had to do was let go, drop out from behind the tank as it rolled on, and signal for med-evac. He'd go into hibernation mode and wake up in a field hospital, patched up, with another medal on his chest—and his discharge papers on the bedside table. Then, back home to Indiana and a job with . . .

It was a no brainer. He waited until the tank was rolling up and over a hill of rubbish. As one tread skidded and the tank slewed, he watched for the moment when it cut back across the face of the hill. He shifted himself to the uphill side and thought hexagon-white-white, then had to repeat it.

◘ ◘ ◘

"What the fuck was that," Steenberg barked from a point directly behind Kenny.

"I didn't see," Kenny answered. "Hamilton, did you catch what that was?"

"Something erupted under the tank, like an oversized anti-tank mine, and the damned thing rolled over on its side. Then there was another explosion and another. I think their ammo cooked off. Hey, wait, Witt's not showing on my heads-up. He's vanished."

Kenny was about to say something when Steenberg jumped in. "Witt's out, blown. He must've been stuck to the tank belly, I guess, maybe trying to fix a limpet. Got caught by his own limpet mine, I suppose."

"Is that what will go in your report?" Meacham asked.

"Yeah. I got a micro-spotter flying around the other side of that garbage mound. I can see pieces of his SUIT—not much, but enough. He blew. The limpet must have somehow triggered his self-destruct. The comms dump will confirm that, I'm sure. Otherwise, it doesn't make sense."

Hamilton, the skeptic, wouldn't let it go. "Witt was not big on limpet mines and was too smart to waste one on a tank from below."

"Arty, I'm saying he went out a hero, risking his own life to take out that tank, maybe saving all our butts. Let it rest at that. We gotta finish our mission. We're still short of the Brassie base and running out of daylight. Let's start walking." He stood up and started moving off

44

to the northwest, away from the coast.

¤ ¤ ¤

Kenny fell behind the three other suit walkers and then, preoccupied with other matters, managed to stagger against the corner of a scrap-wood shack, bringing the whole thing crashing down. He was thinking black and flipping through help files to find out how to erase the last point-to-point message he had gotten from Elach.

He had answers now, and a report to write when they returned to base, but Kenny Osmore was too busy mourning for his friend and thinking of Elach Witt's last words: "Fuck wheelchairs."

Finding
Francine

ONE

Wrenched out of a dreamless afternoon nap, I rose from the living room sofa and answered the call with drowsy impatience. "Yes?"

"They found her."

"What?" I was not sure I had heard right. The voice on the other end was hesitant, halting, with a middle-European accent muddled by the underwater distortion of a bad connection. "What did you say?"

"They found your wife. They found her." The slow, distinct syllables reverberated, sounding almost like a remembered call, the echo of a particular conversation.

"You mean they found the body?"

"You need to come here, Dr. Andberg. Right away. L'hôpital des Frères de la Montagne."

The request, the demand, confused me. I was, by this time, leaving the present, still holding the telephone tightly against my ear but already sliding down a steep slope into the recent past, the past of that other call, so much like this one, the bookend to my months of personal and parental purgatory. And by way of that dark slide, I was slipstreaming through time, past a still more distant, dimmer signpost.

◻ ◻ ◻

The tornado that tore the heart out of Moorefield had been the marker that divided the epochs of my childhood, as it had been for so many of my acquaintances and chums whose childhoods had not been ended by it. The funnel had touched down at the far end of Main Street, sparing the hardware store but ripping the front off of Pierce's Drug and ending the romance between the starting quarterback of the high-school varsity squad and the pretty blonde who should have become the next homecoming queen. I didn't really know them, but they went to our church, so they were members of our tribe, suddenly made prominent and personal in death.

Our small congregation, a non-denominational church a block off Main Street in a converted two-family, was spared, but the twister careered down the center of town like a giddy toddler tromping through six inches of a first snow. It gutted the large Presbyterian church, mercifully empty on that Saturday afternoon, turned the half-renovated library into a refuse heap of benches and books, and lifted again after destroying the movie theater at the far end of town. The Saturday matinee had just started, and most of the kids in town who could spring for the five-dollar admission were there. Had been there.

I was not in town when this happened because I was staying on my uncle's farm to the north. Still, I can see the imagined video in my mind, the tornado spinning like a blender, turning a third of the kids in my school into slurry. This was the nightmare that divided my before from my after and that pushed Jody Sebastian into my arms on the following Monday morning. She cried.

And I held her like I had seen my father do with my mother when she was alive, not moving, not speaking, just being. "A solid something to hold onto," he had once said to me in an uncommon moment of candor. "That's what a man has to be sometimes. No more."

I was that solid something for Jody that day: at fifteen, a man for a morning. A week later we stood holding hands, looking up at the only wall of the theater left standing—an ugly, massive headstone for the young people who were buried elsewhere—and we watched as a wrecking ball started its swing. The operator was an artist with a crane, and the ball struck the very center of the wall with such force and precision that, in a thunderclap, an enormous hole was punched clear through the solid concrete just below the jagged arch of the top.

An ellipse of blue sky showed through the picture frame of what had been the back wall of the theater. Then the bridge of rebar and fractured concrete across the top sagged, and an instant of magic was transformed into the tedious work of finishing a job: making rubble from a local landmark.

Jody cried again, and I pulled her toward me, but I failed to be a man that time and had to fight off the sobs that shook my skinny body. The list of those I knew who had been watching the movie was long, but only two names mattered to us in those moments, because each of us had lost a brother the week before.

Was it that? Shared grief, a link forged of loss? Or was it because we were the two smartest kids in the district and already growing too big for the town of our birth? Until we left for college—Jody for Stanford and me for the University of Minnesota—we were "The Two," Luke and Jody joined at the hip. She never wanted to be away from me, which was mostly just fine with me because she was so physical, pressing her hip against my crotch or warming my arm with her breasts.

It was a delicious game we played, one that kept me in a state of near perpetual arousal, an energy that she seemed to feed on. When we finally did the deed in the autumn of our senior year, she rode me with such hunger that I had images of being consumed. My climax was a relief in ways that I would not then have been able to express.

In college, reunited for a weekend, we laughed at the comedy of that scene in the backseat of my Volkswagen, the passenger seat tipped forward and her head banging on the ceiling as she straddled me and shouted, "Okay! Okay!" and then kept moving and shuddering long after I thought it was all over. It was as if there were still this circular nothingness punched through a wall by that wrecking ball, a void left in her that no amount of presence or love or orgasms could ever quite fill.

This is what, as a young man, I thought love was, and even as my world widened and I learned that not all love was hunger, not all relationships defined by inseparability, that was what I knew best, a template imprinted on my soul, a form waiting for other names to fill the blanks, a model to which I returned again and again in my relationships with women. Until Francine.

We both dated others while separated—Jody with hunger and determination, me with curiosity. Some of my dates qualified by the criteria of my unconscious application form, but few returned for a second interview. Some even sensed that I was looking for somebody, a specific somebody. Over the summers, my Somebody would return to the Midwest and The Two would re-form for a couple months of coupling that reminded us of who we were and who we wanted.

Jody transferred to the U. of M. in her senior year—to be with me, of course, but also because I had twice been turned down by Stanford. The move was easier for her than she admitted. The small town Minnesota girl had never fitted into the urban California scene, and she slid effortlessly into life in my small apartment near the edge of campus and into the less demanding classes at the U.

We were married right after graduation, and Amy Joyce, AJ, was born that October. To the deep disappointment of Dr. and Mrs. Sebastian, Jody did not pursue graduate studies and instead dropped out of school to devote herself to devotion. Whatever it was that Jody needed to complete herself, neither I nor her daughter were enough. Even as a toddler, AJ was adventuresome and independent, dashing across the playground to the farthest installation, yabbering with strangers at the mall, and insisting that, whatever it was, she could do it herself just fine. As AJ aggressively resisted being smothered, Jody's hunger for me escalated to the point that she even resented when I had classes to attend or research to finish.

"Do you have to go to the lecture? Can't you just read the book? It seems like I haven't seen you all week."

I tried to explain to her what she surely already knew. "It's not a lecture. It's lab work, my dissertation research. I can't fake it or get it from a book."

In the end, I did fake some of it, getting almost exactly the results my theory predicted with just enogh carefully introduced random error, all the time praying not to be found out. Even with all the world watching, it had taken two-hundred-and-fifty years for Sir Isaac Newton's fudged results to be exposed. Perhaps I could win a few decades. In retrospect, I think my advisor was complicit, turning a blind eye to small inconsistencies and never rechecking my results. He knew I was no rising star, that I would not be going on to researcher greatness, and he was relieved to be rid of me.

Tommy's arrival three years and two failed pregnancies after AJ should have finally been enough for Jody, but it wasn't. Unfulfilled emotionally, she began to withdraw physically. My long-married friends assured me that lagging libido came with the territory of young motherhood, but I knew our failings were far deeper, as deep as the emptiness at the center of our relationship.

Like my father, I was stubbornly stoic. My determination to bear what Fortune had bequeathed to me merely contributed to Jody's hunger for something more from her husband. Perhaps, had I more often broken down as I once did behind the destroyed theater, things might have been different. But I didn't. I didn't fall apart, not even when the affairs started, not even when they became florid, in-my-face declarations of my failure. I was an Andberg, and Andberg men did not fall apart, did not whine, and did not tantrum.

As the perfect couple, the childhood sweethearts whom everyone in town had known were meant for each other, we endured nearly a decade of perfect desperation until, in imperfect synchrony, we both gave up. She found Owen Cargill, and a year later I met Francine Demeter.

We were, the four of us, a contorted cliché. I was the one being dumped for the younger man. Owen and Jody were complete in some way that I would never understand. It was frighteningly easy for Jody to move on from Tommy and AJ, neither of whom had ever needed her enough, and Owen at that point was too immature to have any interest in children.

With the perverse logic of modern divorce, Jody and Owen got the house in Edina, I got the kids, and I ended up paying alimony. I was suddenly a single parent with two school-age children living in an apartment that was all we could afford on my salary less the alimony. Only AJ's independence and Tommy's easygoing temperament made that first year possible. That and my stoicism.

AJ fooled her school peers with inventive outfits assembled from pieces picked up at the Salvation Army Thrift Shop. Tommy buried himself in books, becoming the grade-school genius on Greek myths and Ursula K. Le Guin. They studied on the unsteady kitchen table, doing their homework with silent determination while I hand-washed the dirty dishes. None of us complained, each drawing on different drives, each sustaining the performance for our own reasons.

I allowed myself to cry only after they were on the school bus and only for the minutes before I left to catch the bus to the lab. I was, the rest of the time, something solid for my children, for us all.

TWO

If I had been able to keep up the car payments, I would not have met Francine, but one day the regular bus that I boarded four blocks from the lab was late. The growing line of commuters started to include passengers trying for the next bus, one that ran on a schedule more suited for people who worked the later, more conventional hours that my single-parent lifestyle would not permit.

I was looking up the street, trying to spot the approaching bus, when she emerged from the pedestrian crowd in long-legged strides aimed straight toward me. Even from a block away, she stood out—her long, auburn hair catching the late sun, her smile one of supreme and centered confidence. The smile broadened briefly as she neared, then suddenly went flat.

"I am sorry," she said as she stood in front of me, "but I thought you were someone else."

"At this moment you have me wishing I were that someone else." It was so bold, so out of character for me, that I could not believe I had said it. I could feel my face redden and hoped she would not notice.

"No you don't, not really. He's quite a bit older and a bit of a jerk. You do look a bit like him, though, with the sun at your back." She held out her hand. "I'm Francine Demeter. You're not one of the regulars, are you."

"I'm Luke Andberg," I said, taking her hand. "One of the irregulars."

Why had she introduced herself? I had no way of knowing that she had singled me out in the way she singled out prospects, potential consulting clients, merger targets. She took aim, and I fell.

We never actually dated. I was simply drawn into the cyclone of her life, meeting for lunch, attending lectures, being brought in for expert testimony on a possible acquisition of one of the local agro-chemical firms. One day I was a single-dad with no life; a month later I was part of Francine's life. Caught in the blender.

With Francine, it was my turn to cling and to hunger, trying to fill a Francine-shaped hole in me during the weekends when she passed in and out of my life or in the weeks when she was not on a trip chasing new investments or lecturing at some conference. Francine had a drive to live, to be self-sufficient without qualification, like no one I have ever known. Sharing an apartment together made no difference, because she was still independent, self-contained, and I still wanted more. Marriage and the move into a house purchased on the arc of her soaring career made no difference either. It was the same life with more rooms, more furniture. Until the baby.

Babies are sorcery in a pink package, making changelings of their mothers and fathers.

"I've been interviewing midwives," Francine announced as she chug-a-lugged the last of her morning coffee and stood to go.

"At the birthing center?"

"No. It's all too . . . too managed. It's routine for them. I mean, they've done it all a thousand times. Makes you feel like the mother is just a box in a flowchart. I'm the one who is having the baby, not them."

"So, what exactly does this mean?" I knew that whatever it was, the matter had already been decided. The discussion was merely to inform me.

"We are having a home birth. With the help of a midwife, of course."

Of course.

Always professional and practical, Francine had the

baby in our living room. "The floor is tile, the rugs can be rolled up, and there is an acre of room for everyone."

For everyone? To my small-town horror, Tommy and AJ were onlookers to the final moments, AJ posturing in adolescent nonchalance and Tommy standing stiffly to cover his terror, another step toward the Andberg manhood that was coded in his genome.

"I want to start from the first moment, the bonding," Francine had said. "I want to be there to hear his first cry." We didn't know it would be a girl. How old-fashioned of us; it would have been so easy to know. "I don't want to be woozy or wacked out. This is, like, one of the most important moments of my life. I don't care how much it hurts."

Now, that was my Francine. Pain was high-octane fuel for her. She finished her first marathon fighting through the pain of a broken toe. When she discovered she wasn't going to end up crippled by that experience, she scheduled back-to-back marathons on the East and West coasts separated by only a week. Whenever we skied together, she was always first to the bottom of the hill and last to leave the slopes at the end of the day.

"My knees are like rubber," she would say. "I should have packed it in for the day an hour ago."

"But you didn't."

"No. I'll probably pay for it in the morning. I am so sore."

In the morning, she always paid the price—and counted it a bargain. So, only natural childbirth would carry the properly painful price. And Pia was, for Francine, a worthy return-on-investment, a tiny piece of perfection in our messy, imperfect lives. Both of us fell in love again, with each other and with Pia. Life was transformed, not only because we had a baby, but suddenly we were together, not on weekends or two weeks out of the month, but around the clock. We both took parental leave. True, Cassidy and Dorn, LLC, were less than happy to be without Francine, their star quarterback, for two full months of maternity leave, but their meticulously constructed public image was at stake. They were a progressive, equality-promoting economics consultancy. In word and deed.

Neither I nor the lab really cared about my absence, because we all understood that I was going nowhere anyway, so I was not being derailed from some promising career path. By title and salary, I was a "Phase Transition Chemist," but it was a silly title for a glorified and over-specialized lab technician, and my modest salary exposed the silliness. I have never been ambitious or hungry enough to chase a brass ring. My only real hunger was for Francine, and parental leave was an all-you-can-eat Francine buffet, my chance to get my fill.

I should have known better. By the time Francine had used up her eight weeks of maternity leave, she was a caged lynx prowling for a way out between the bars. The second week back at Cassidy and Dorn she was off to Zurich for a conference at some retreat in the Alps.

The night before she left, she wrapped her long legs around me and stared into my eyes without so much as blinking as she climaxed. I could feel the squeeze and a flutter, but she didn't make a sound.

"I want to try for two," she said. "Can you keep it up?"

I smiled down at her. "Hungry, are we?"

"No, I just want to try. I always wanted to know what

multiple orgasms were like. And I sort of thought of like . . ." She closed her eyes in concentration. "Mmm. Yes. That way. Don't stop." She opened her eyes again and stared, unblinking, at my lips as she licked hers and her breathing got deeper and faster again.

As she concentrated, I tried not to concentrate. Then she climaxed and I went into overdrive.

"I wanted to sort of, store it up," she said afterward. "Your energy. It will be awhile before I can get more of it."

She left that Sunday, and on Tuesday I got the call, the one that brought back the mental movie of the wrecking ball. The baby and I were asleep. At first my sleep-deprived mind thought it was the alarm, but the digital alarm clock makes this synthesized sound of a tiny tri-angle being struck by a small metal bar, and this was the brrrip-brrrip-brrrip of my cellphone. My first impulse was to turn it off, and that impulse was reinforced when I saw that it was not yet five o'clock.

Pia was cuddled up next to me. Francine, along with her conversion to home birthing, had jumped on the trendy bandwagon of co-sleeping. I was a skeptic at first, but I had to admit, that as long as we were not having regular sex anyway, sleeping with a baby between us was its own delicious little experience. It certainly made night feedings easier on all of us.

I slid away from Pia and sat on the side of the bed as I opened the cellphone and grunted out a sleepy, unhappy hello.

"Mr. Demeter?"

"Yes?" There was no point in explaining that I was Dr. Andberg. Mr. Demeter was an acceptable alias that I was accustomed to by then.

"It's about your wife."

"What?"

"Your wife. Dr. Demeter was attending the European Econometrics Modeling Workshop?"

Was it a question or was he telling me what my wife was doing? "Yes, yes. What is it? Why are you calling me?" I was still more annoyed than anxious at that point.

"There has been an accident, a terrible accident."

The wrecking ball started its swing as the voice on my cell phone droned on. It struck the center of my chest just as the words "presumed dead" filtered through the buzz on the line. Or was it in my head? I was enough of a technician to fumble for paper and a sharpie and to record the contact details, but I didn't actually understand what had happened until I pulled the story from the Web after getting the kids off to school. In between, there had been lunches to be made and breast milk to be given to Pia and an hour of staring at the wall while Pia gurgled and then drifted back asleep in the playpen.

They had recovered only seven of the bodies. Nine were still missing: six villagers plus three from the workshop. The avalanche was unexpected, the result of anomalous softening of the snowpack that the professional chatterers were all too ready to attribute to global warming, with or without evidence or analysis. I didn't know and didn't care. Francine was gone.

Her family will never forgive me for not flying immediately to Switzerland, but there was no point. There was no body to claim, only paperwork to complete, and that could be done through forms on the Web and by a visit to the embassy. I had a baby and two kids to take care of, and I was a single parent again. I saved several thousand dollars in last-minute airfare, too, which I imprudently mentioned to her parents as a closing argument for why I was not flying over. Why should I go, only to have foreign strangers stand around awkwardly expressing their sympathies and apologizing for their inability to recover bodies under fifty-thousand tons of snow and ice? Margarit Demeter accused me of being a heartless cheapskate, and I was only able to protest the first part of the accusation, which clinched things in their minds.

"You never really loved her," her mother said. "It's obvious. You married her because you thought her career would give you a free ride."

I married her because I was carved to fit, because the gods had destined it, because I could never get too much of her. But I said none of that to her parents. They finished that phone call by announcing that they were striking me from their wills and would leave it all to Francine's brother and his children. I pointed out that Pia was their granddaughter, which left them flustered and without an immediate answer. But I knew they would devise one. Or their lawyers would. There seemed to be no end to what their lawyers could do, which I would learn in the coming weeks after that day of painful phone conversations.

We muddled through the first weeks and slowly settled into a new routine that was not that much different from our old one. It was not that Tommy and AJ didn't care or didn't feel the loss, but theirs was nothing like my loss. Francine was not their mother. Their mother was the woman who lived in Edina and sent them cards on their birthdays. Francine was my wife—not even their stepmother—somebody who, up until the last two months, breezed in and out of the house. I was the sea anchor in their storm-tossed lives, making lunches, helping with homework, and meeting them at the bus returning from after-school programs.

I was the one who had lost my anchor; the center of my universe was gone. I had never prayed before, but I took to asking an unseen god for her return, for awakening from a nightmare to find the center restored. With time and the demands of parenthood, my ache diminished, but it never disappeared.

Pia's problems were intense but short-lived. When the stored breast milk ran out, the transition to formula was a two-day crisis that vanished after I switched brands. For the first week, she slept fitfully without the smell and feel of her mother on her other side, but the co-sleeping was a godsend, and she quickly adapted to my body wrapped around her. If her infant psyche experienced the loss, there was nothing on the outside to show.

AJ cried at the memorial service, which had taken me unconscionably long to organize, but Tommy kept his composure, yet more practice for becoming an adult Andberg. "Will we have to move back to an apartment?" he asked me as we left the church.

"No. Francine took care of that. We can keep the house." Eventually, I would have to go back to work, but for now, we were well covered by Francine's passion for preparation. The house in her name was suddenly paid off by the mortgage insurance, her life insurance with me as beneficiary was a cushion for the short term, and her already substantial retirement accounts were protection for the longer term. For a while, at least, I could concentrate on filling the pit in my life by being a fulltime father to my three children.

Until the afternoon phone call and the incomprehensible message.

"They found her."

"What?"

THREE

"You need to come here, Dr. Andberg. Right away. L'hôpital des Frères de la Montagne."

The man on the line, a Dr. Tannenbaum, would say no more, no explanation, nothing, only the repeated insistence that I come to the hospital as quickly as I could.

It was a nightmare, not knowing what awaited me, wanting immediate clarification. I did not know what to think, and I found myself holding my own thoughts at arm's length. It was not easy making short-notice arrangements for the kids, either. Jody was willing, reluctantly, to take Tommy and AJ for the weekend, but was adamant about Pia.

"She is their sister," I pleaded, "surely you can take her for three days."

"Half-sister," Jody snapped. "No. Absolutely no. Owen and I have our hands full as it is. It will be hard enough taking the kids on such short notice. A baby is impossible. No."

"Pia is not just a baby, she is Tommy and AJ's baby sister. And she is really an easy baby."

Jody would not budge. She had moved on, and any connection she may have once had with me was buried beneath a new, all-consuming life with Owen.

It was AJ who stepped up to the plate. "Daddy, I'm fifteen, I can take care of the baby. We don't even have to go to Mom and Owen's. I can handle it."

I turned from the phone and looked at my daughter— her face with her mother's intelligence and vulnerability, her eyes with her father's determination to meet life's demands—and I knew that she was right. "Where?" I asked.

"Here," she answered. "We'll be all right. It's only a long weekend. I can keep the door locked. Really. I won't have any friends over and won't even tell anyone. We'll be fine. We can both afford to skip school one day. You can, like, write us an excuse when you get back."

I lifted the phone again and said, "Don't worry, Jody, AJ can handle things. You don't have to take the baby or the kids." It was a bluff, but neither AJ, who was grinning in triumph, nor Jody, who started ranting on the phone, knew that.

In the end, Jody took all three of them with the explicit understanding that AJ was in charge of the baby. I reminded AJ that this included changing diapers, to which she replied with exasperated insistence that she knew how to change diapers.

With those logistics settled, I booked a flight to Zurich and a rental car for the drive up to the hospital. After packing and repacking everything for the baby, I ran down my checklist with Tommy and then AJ, then drove the three of them to Edina. As we stood inside the foyer of what had once been our home, Tommy leaned over to me and whispered, "They've changed everything."

I nodded and gave him a squeeze. "They sure have."

As I reached my car in the driveway, I looked back to

see Tommy and AJ peering out the sidelight of the front door. I waved. AJ lifted Pia up and waved the baby's hand in my direction as she mouthed bye-bye; Tommy stood stiffly, raising his hand, palm angled down, just above waist level. He was an Andberg.

¤ ¤ ¤

It was late afternoon the next day when I reached the hospital, a sprawling complex of gray stone buildings connected like the fingers of an open hand. If it was meant as metaphor it succeeded, but more as a warding than a welcome sign. It reminded me of a monastery, which it most likely had been at one point in its history.

I was greeted in the high-ceilinged entry hall by Dr. Tannenbaum and a man introduced as Prof. Mecklinberg from the ETH, the Technical University in Zurich. Tannenbaum was not as I had pictured him from his voice on the phone, which had been high-pitched and pinched. He and his colleague were both squat and muscular, like tag-team wrestlers with scruffy moustaches.

Once more, I pressed for an explanation of what this was all about, and, once more, Dr. Tannenbaum demurred. I turned to Prof. Mecklinberg for help, for some kind of clarification.

"I am sorry, but I think it best if you come with us and see for yourself."

They led me down a long hall that seemed devoid of shadows, with white marble floors, white ceilings and fixtures, and even white porcelain doorknobs. At the end we turned at an acute angle into another similar hallway, past open doors and closed-off corridors until we stood outside a closed door posted with a hand-lettered sign in French, Italian, and German.

"Please," said the doctor, opening the door and gesturing me in.

The windows in the wall opposite were wide open, and the room was chilled by the cool spring air rolling off the mountains. Francine lay on the bed to my right. If I was expected to be instantly enlightened, I was not, because it was impossible for me to tell whether I was looking at a corpse or my sleeping wife.

I turned to Dr. Tannenbaum for an explanation, but he only nodded toward the bed. I walked over and looked down into the pale face of my wife. Her frizzy blonde hair was tucked under a paper surgical cap. Clear plastic tubes, no doubt carrying oxygen, passed below her nose, and around her head was a puzzling halo of bright blue packets.

"She's . . ." I couldn't get the words out.

Tannenbaum nodded. "But come to my office. We need to talk."

I reached to touch Francine's face. It was cold, as if she were still buried under the snowpack. Then I noticed the lumpy rolls of bedding running alongside her. I assumed they were to help support her body, but when I touched one of them, I realized they were packed with ice.

"What the . . ."

The doctor placed his hand on my arm. "Please, come with me. We will try to explain."

Just off the cavernous entry hall, Dr. Tannenbaum's office, with its glass-top table, Danish-modern couch, and white-LED lighting, was a sharp contrast to the prewar decor of the rest of the building. He gestured for me to sit in a bright blue office posture chair, then perched on the edge of his teak desk while the professor paced as if lecturing a class.

"They found the car, a minivan you would call it," the Doctor began, "when the lake below the village began to thaw. It's been warming . . . warmer in the recent years. Otherwise it might have been another month or more before it would have been visible. When they raised the car, they found your wife, and when they went to pull her body out, one of the divers thought he detected a pulse—faint and slow, but a pulse. I was called because I was holding a surgery—a clinic—that day in the village, and I told them it was impossible. Still, I told them to support her head but not to move her or do anything else until I arrived.

"The diver was right. There was a pulse. Bringing the car to the surface, perhaps, or the sun on her face, who can know? But her heart had restarted."

My heart was a timpani in my ears. "How is that possible? She was at the bottom of a frozen lake in a flooded van. She would have drowned."

"Yes, she would have drowned when the car was swept into the lake. I am telling you that we do not know exactly what happened. It seems she was driving past the lake when the avalanche hit. The car was pushed into the lake, then forced to the bottom by the weight of fifty meters of snow and ice above. The car had been spotted in the clear waters the week before. When the divers reached it, it was standing at an angle, almost on end, with your wife in the driver's seat. Her head was tilted back and held that way by the shoulder belt. There was a bubble of air above her face.

"I know it seems impossible—it does to us also—but your wife is alive, at least in some vegetative way. I brought in Prof. Mecklinberg to help with the diagnosis and disposition. He is an expert on what is known as the mammalian diving reflex. Do you want to try and explain, Professor?"

"I will try. Please bear with me, as I am not used to speaking in English."

I told him to please proceed. "You are doing just fine." It was not his English that was the problem for me at that moment, but the ringing in my ears, like the whine of an ambulance siren screaming just over my left shoulder. The room swam in time with the rise and fall of the siren, and I felt as if, any moment, I would lose the greasy breakfast that I had wolfed down before my plane had landed in Zurich.

"Mammals," the professor was saying. "including humans, have this reflexive response to cold water, specifically on the face, that induces bradycardia and vasoconstriction."

Dr. Tannenbaum interrupted to explain. "The heart slows and the blood vessels constrict, thus reducing the need for oxygen."

The professor tag-teamed. "But the brain can only survive this way for a limited time. There are cases, cases on record, young drowning victims who were revived after a few hours, but your wife . . . Months underwater is impossible." He studied his hands. "I have never seen anything like this."

It was the doctor's turn. "We must assume that what we are seeing is only a primitive, physiological response, that the brain must be . . . gone. Still, the patient is breathing on her own, which suggests a functional brainstem. We don't know. We have done scans, but they only tell us that there is no visible damage, no trauma or . . . or tissue death. We have kept her cooled, her head especially, with ice packs to reduce the oxygen load until a decision could be made. Which is why we have brought you here, to decide. We have kept her in this state of induced hibernation, you might call it, until you could arrive."

The doctor stood up. "You are the next of kin; it would be your choice how we proceed."

"You are saying that my wife could be a vegetable."

"We do not know what brain functioning would be present if we bring her out of this state. She might not regain consciousness, and even in the best of outcomes, she is likely to be severely impaired. Even less extreme cases have resulted in brain damage with dramatic consequences."

"What is the alternative to reviving her?"

"Given that she survived over two months underwater, it seems reasonable to assume that she could remain in her present state indefinitely, perhaps for years. It is unlikely that the induced hibernation would be sustainable, however, simply as a practical matter. In any event, you will need to arrange for a medical evacuation, as she cannot be maintained any longer at this facility."

"Your wife seems to have a most remarkable drive to survive," the professor added, "something too powerful to be called merely the will to live. It is something more primitive, an unquenchable spark."

Dr. Tannenbaum held up his hand and shook his head in disagreement. "I think it a mistake to romanticize. This is just an extreme and anomalous reaction to cold and oxygen deprivation. We can't let our feelings cloud scientific judgment."

My feelings were focused on the hole in my being that ached to be filled again by Francine. I told myself that I didn't care if she were retarded and wheelchair-bound, that I wanted her back regardless. I told them what I wanted, and they agreed to start the cautious warming process. Six days later, Francine was in the seat beside me on a flight back to Minneapolis.

FOUR

The doctors had not known what to expect, but they were completely unprepared to have a patient open her eyes, glance around, and try to raise her head as her internal temperature approached normal.

"A remarkable woman, your wife, but we must not jump to conclusions. There still could be extensive damage, cognitive impairment, personality changes, even paralysis that is not yet evident."

But Francine continued to astonish us all. She recognized me from the first moment she saw me, which seemed a good sign. She was weak and uncoordinated in her movements, and at first could not talk, but she made rapid progress. By the third day she was sitting up, responding to questions with single-word answers, and smiling whenever she saw me. By the fifth day, the doctors were reluctantly ready to discharge her for the trip home.

The press on both sides of the Atlantic declared it a miracle. I was not prepared to argue too vigorously with them. I had stopped believing in miracles after the Moorefield tornado, but miraculous was still in my vocabulary, and hers was certainly a miraculous recovery. I made the mistake of granting one interview, then nothing I did could rid us of the media vultures. For a week we had the Star Tribune and the TV channels camping out in front of the house. Doctors at the University of Minnesota med school wanted to study Francine, but she and I presented a united front, turning down both research requests and bids for book rights. I knew we could outlast them, that eventually the world would tire and turn away to other trendy developments. The important thing was that I had my wife back, Pia had her mother back, and we were a family again.

I am not saying everything was normal. For one thing, Francine needed a lot of extra attention and special care. She was still very weak and had trouble sleeping. I went from being a single parent with three kids to having four people dependent on me. I was exhausted from taking care of her, and she was exhausted from lack of sleep and trying to cope. She was easily confused and often discouraged. Some days she spent shuffling slowly back and forth between the living room and the kitchen, looking around as if something or someone had called to her, then leaving to resume the endless elliptical journey. Most days she spent in her flannel pajamas and wool bathrobe with her ski jacket on top.

One morning I returned from seeing the kids off to the bus to find her standing at the stove staring at the newspaper spread open over the burners. "This word," she pointed, "what is this word?" I leaned over to see where her finger was. "Influential," I said, surprised.

"It looks funny. It doesn't make sense. Influent. Not fluent. Why would a senator not be fluent?"

"That's not what it means. It—"

"Oh, I know what it means," she said, quickly covering. "I just never thought how strange a word it is."

It was like that. She could be perfectly logical, but there would be odd lapses, as if her brain had stalled or her memory for ordinary things had become scrambled. Then she would seem to be fine. She could read and write. She recalled things from our past together and from her childhood. Most of the time she did fine with everyday intellectual demands, but it was soon evident that Francine would not be returning to her position as a consultant at Cassidy and Dorn anytime soon. Maybe never.

We had been warned. I had been ready to accept a far greater degree of brain damage. Still, I was not prepared for the docility and the neediness. Nevertheless, I felt deeply grateful that she had been returned to me, intact if not unscathed. I needed her, and, for the first time in our relationship, she seemed to need me. The change in her personality was both comforting and, at times, frightening.

And she complained incessantly of being cold.

¤ ¤ ¤

"I am so cold," she said one night. "Cuddle me." Pia was sleeping in her crib at the foot of the bed, as she had since Francine's return. Francine put her cold feet against my bare legs, sending a shiver through me.

"My popsicle-toes sweetheart," I said. "You really are chilled."

"Ever since. I can't seem to ever get warm. I'm always shivering."

"The doctor said your thermostat is probably still haywire. It could take some time for you to get back to normal temperature regulation. Maybe we should get an electric blanket. I—"

"No!"

"Okay, okay, we don't have to get an electric blanket. But let me grab an extra wool throw from—"

"No! Don't leave me. I need you to keep me warm." She hugged me with a ferocity that took my breath away.

"I won't leave you. Don't worry. Just turn over. I'll keep you warm, spoon-style."

I tucked my knees in behind hers, reached around and cupped her breast in one hand, and drifted off to sleep.

I awoke in the small hours of the morning. The glowing digital clock said it was nearly four. I was under the duvet, still curled up against Francine, and this time I was the one who was cold. I tugged up closer to her and tried to go back to sleep, but my head was hurting and my arm was tingling. At five, I gave up and left the bed to start making breakfast. When I returned with the mug of hot cocoa that had become Francine's preference for starting the day, she had Pia in bed with her. The baby was asleep in the crook of her arm as Francine lay on her back, mouth open, snoring at full gale. I lay down beside them atop the blankets and fell almost instantly asleep.

FIVE

In the coming weeks, I could not overcome my fatigue. Since I was long overdue for a physical, I made an appointment with Dr. Townsend. I told him that I was exhausted, run down, and perpetually fighting off a cold or the flu or something.

"You have been under a lot of strain and stress," he said, as if it were a brilliant diagnosis rather than an empty template. "First you lose your wife and suddenly find yourself a single parent with two kids and an infant. Then, just as suddenly, you get your wife back and you are taking care of her, too. It's wonderful, but that does not mean it is not another stressor to manage. If you weren't exhausted, physically and emotionally, I would think there was something wrong with you.

"There is something wrong with me. That's why I'm here."

"You need to pace yourself, Luke, not act as if the whole world depended on you. I'll prescribe some extra vitamins, but what you really need is to let yourself off the hook a bit. And get some sleep."

Easy prescriptions, I thought, impossible in practice.

¤ ¤ ¤

Where I had once been used to leaning on Francine, drawing on her vitality, now Francine was dependent, drawing energy from me. Eventually, it all caught up with me, and I developed a cough that I could not shake. One night, despite loading myself up with dextrome-thorphan, my coughing continued and was keeping Francine awake. I dragged myself down to the living room couch and pulled my winter coat over me. Once the coughs subsided, I slept through the night.

I awoke to find AJ standing over me. "Are you all right, Daddy? Are you and Francine all right?"

I gave her a sleepy smile and pulled her down next to me. "Francine and I are just fine. My coughing was keeping her awake, so I came down here to sleep on the couch. No biggie. Get yourself some breakfast and get ready for school."

I padded upstairs to our bedroom and found Francine

curled up with Pia in bed with her. Pia was just awakening and starting her morning hunger whine. I reached to pick her up, and Francine's arms shot out, grabbing my wrist.

"No!" she snapped.

"Pia's hungry. Unless your milk has suddenly and mysteriously come back in, I need to feed her. Okay?"

Francine looked up at me and frowned as if she didn't recognize me. "Get me her bottle and I'll feed her. I want to keep her here with me."

"Okay. I'll be right back."

"How are you feeling?" she asked as I reached the door.

"Better, much better."

"Good. Pia is sweet to snuggle with, but she is not you, not nearly as good as you." She sent me a still-sleepy grin and pulled Pia closer, which Pia protested loudly.

"I'll get your ba-ba, Pia. Just hang on a couple of minutes." As if on cue, Pia stopped crying and relaxed her body. When I returned just minutes later, she was asleep curled up against Francine.

"She's become a sleepy baby," I said. "Have you noticed? I wonder if she is all right."

"She's fine." Francine swung her legs out of the bed. "It's just a growing spurt or something."

"Now that is a scientific explanation. A growing spurt. Maybe that's what I have, too. Not whooping cough or some bug going around, just a growing spurt."

Francine gave me a look that said she didn't understand, and I didn't feel like explaining. I had lunches to make and, when she reawakened, a baby to feed. Francine shuffled off to the bathroom as I headed downstairs. Duty calls, I thought. And Daddy answers.

A week of sleeping on the couch brought me to full recovery, with more energy than I had known since Francine's return. In the meantime, the baby had gone from full of vim to listless. I called the pediatrician's office, but my vague description of ambiguous symptoms was hardly considered worthy of an urgent-care visit. I insisted, and the secretary relented, giving me an afternoon appointment with a nurse practitioner.

¤ ¤ ¤

"You were right to bring her in," the nurse told me after running through her check list. "She has lost weight since her last visit. That's not good, Mr. Andberg. Has anything changed at home? What are you feeding her?"

"Everything has changed since her last visit. My wife is back, for one, Pia has started on solid food, for two, I've been sick, for three. What else do you want to know?"

"Your wife is back? I thought she was . . ."

"She was. She's the Lazarus Lady. You must have read it in the papers."

"Oh, my God. That's right. Now I remember. That was amazing. You must be thrilled. A modern miracle."

I was thinking about miracles and wishes and the cautionary folktales about wishes coming true. I got a prescription for baby vitamins and a new regimen for introducing solid food plus a redundant pep talk about babies and TLC. When I got home, Tommy was in bed with Francine.

I reminded him of homework and shooed him out of our bedroom. As the door clicked behind him, I turned to Francine. "He's twelve, almost a teenager, Francine. It just isn't right for him to be climbing into his mother's bed—or his stepmother's bed. It doesn't look right."

"I was cold, and he just climbed in for a few minutes to snuggle. It was completely innocent. Besides, you weren't here and Pia was with you. AJ had band and is taking the late bus. What was I supposed to do?"

"Is that what we are? Bed warmers? Nothing but living heaters to keep you warm?" I regretted saying it as soon as the words were formed, but I also heard the ring of an uncomfortable truth in it.

She had no answer.

¤ ¤ ¤

I asked her once, only once, if she remembered what had happened, if she recalled anything about being under the water.

"I really don't know. I suppose I do, but it always seems to run away from me when I try to think of it. I seem to remember the world tumbling, and I remember being scared. I think my head hurt, like an ice cream headache, at least for a while. Then they were warming me. They gave me a shot, I think. That's it. Except for the cold. I remember feeling the cold pouring into me and something, the life, being drained from me, like the water in a sink when you open the drain. Or, no, I think I made that up after. I don't know. Maybe I dreamed while I was . . ."

She looked at me with pleading eyes. "I remember flying home with you. That I remember."

SIX

We had been naïve, surfing a wave that was about to crash on a rocky shore. I had been able to stay home and take care of Francine and the kids because of Francine's death. But Francine was not dead. We started receiving blue envelopes from the bank with requests for overdue mortgage payments, and an insurance adjuster arrived one day to lecture us about insurance fraud and to present us with an invoice for repayment in full of the death benefits from Francine's insurance.

In the course of weeks, we went from financially comfortable to courting insolvency. It was obvious to everyone but Francine that she could not return to work. She insisted that she was fine, but she would also lie for hours on the couch, watching television programs that she was not able to explain at the time and could not recall later. Her clinging insecurity did not abate. If she was not actually curled up with one of the family, she had to be sitting with thighs touching or holding hands or with a leg crossed over.

The lab, as it turned out, was more than happy to take me back with a small salary increase. I may not have been a stellar performer, but they had finally realized that I was reliable. My analyses never had to be redone, I never botched a procedure, and I was more efficient than two-thirds of the staff. I called my old supervisor on a Thursday and on Monday was back working full-time at Twin City Chemalytics. I spent much of the first morning answering questions about Francine, then it was back into the routine.

For a week, I would tear myself away from Francine's arms, change and feed Pia, get the kids off to school, then head for Saint Paul. Francine was still at home to take care of Pia and to greet the kids when the bus returned them from school. We were fortunate that both the middle school and the high school were on a single campus, so the kids could take the same bus, despite slightly different schedules.

At the end of the week, AJ pulled me aside. "We need to talk."

"Okay, what's up, Pumpkin?"

"I think we need to do something. Every day when I come home I find Francine and Pia sleeping in your bed. It's obvious as soon as you walk into the room. You can smell it. Pia hasn't been changed for hours. And I've been checking on Pia's formula. I'm not even sure she is being fed during the day. She doesn't seem to have any energy."

"Are you talking about the baby or Francine."

"Well, both. But I was really talking about Pia. I'm worried. I don't think Francine can handle taking care of her. I hate to say this, but . . ."

"You may be right, but I hope not, because I have to work. We are up against the wall with the insurance company."

"Can we get somebody to come in? Can we put Pia in infant daycare? I'm worried about her."

It was genuine. She was suddenly not just AJ, my teenage daughter, but an almost adult, another member of the household trying to work with me to solve our problems.

"Okay, here's what I can do; I'll start looking into part-time daycare. We certainly can't afford a nanny at this time. And I'll talk with Francine, try to get her to understand how much Pia needs her. I can also call to check in with them during the day. After I get back from Cincinnati—"

"Cincinnati? You're going on a trip?"

"Yeah. The lab has new equipment that I have to be

trained on. It's only a week. Grandma Demeter will come and stay with you."

"No way. She hates us."

"She doesn't hate you; she hates me. And I won't be here, so everything will be fine. She can get more acquainted with her granddaughter—and reacquainted with her daughter—while keeping an eye on you and Tommy. It's only a week,"

"A week with her is forever. You don't know how she is with us. 'Do this! Don't do that! Can't you ever? Why, oh why, I ask! Do I deserve this?' Daddy, it never stops."

I knew this was an exaggeration, but I also knew there was a truth at the bottom of it. "I'm sorry. Just this once."

I called every night that I was away. Margarit Demeter would not talk with me; as soon as she heard my voice, I would hear her call to AJ: "Amy Joyce, it's your father again. Don't talk too long, you have homework to finish." Or it would be nearly bedtime or Margarit would be expecting a call, but always the warning not to talk too long. If AJ and I talked for more than ten minutes, I would hear annoyed throat-clearing in the background, and AJ would apologize and say she had to get off the line.

I ended up having to stay an extra week for a second course. Now I had both my daughter and my mother-in-law furious with me. I told AJ that I would make it up to her. I told Margarit that I couldn't thank her enough, and she said, "You're damn right."

I flew back late on a Friday, arriving after ten. Margarit had already decamped, not wanting to spend even a few minutes in the company of her despised son-in-law. In some twisted illogic, she blamed me for the avalanche and for her daughter's condition. AJ, still awake and waiting for me, ran to the door when she heard the key in the lock. She threw her arms around me and hugged me in a way she had not done for years. "I am so glad you're home, Daddy."

"I am so glad to be home, my Amazing Amy."

She pulled back and grinned up at me. "You haven't called me that since you were coaching my girls' soccer team."

"Well, you're still amazing. Is there any coffee left? Want to sit and talk for a while?"

"Yeah, let's."

She told me about her week, about her struggles with Margarit, which I already knew from our nightly debriefings, about her worries over Pia, who was not running a fever but who had just not been herself for days, and about the new boy in calculus class. Then she kissed me goodnight, which she never did anymore, and left me to wonder at what had happened to my little girl.

I sat there for a few minutes before turning out the lights and heading up to the bedroom. By the light from the hall, I could see Pia in bed with Francine. I left the door cracked, undressed, and got into my pajamas. I slipped in beside them as quietly as I could. As I kissed Pia's head, I placed my hand gently on her chest.

She was cold and not breathing.

SEVEN

I had thought Francine's death was devastating, the nuclear destruction of my world. I had no idea what devastation was until the death of my little girl, my tiny, perfect Pia, who had sustained me through the months without Francine by her giggles and burps and her tiny fingers closing around mine and by the sweet smell of her breath as she slept beside me. Her life had ended before it started. I plummeted so far and fast that, were it not that AJ and Tommy still needed me, were it not that Francine was back and so dependent, I might have ended it with a midnight swim across Lake Minnetonka. A lake as a final exit felt like a fitting coda, almost a reprise on an earlier theme, except Minnetonka was not covered in ice and I would not be saved by some freak primordial reflex. This I knew, but I kicked the idea away and doubled over in painful sobs instead. Then I shut off the shower that I hoped had masked my crying, dressed, and readied myself for the funeral.

To my surprise, Jody was there, without Owen, and she generously said nothing as she took my hand and held it for a few moments. As we sat on display in the designated pews, AJ cried and clung to me as if it were her baby who was in the tiny casket at the front of the church. Tommy wiped tears from the corner of his eye, but sat stiffly still through it all. And on the other side of me, Francine chewed her lip but said nothing. It was unclear if she understood what had happened. For that matter, it was unclear to me. Other than that my littlest one was dead, that she had died in the very bed in which my wife was then sleeping, we didn't really know what had happened.

They did an autopsy, as required under the circumstances, and we had to endure the scrutiny of social workers from the Department of Human Services, who would have loved to find cause to attribute our tragedy to our out-of-fashion, not-approved-by-pediatricians choice of sleeping arrangements. But they got nowhere. The autopsy ruled out suffocation, finding idiopathic heart failure as the proximate cause and "failure to thrive" as contributing. Idiopathic is doctor-speak for "no fuckin' idea." But, with no evidence of neglect or abuse, the DHS child protection troops were left without recourse, so the file was closed. That there was still a file, closed or not, bothered me at the time, but not enough to try to do anything about it.

I was wrong to think that Francine did not realize what had happened. As we left the church for the cemetery, she bowed her head and said, "My baby." The sorrow and pain in those two words was beyond reckoning, and I turned her into me and held her with her head on my chest as others walked past us or stood in awkward indecision until the minister, a man I did not know but chosen by the Demeters, placed one hand on each of us and opened his mouth to speak. "Not now," I said, and Francine looked up into my eyes with an unrecognizable expression. "Not now," she said, taking my arm as we walked down the steps toward the waiting line of black limousines.

EIGHT

Once again, I was surprised with our resilience as a family. For the fourth time that year, we had been plunged over the precipice, tossed into the frothing rapids of chaotic change: two deaths and two births, if one is willing to stretch definitions, all in less than six months. Yet we slid back into routine, a routine made simpler, in blunt honesty, by the absence of an infant to care for. The kids went back to school, I returned to work, and

Francine returned to bed. It was not that we did not care, that we were not, each in our own way, deeply wounded by the blow, but we had lives to lead. The grief gurus underestimate the power of routine, of ordinary activity to cope with extraordinary pain. Denial may be a defense mechanism, but evolution granted us defense mechanisms for good reasons.

Francine's mode of mourning was the most overt: depression. Her mood blackened into a dusky fog that dimmed the light and dampened spirits, sucking the force from her surroundings. Her mother was the one to work the miracle this time around. I thought her idea to "bring Francine out of this" was loony, but it worked.

It was only Francine's passivity that made it possible for her to be dragged to the Brighter Beginnings Daycare Center that first time, but, by the end of her first week as a volunteer, the transformation was amazing. Her energy was up, there was a sparkle in her eyes, and her conversations had become more focused.

"I have to admit," I told Margarit, "your idea to distract Francine from her grief by having her work with little kids was a brilliant intervention. It would never have occurred to me."

"It would have occurred to you if you gave a damn about her."

There was no answer to Margarit then and never would be.

The daycare center loved Francine, who, they said, had a calming effect on the children. She would sit and read with one or two of them in her lap, and even the most difficult or rambunctious of them would slow down and listen. She took to it as if this were her calling, coming home at the end of the day not tired, but rejuvenated. Her intellect still suffered, and she was given to moodiness and confusion at times, but the work with children seemed to strengthen her and build her resilience. Her strength would be tested later that summer when one of the kids at the center, a boy who was among her favorites, died unexpectedly.

"I loved Jason," she told his parents. "He was such a sweet little boy. He loved books and stories. He would sit quietly in my lap for hours on end as I read to him."

"You are so patient with the children, Mrs. Demeter. Jason talked a lot about you. I think he loved you, too."

In the fall, the daycare group was smaller, owing to a new and less costly operation that had started at the nearby Y. Then the center was hit by another tragedy, as several of the fulltime regulars developed pneumonia within days of each other. There was a full investigation, and no health violations were identified, but the death-blow had been struck. Brighter Beginnings was forced to close its doors and declare bankruptcy, and Francine was back home without a job.

It became clear how important the volunteer work had been to Francine. Within weeks, she had turned morose and possessive, clinging to me and to the children as if we were her life preservers in a storm-tossed North Atlantic. I tried to get her involved in other volunteer work, pushing her into brief stints at the library and at the middle school, but whatever it was that had energized her at the daycare center was missing from the library and the school.

It was only the fact that Francine was recognized as "mentally challenged" that saved her when she was caught cuddling with a twelve-year-old girl on a cot in the school nurse's office. The girl, who had been despondent over the loss of her boyfriend of the moment, had turned for consolation to the ever-friendly Francine. If Francine had been a Frank, mental challenge would have been disregarded and the middle school would have been rocked by scandal. As it was, Francine was hustled out the door, and I was told never to bring her near the school again, even though Tommy was a student there.

For a second time, our family was investigated by DHS social workers, and for a second time, the fattening file was closed without a finding. In the calculus of modern social work, we were not guilty, but we were also not not-guilty.

Whether all the losses and crises were contributory or not, Tommy started having trouble at school in the seventh grade. He complained of headaches and stomach aches, but no clear causes were ever identified. Our pediatrician started cutting out gluten, then lactose, then tree nuts, but changes in his diet had no effect.

"I just can't do it anymore, Dad. It's all too hard. Everyone hates me. My teachers hate me. I'm a failure and I'm only twelve."

"You are not a failure, son. You're just having a tough time right now." Naturally, my attempted reassurance had no impact, and Tommy continued on a downward spiral. He started being sick more often than he was well, staying home or coming home early two or more times a week. His grades plummeted, only confirming to him his sense of hopelessness. I would come home from work to find him curled up with Francine on the couch, with the television on but the sound off.

"Our poor Tommy," she would say. "He just gets so tired and discouraged. He seemed like he needed a mother's hugs."

Some part of me was growing wary, afraid of something that I could almost but not quite put my finger on. Sometimes it felt as if God were punishing me or balancing the scales for having given Francine back to us. That I did not believe in God made me no less ready to attribute agency to Him and to see intention in our misfortunes. I became more vigilant, determined that nothing more would happen to my two remaining kids.

When I came home to find Tommy with his head in Francine's lap, his forehead as hot as an iron, and his breathing ragged, I carried him into the car and drove him to the emergency room without pausing to discuss the matter with Francine or to call ahead to the hospital.

It was pneumonia. They caught it in time and turned it around. In a week, he was home again, a new kid with color in his cheeks and determination to turn around his record at school. He started staying late at school to work with teachers and working into the night in his room with the door closed. In defiance of ordinary logic, the harder he worked, the less tired he was. He was on an upward spiral that kept reinforcing itself all the way until Christmas vacation.

It was no vacation for me. I had been picked to temporarily take over for a manager who was out on maternity leave, and I was having trouble staying afloat. As the holidays approached, my hours at the office increased. I had, of course, noted that Francine had returned to her slovenly routine of wandering around in a robe and ski jacket over her pajamas. I was not aware of how much time she and Tommy were spending curled up on the couch watching television.

Two days before Christmas, I came home late in the evening to find Tommy and Francine stretched out in our bed. "He was so tired. He said he was cold and felt like he was coming down with something, so I told him to come here, that I would get him warm again."

I said nothing of my annoyance as I felt his forehead. "I don't think he is running a fever, but I'm going to take his temperature, just in case." I got him to turn on his side and stuck the digital thermometer in his ear. "This thing must be broken. Let me try it again." I got the same result. "This doesn't make sense. It says his temperature is 94, which seems impossibly low. I'm going to call the clinic hotline."

The nurse on duty told me to check with an oral or rectal thermometer. She waited on the line as the old-fashioned glass thermometer sticking out of his mouth slowly inched up. I twisted it in the light to see where the red line ended. "93.6," I said over the phone.

"That's hypothermia. We need to warm him up. Put him in a hot bath. I'm sending an ambulance."

Tommy didn't make it to Christmas. Tommy didn't even make it through the night. The doctors said they did not know what happened, but his body just shut down. Despite their efforts, his heart rate and breathing kept slowing until he just stopped. They tried to resuscitate, but it was fruitless.

This time, the police came to the house. AJ and I were interviewed repeatedly, and Francine, who was having trouble keeping her story straight, was taken away for observation. Francine was judged dull normal, and neither the police nor social services found anything, because there was nothing to find. By now, though, our file had grown to fill a bulging folder.

A side effect of all the suspicious attention was that we were distracted for a while from having to fully face up to what was happening to us. In less than a year, we had lost two children. It was more than any parent should ever have to bear. Only AJ was left. Although it made no sense, I was terrified for her, and, under her brave exterior, AJ was scared as well. We were all almost ready to believe in vengeful gods that we had somehow offended.

Human Services and at least one of the detectives were convinced that we were in some manner or for some reason poisoning our children. They said outright that they wanted to take custody of AJ but had no legal grounds. Then the bank foreclosed on the house, and we were homeless. Before Human Services could step in, I begged Jody and Owen to take AJ while Francine and I found a cheap apartment.

"I am not going to have some insolent teenager living in my house," Owen fumed, as we sat in the kitchen of the house that had once been mine.

"AJ is not insolent," I said. "She is quiet, studious, and responsible. She cleans up after herself and does not need to be reminded to do her homework or her laundry. She will not be any trouble."

"You make her sound like a fifteen-year-old saint."

"Sixteen-year-old saint. She had a birthday the end of November."

Jody, her tongue poking into her cheek, looked at Owen expectantly.

"I suppose," he said.

I thanked him profusely and was surprised at both my gratitude and my sense of relief. For some reason, I had a feeling that AJ was out of danger, at least for the time being.

Francine and I moved into a crummy little apartment south of Bloomington while we tried to sort out our legal and financial mess. Francine's parents were furious when they found out. Of course, the blame fell on me rather than on Fate or financial institutions. They did not offer to help, in part, I think, because any help they gave would be to my benefit as well as Francine's.

Life in the tiny apartment was hard, particularly on me. My commute had suddenly grown by twenty-five minutes each way, and my health started to fail. Whether it was because of the air in the musty apartment, bad eating habits, or the simple accumulation of stress, I was getting more and more run down. I caught a cold, then some virus, then the flu, and then another cold. It seemed I was no sooner over one thing when I came down with the next.

One bright spot was AJ, who was thriving while living with Jody and Owen and had quickly adopted to the new school. She confided in me that not having to go back to the same campus where Tommy had been made it easier.

Then, as abruptly as we had been evicted, we were back in the house, thanks to the Demeters, whose change of heart, their connections, and their finances enabled them to convince the bank to sell the house to them—at a substantial discount from what we had paid, needless to say.

We agreed all around that AJ had endured enough disruption and that she should be allowed to finish out the school year in Edina. She would move back in with us for the summer. What happened after that would be decided farther down the road.

NINE

For just the two of us, the house was a baronial estate, with rooms we never visited and furniture we never used. We recovered only some of our furniture, a few of the best pieces that we had put into storage at a self-store facility owned by Owen, a gesture that he reminded us of on every one of the few occasions when we met or talked. The rug that had been in the living room, a moderately expensive oriental that had been given us by the Demeters, was one of the casualties of the storage arrangement, the victim of a pernicious mold that would have required expensive cleaning and rehabilitation that we could not afford. When the Demeters learned that we had dumped it, they were furious.

"Why do we give you things if you don't take care of them?"

It was a rhetorical question, as I recognized, but I countered anyway. "I don't know. So, tell me, why do you?"

Arnold rolled his eyes and Margarit shook her head, but neither spoke, and I was at a loss for sufficiently clever words. I had learned that the Demeters respected only two things: money and verbal skill. I had only the latter to trade on, so there was no point saying anything unless it dripped with wit, sarcasm, or, at the very least, vocabulary.

Francine broke the silence. "Decay."

"What dear? What are you saying?"

"It was decay, Mother. Luke didn't do it."

Her defense of me was surprising, especially against her mother.

"Precisely my point, dear. How did it get overrun with black mold? Because it was not properly stored in a climate-controlled facility."

"Climate control. We need that. The glaciers are melting." Francine had developed this way of free associating to isolated words and pieces of a conversation. She could sometimes show flashes of her earlier self, but never for long. She had become slow, in the now archaic sense of the word, as well as in pacing.

"We were talking about rugs, dear, the beautiful oriental that used to cover the bare floor of your living room."

"Yes, I know. The tile is cold, like ice. I don't even like to go into the room anymore. It sucks up the heat. We should have kept the rug. But it smelled."

Arnold made a silent show of checking his Breitling chronograph, and Margarit supplied the voice-over. "It is getting late, and we have so much to do. We really just wanted to drop in and see how you were doing, dear."

It was not true, of course. They had dropped in with high hopes of humiliating me and fantasies of witnessing sensational progress on the part of their daughter. I, however, had grown immune to their disdain, and Francine's progress was limited to the pounds she had accumulated. During the visit, the Demeters had commented about Francine "finally filling out," an allusion to dinnertable struggles of the past that Francine had recounted in our early days together.

She was taller than me by an inch, and now she out-weighed me as well. Her frame could carry the weight, so no one would call her fat, but she had gone from svelte before the accident, to skinny after, to simply big as she recovered. Despite my best efforts as cook and caretaker, her diet was supplemented by a disastrous blend of chocolate and carbohydrates that she would order delivered from Lunds and Byerly's while I was at work, to be consumed before I returned. Her sharply re-duced mental capacity did not seem to prevent her from mastering online shopping, which was, thankfully, large-ly limited to satisfying her dietary cravings.

My own diet was nothing to brag about at the gym, alt-hough somehow I was not gaining weight despite pig-ging out on breakfasts of bacon-and-cheese-double-sausage sandwiches and lunches rounded out by carrot cake with cream cheese frosting. I was perpetually hun-gry, with a noticeable and uncharacteristic craving for fat and carbs.

With nothing more to offer on any topic, Arnold stretched his arm again to verify that his chronograph was still ticking with Swiss precision. Having announced their departure, the Demeters simply waited impatiently for confirmation that their visit had not been in vain.

Francine, suddenly catching on that it was her turn to say something, turned toward her parents with a trapped look. "I'm fine," she said, flatly. "Well."

"Yes, Mrs. Demeter, Francine has been doing well. She has gotten over her cold. Although it seems that I now have it." That was the way it went those months without AJ. Francine would get sick, begin to recover, then I would get sick. I couldn't remember a single time when both of us were healthy at the same time that summer. I said as much to Margarit.

"I was talking to my daughter." Snap.

While I was working on a retort that would not crystallize, Francine got up and stood looking down on all of us. "I like your new watch, Daddy." It was either very clever or quite clumsy, but it had the necessary effect. After goodbyes all around, and the ritual of watching their car depart, Francine took me by the hand and led me to the bedroom.

Our sex life had taken a strange turn. Francine, whose approach to sex had once been casual and utilitarian, had become passionate, driven. She did not want to go more than a day or two without making love, and she would milk me for as much as she could get from me, then insist on cuddling and petting long after I was emptied. It was, I suppose, the dream of every middle-age American male, to be the sex object of a demanding partner, but it had become, like breathing or bathing, a necessary but joyless ritual. I began to feel that I had to be ready to perform regularly, and the expectation began to spoil the performance.

"I don't want that. I want you in me." It was not an expression of desire; it was a demand.

I lifted my head from between her legs. "I just wanted to give you some loving."

"Then come in."

"I . . . I'm tired. Work. Taking care of kids. Everything."

She slipped out from under me, turned me over, and climbed on top, stretching out, covering me with kisses, and squirming as if trying to mix her body into mine. I let myself become lost in the purely physical, the sweaty heaviness of her above me. That time it worked. Sometimes it didn't, and I would fantasize about Sondra, the cute receptionist at the lab. Sometimes I would collapse.

Donald was the messiah and the devil of our impasse. Donald was retired, a fit seventy-something neighbor who spent his days playing golf and making online trades. He was twice Francine's age and deeply flattered by her attention, which I kidded myself about at first, living the lie that it was their shared interest in economics and markets that accounted for the time they were spending together. At least Francine was getting dressed and leaving the house, I told myself. It's nothing. Besides, the man was old. Beneath the salon tan and hair dye was a geezer.

The pressure was off me, enough so that I began to feel rejected when Francine would show no interest. Still, I had to admit that the affair was obviously good for her. The color returned to her cheeks and a bounce entered her steps. That she was no longer sleeping like a puppy draped over me was actually somewhat of a relief.

I remember the day I rounded the corner from the bus stop to see the flashing lights of the fire department ambulance at the house two doors down the street. Francine was standing beside the ambulance, arms folded, rocking. I rushed to her side.

"What happened?"

"He died. Let's go home."

The local weekly carried the story of this prominent community member who had died of congestive heart failure and whose body was discovered by a neighbor.

I finished reading the story. "The man was a ticking time bomb. His heart . . ."

"He was full of energy. Was."

I didn't want to pursue that line of conversation any further, so I dropped it.

At first I thought that it didn't matter to Francine, that Donald had just been a fling, a sexual outlet, but then she started into another downward plunge, her moods darkening and her clinging demands on my attention escalating. I began to wish for another Donald to come along, to bring her alive again, but no one stepped forward to volunteer.

Then AJ returned to start her last year before college back at her old high school. She did not explain what was behind this sudden reversal—I had thought she was doing fine with Jody and Owen and her grades had been solid though not spectacular—but there was more to the story that I would not learn until much later.

TEN

The three of us together still did not fill the emptiness in the house, at the center of which were two huge holes, black pits of loss. We were seldom all at home at the same time, and when we were, it was for brief pit stops. Francine had resumed volunteering, this time at a retirement community where she fed and bathed the elderly who could no longer care for themselves. It was not as gratifying to her as her work with kids, but it gave her a life beyond the walls of the house.

AJ was busy with band, debate club, and boys. And I was, to my complete surprise, being nudged up the ladder into management. That meant longer hours, more responsibility, and night courses in an MBA program for guys like me who didn't know ROI from royalties.

We were all three, for the first time in a long time, relatively healthy at the same time. Relatively is relative, of course, and it seemed we were always teetering on the edge of another cold or infection. Then the retirement home let Francine go, and another slow spiral began.

The homebound Francine reverted to her slovenly ways of late rising and hours reclined in front of the television. Then came the mounting pressure for me to spend more time with her along with sullen criticism of AJ and her lifestyle.

"There is more to life than boys, young lady. Just one weekend. Spend time. It would be nice if you spent some time with your family. With me."

"It's a road trip, the band, not boys."

"Yes, and that's the same. You spend more time talking with your friends about this boy or that than practicing your trumpet."

I would try to intervene, but AJ had a guilt button as big as a frisbee with a flashing sign that said "Push me!"

Francine took to pushing it. "I miss you. And it's lonely with your father gone. All the time now. Come here. Snuggle on the couch for a while before you go out. Tell me about what's up." She patted the spot beside her.

The telling would quickly taper off—what teenager can sustain a casual conversation with a parent?—and the two of them would end up watching some mindless show on cable, stretched out together on that now well-worn couch.

Then AJ caught a cold and stayed home for a few days. Each night I would come home to find the two of them lying together, asleep in the living room, with the television blaring in the background. Except the last time.

Francine was standing over AJ, looking down at her sleeping form. She turned as I closed the front door. "How was your day?"

"Filled with chemicals that alter and illuminate our times. How are you?"

"Feeling . . . better. A few days of doing nothing with AJ around. I think it's been good for me."

"How's AJ?"

"Oh, I don't know. Tired I guess." She reached down to tuck in the edge of the Navajo blanket covering AJ. "We should just let her sleep."

I went and knelt down beside her. My first born, now so big, sleeping like a baby. I brushed the hair from over her face and jerked my hand back. She was cold. Her breathing was shallow, with a flutter in it. "Call an ambulance."

"What?"

"I said call an ambulance. Now."

"She'll be fine. She's just a little run down."

I shoved Francine out of the way and grabbed the cordless handset from the table by the door and made the call myself.

"She'll get better. I did."

I looked at Francine as though she were some other species ignorant of human life. "You get better, she gets worse." I heard myself say the words as if some announcer on late-night TV had just spoken them. Then: "She gets better, you get worse." The punch line, a punch in the gut. Impossible to ignore. Francine, oblivious to what I was saying, drifted away toward the kitchen.

The ambulance arrived and I accompanied AJ to the hospital. It was pneumonia. That they deduced right away, but it took them days to piece together the puzzle.

"It's PCP, pneumocystis pneumonia, which is most often associated with AIDS, but your daughter tests negative for HIV. Something is weakening her immune system, making her vulnerable to opportunistic infections. We're going to have to keep her here for a while."

AJ recovered quickly in the hospital as Francine started on a slow, downhill slide into depression and ennui. I could not resist starting my own experiments, a time series analysis, as it were, in which I would sleep with Francine for three nights, then invent reasons not to for three.

Why did it take me so long to figure it out, to be certain? Denial? Or because it was impossible, of course. It made no sense. But what in life does make sense? What do we know, anyway? Everything we know is only theory, working hypothesis, awaiting revision or rejection. We guess our way through life and assume our way from one day to the next. Maybe God does exist. What do I know? The Devil, that is a different matter. Evil, yes.

I decided that AJ would not return to us from the hospital. I called Jody and Owen and asked them if they would be willing to take AJ in again. Owen said sure but Jody hesitated before finally agreeing, "for now." It was AJ who refused the offer.

"I can't go back, Daddy. You can't make me."

"What is it? Why not? You can go back to your old school, live in a nice house, be away from all the drag around home."

"You don't understand. I have my reasons."

"And those would be?"

"Never mind, I just don't want to be in the same house

with Owen . . . and my mother."

Owen. Not with Owen, she had said. Not in the same house. "What did he do?"

"Oh, Daddy." She put her arms around my neck as she used to when she was little. "I don't think I can talk about it right now. But he only tried, that's all. Once. I just don't want to give him another chance."

"You don't have to. You don't have to go back with them. I'll find a way."

ELEVEN

She was my last and my first, my first-born, my Amazing Amy. I had lost too much already. I could not face losing her, too. My hand was being forced. Impossible choices, even for an Andberg.

I knew what I had to do. It was not just about AJ; there could be others. I became obsessed. I had to plan and prepare, but I could not take my time. If I waited too long, the seesaw of my life would tip the rest of the way, and then who would right it?

I waited until after two overtime shifts had kept me away from Francine for the better part of two full days. On the first night back, she insisted we make love, which dampened my determination and left me drained. I drifted into a restless sleep but awoke with a start sometime after midnight. My right arm, pinned beneath her head, tingled. I slid it out and flexed my hand to restore feeling, to pump strength into my fingers. I would need both hands.

A gibbous moon cast its wan light through the sheers over the window, spreading a cold, soft glow across her face. So beautiful. As I studied her profile, my resolve weakened. What if I was wrong? I was not wrong. I closed my eyes, squeezing them shut against the reality beside me, the reality ahead of me. I could not watch. I tried to channel Mathew Andberg, my steel-stiff father, who had once calmly extracted his mangled foot from a combine and had limped all the years I had known him. I straddled her, pinning her arms, then closed my fingers.

I had no idea how strong she was. She bucked and twisted and almost threw me off. I squeezed, crushing, my large hands completely encircling her throat. I poured what power I could summon into my hands, every current left of my energy focused as she tried desperately to escape my grasp. She pulled one arm free from where my legs pinned it and clawed at my face, then tried to wrest my hands from her throat. I pumped one last time with all my might and something gave way beneath my hands. I had crushed her windpipe. Her thrashing grew wilder, then became spasms, then tremors, then nothing.

I counted slowly to one hundred before releasing my grip. My hands were aflame, aching, and I thought I might have torn something in my thumb, which did not want to straighten out. I felt for a pulse with my fingertips, then placed my head on her chest and listened, terrified at the prospect that I might hear something, terrified that I would hear nothing. I placed my cheek above her slack mouth praying not to feel a puff of air. I held both hands tightly over her nose and mouth and kept them there until my arms ached.

She was dead. My wife, my beautiful Francine. The wrecking ball was in full swing once more.

I went to the kitchen to retrieve the big carving knife,

to be sure, to end it unambiguously, with a gaping hole. I hated this, all of it, but it seemed necessary.

It was less messy than I expected. With no heart pumping, she did not really bleed. The blood pooled and leaked, but it was not spurting and running everywhere as it had in my nightmares.

I wrapped her in the gravel-filled duvet cover, tightened the luggage straps I had collected, then stuffed her into the makeshift body bag that I had prepared from an old tarp and tied the whole thing with nylon rope. The bedroom was a mess and the sheets were bloody, but I had no intention of covering my tracks, just of taking care of Francine as quickly as I could.

I drove out to the Demeters' summer place on Lake Minnetonka and found the keys in the boathouse just where I expected. I almost ended up sending Francine with me in tow into the shallow water off the dock, but was able to wrestle and heave us both into the little Alumacraft speedboat. I was already anticipating trouble out on the lake, but I could always just flip the boat if need be and ride it out until somebody picked me up. It was not like I was trying to get away or anything.

They will never find her body. Lake Minnetonka covers some twenty-three square miles and in places is well over a hundred feet deep. Even I don't know exactly where I dropped the body. I almost capsized the boat in the process, but managed to get the heavy bundle over the transom without throwing my back out or snagging anything on the outboard.

¤ ¤ ¤

The trial surprised me. I had expected that my confession, the knife, and the bloody mess left in the bedroom would be enough for them to just cart me away, but justice is not only blind but stupid and inefficient as well. Owen, for reasons I can only guess, hired me an attorney who immediately entered an insanity plea. He was good, that lawyer. The more I simply told the truth as I knew it about Francine, the more he had people convinced that I was insane. I told them that I had to do it. It was a moral imperative. If I didn't act, what or who would have stopped Francine? And that makes me crazy? Maybe.

Matters so simple and straightforward seem to be beyond the reasoning power of juries and judges. I told the examining psychiatrist that Francine lived on the life energy of others, that if I hadn't killed her, she would have been the death of me and of AJ, exactly as she had been for Pia and Tommy and Jason and the others. In their testimony, guided by Owen's trained pony-at-the-bar, this was turned into definitive proof that I was *non compos mentis*. I was delusional, criminally insane.

Not guilty by reason of insanity. Even that is an absurd concept. If anything, it should be guilty by reason of insanity. But, of course, in my case I think I was both guilty and sane.

TWELVE

It was and is the rest of the world that refuses to face reality. I am sympathetic. Reality is not always easy to face. I first learned that the summer of the tornado. I learned that on the many occasions when reality called for me to man-up as an Andberg. Now I shuffle around in a robe and slippers, and there are no other Andberg men to stand tall. My brother was sucked into an EF5 tornado, my father limped into the path of a drunk driver not far from the site of the old movie theater, and my son had his life force sucked from him in his parents' bed.

In the end, the verdict makes little difference. It's life. Minnesota abolished the death penalty in 1911. Jailed for life or institutionalized for life. Tough choice. I am told the food is better here, but there is no parole and you have to put up with idiot doctors who want to help you gain insight. Insight.

Oh, yes, and I am surrounded by crazy people. They seem to think I am not one of them, but they also find that the explanation for why I am here strains credulity. Only Jacob Werman, who hears voices, believes what I tell him about Francine, but he also believes God told him his children were possessed and had to have the Devil burned out of them with a red-hot poker. God didn't tell me to kill Francine with my own hands; my own conscience did. But maybe I am as crazy as old Werman.

Sometimes I think AJ almost believes me. She is doing well at St. Cloud State, thinks she wants to be a teacher. She has a boyfriend who has a tendency to smother her, but she is adamant in asserting her independence and told me she does not think it will last.

Nothing lasts. Even my life sentence will someday run out. In the meantime, I amuse myself by playing games with the staff and inventing new chemical tests by dry-labbing. I have two patents and three more pending. Twin City Chemalytics is assigned the rights and the royalties go to AJ. All that practice in grad school finally paid off.

¤ ¤ ¤

"Luke, Luke Andberg." It's Dr. Spearmint, calling to me

from across the Day Room, the shrink with the breath tabs that almost cover his halitosis. Dr. Spearmint has a name that I can't be bothered to remember. He is new. They come and go, these doctors in their white coats, even though none of them is a real doctor, not doctors of medicine. Still, they wrap themselves in the disguise, a medical costume, something like a haz-mat suit, protecting them from the contamination of mental illness. Without their armor, who could tell them from the inmates?

None of these well-protected doctors carries a stethoscope, none ever checks my pulse. They are like the social workers who are not social and busy themselves with activities that are not work. Doctors who do not doctor. Things are not always what they seem. This I know. This Francine taught me.

Dr. Spearmint has just finished talking with leatherfaced Dr. Currypowder, who might be from India or Pakistan or Bangladesh and who was here when I first arrived. Dr. Currypowder stands apart, as he always does, and pushes his words out with resonant consonants. I could not hear what they were saying, but Dr. Spearmint is working his mouth like he does when he is leading a therapy group and doesn't know what to say. When his lips become like worms after a rain and his eyes search the ceiling for inspiration, I always say something. "As you were saying, Doctor . . ." Or, "I can tell you have this one figured out." Or, "Just say it. Go ahead, say it." He always coughs or twirls his Mont Blanc, desperately hoping that the words that weren't there when he looked heavenward will now come to his rescue. It is a little game I play with him. Little games, each one tailored to the other player, are my occupation, have been for the past two years now. That and doing mental chemistry.

I am alone in the Day Room, which strikes me as odd, but not odd enough to worry over. What is odd, is the noise, louder than usual. The liquid whoosh and metallic squeak of the ceiling fans high overhead, the thrumming of traffic in the distance, a gurgle of talking in the hallway, and the rattle of a cart with a loose wheel. These sounds are loud enough, but not as loud as the muffled screeching in my ears. Tinnitus, they call it, my constant companion, like a woman's scream beneath a down pillow. Always there, just behind me and to the left.

Dr. Currypowder stands, with his arms crossed, perplexed or displeased, as Dr. Spearmint approaches me. Currypowder is the supervisor, the boss of the other doctors, or at least he acts as if he were, which is much the same thing. He is the one who never agreed with the diagnosis, who believes I am dissembling, faking insanity. He is wrong, of course, because I do not claim to be insane. Just the opposite. I told them that in court, but they chose to believe otherwise. I tell them that here, but they choose not to believe me. All except Dr. Currypowder, who believes I am sane but does not believe what I tell him.

Dr. Spearmint is now in front of my chair, the metal institutional chair with the missing pad on the right arm. It is mine, my chair, my place in this room, with or without the others. I stand up, but he is too close and I have to push the chair back to make room for his mint-and-garlic breath that fills the space between us. His lips stop squirming and his mouth opens. He is saying something, but the screaming behind me and to the left is too loud.

"What?"

"I said, they found her. They—"

The screaming intensifies, and I can't hear what he is saying. "What? What did you say?"

His mouth opens wider and he forms the words more slowly, exaggerating the pronunciation. "They found her."

"Who?"

"They found your wife."

"What?" The screaming and the susurration fade momentarily.

"They found your wife. She's—"

I can't hear his last word. The muffled scream is now a siren in my ear, an avalanche warning.

Innocent
Slaughter

It was show time.

Habib straightened his black apron, picked up the two plated entrees, peeked through the glass oval in the double doors from the kitchen, and hip-checked his way out. The dining room, a buzz of conversations in a half-dozen languages, was quickly filling as the evening exo-tube traffic from Milan started spilling into Munich. It would be a good night.

Distracted by the din in the room, Habib looked down at the plates in a moment of disorientation. Which hand? Left? Yes. The green rimmed plate was for the *fräulein*—no surprise. He delivered the food with his usual pleasant panache, then scanned the room full of moneyed multinationals.

In the decades of fallout since Brexit, Europe had closed ranks and made massive investments in infra-structure. With the vacuum transit exo-tubes that now interlinked cities in France, Germany, Italy, and Spain, a multi-ethnic culture was on the ascendant, enabling those with the time—and means—to dine in one country before attending the theater in another. Habib was happy that his parents had the foresight to have left Syria for Germany and that he had the foresight to attend culinary school. Yes, he was a waiter, but someday, in the New Europe, he would have a restaurant of his own.

It was not difficult to see that the two couples just being seated at table number eleven were in the early days of friendship. Theirs was an exaggerated *gemütlichkeit*: too loud, overacted, covering an unspoken awkwardness. A good waiter could read the table and play it for the best result: smiling, satiated patrons who would over-tip and ask for him by name on their return visit.

In this case, they were all speaking German but with competing accents. The slightly older couple nearer the door were evidently natives, most likely from farther west, Karlsruhe perhaps. The slightest hint of a French *R* was the tell. The other pair—younger and most likely not yet married—were American, or possibly British. By contrast to the bulked-out Bavarians around them, they were ascetically thin, with smiles meticulously drawn across skeletal faces. Habib instantly concluded they were veggies, probably vegan, and likely practitioners of Achrono-Yoga, the latest passion of the orthodox pantheists and animal rights fundamentalists. Even before he was close enough to pick up on their conversation, he knew what the subject was. As the intensity of the exchange rose, they switched into English. No problem, Habib thought.

"Trust me, you are going to love this place." It was an American expression in the mouth of a German man. Habib guessed he had spent time overseas or worked for one of the multinationals with offices in Bavaria.

"But, I told you, we are—"

"I know, Julian, I know. You're vegetarians. Okay, vegans. I understand the distinction. Not a problem. This place, Café Zweigelt, does it all: bio-dynamic wine from Austria and Spain, organic fruits and vegetables from Italy and Portugal, and the finest factory-grown meat analog from right here in Bavaria. It starts as, like, a clear broth and some genetically engineered cell culture or something. Well, that's one side of the menu, as it were. On the other, we have beer-fed Kobe beef from Japan and grass-fed free-range from Argentina, spring lamb from New Zealand and succulent goose from Greece."

"Oh, please." The asthenic woman across the table screwed up her face in studied distaste. "You don't have to be so explicit, Karl."

Her counterpart, the woman seated cattycorner from her, jumped to her husband's defense. "Just be glad Karl didn't go into the details of ritual slaughter. They have both hallel and kosher meat here, you know. I'm not sure if you understand the distinction, but Karl can en-lighten you, I'm sure."

"Ew, no, thank you, Greta."

"I'm with you, Kristin," Greta said. "I'm neither Jewish nor Muslim, and I definitely don't want to know how my dinner spent it's last moments."

Kristin shook her head and tightened her lips into a disapproving slash. Her husband put his hand on her arm as he turned to the German couple. "Look, Karl . . . and Greta, we already heard about this place. I under-stand the premise. Both/and, as we say in the philosophy department, not either/or. Something for everyone."

Kristin was not ready to let go of her point. "I don't know, Julian." It was a plaint. "I don't know whether I can actually do this. I mean, with animal flesh actually on the same table. Like, I mean . . ."

Karl filled the silence. "Oh, here's our server. Let's get his recommendations."

"Madams. Sirs. Good evening. My name is Habib." He bowed, a measured four-centimeter nod of the head. "How may I help you this evening? We have several excellent specials tonight. I could—"

Karl cut him off. "Just help us out here. We have a difference of opinion, as in totally different takes on what food and eating are all about. We—"

Kristen sighed loudly. "It's not about either food or eating. It's about ending the suffering of living creatures and about respecting the living world, our planet."

Karl looked up at Habib. "Right. Like she said. On the other hand, my wife and I are realists. The human species evolved as omnivores—don't you agree?—and it makes sense for us to eat dumb creatures raised for one purpose: to feed the human race and keep us alive."

Habib, well-versed in this opening gambit, simply smiled. "I wouldn't know and wouldn't presume, but we at Café Zweigelt can cater without prejudice to every taste. Our lab-grown synthetic animal proteins are the finest in Europe, in the world, engineered to be indistinguishable from, shall we say, traditional resources." It was virtually a quote from the staff training manual. "On the other side of our color-coded menu, we have everything to satisfy the most discerning carnivore palate."

"And what would you recommend, if you were as hungry as we are, after a tube-train ride that took forever. I tell you, I tried to convince them to fly, but, quote-unquote, 'It's not ecologically defensible.' How can you argue with that? Am I right?"

His idioms were as American as those of any Post-

Trump politician, Habib noted. He must have studied in the States. "I wouldn't know, of course, sir. But . . ."

"Then, what would you choose from the menu for dinner now?"

"Well, sir, I've had dinner already, thank you, but I could certainly recommend the filet mignon, finished to perfection, from either the green or the red side of the menu and decadent in either case." It was sleight-of-hand, like a magician's forced card, a pricey selection inspired by their accents. "We serve it with field mushrooms in a beetroot wine-garlic glaze alongside haricot vert sprinkled with peppered pistachios."

Julian grimaced. "Can you do the green beans without the nuts? My wife is allergic."

Aren't they all, Habib was thinking. "Of course, sir," he said.

Karl held up his index finger. "And, can I have the filet kosher, without the usual bacon wrap?" Habib smiled, noting for the first time the man's decidedly Semitic features and feeling an instant kinship. He was thinking that it was easy to respect a man who avoided pork. "Yes, we can substitute lattice-grown faux bacon. The connoisseurs cannot tell it from the real thing."

"Excellent. For you also, dear? Yes? Okay, make that two."

Julian, grinned in triumph. "And two of the same from the vegan side for my wife and myself."

"Most excellent choice. I'll send the sommelier over." Habib swallowed an inward laugh. So much had changed in the technology of food and so little had changed in the gender politics of dining out.

¤ ¤ ¤

Karl was first to clean his plate. "Good, right?"

Julian finished a bite of his faux beef and looked up. "Mmm, yes. It's been years since . . ." He glanced at his wife. "I . . . well, a good hunk of rare beef, I mean, this is, like, well, virtually the real thing. Okay, not really, but you could have fooled me."

Kristen's eyes narrowed. "I wouldn't know. I've never eaten meat. Never. The very thought turns my stomach." She pushed her plate away, half finished.

Her husband struggled to recover. "But this, I mean, it isn't actually meat. But admit it, wasn't it good?"

"I suppose," she said. "The beans and the mushrooms were certainly tasty."

Karl leaned forward. "Are you finished, Kristen? You hardly touched the fillet. Not to your liking?"

Julian set his fork down. "She doesn't eat a lot, you know. But, trust me, the ersatz fillet was amazing."

"Really? Would you mind, Kristen? If you've had your fill, of course. Could I have a taste of yours?"

"Be my guest. I've had enough." She slid the plate across the table.

Karl sliced off a wedge with his steak knife and sampled it. "Amazing, utterly amazing. This is indistinguishable from the real thing. Here, darling, try a bite." He sliced off another small piece and offered it to his wife. She nodded in vigorous agreement. "You know," he said, gesturing with his fork, "this raises an interesting philosophical question. Right up your alley, Julian. Is pretending to eat flesh or eating pretend flesh really any different to eating meat? Aren't you still a carnivore?"

"Interesting. The cell lines that are used for vat-grown meat are ultimately of animal origin, but—"

Kristen bristled. "I really don't think we have to pursue this, Julian." She twisted her head and angled it in almost comic disapproval.

Karl raised his eyebrows. "Seriously, Kristen. So, indeed, no animal died for your dinner—at least not any in recent decades—but weren't you, ultimately, eating flesh? Under a microscope or in a biochemistry lab, could anyone tell the difference between what was on your plate and mine?"

"It is just not the same!"

"Ah, but it is, it is. I think you are playing semantic games with yourself, the payoff being that superior smirk you are trying so hard to suppress."

Greta cleared her throat. "Probably we've all had enough about carnivores and herbivores and philosophy, wouldn't you say, Karl? Anyone else interested in dessert?"

¤ ¤ ¤

Habib was waiting for a double order of vegan shashlik when Vasilli, the Greek busboy, crashed into the kitchen. "Who has table eleven tonight?"

"I do. Is there a problem with the order."

"No, but there is a problem with the customers. I think it's getting out of hand."

Habib hurried to the table. The two men were standing up, angled inward, on opposite sides. The *maître de* was doing his best to calm them. "Sirs, I must ask you to lower your voices, or I shall have to insist that you leave."

Both Habib and the *maître de* moved to restrain the men, but it was too late. In a flash, each of them brandished a steak knife in a posture of threat that bordered on the comical.

"Insult my wife, will you? I'll show you who's a fucking carnivore."

"You started this, you arrogant vegan evangelist. The goddamn converts like you are always the most sanctimonious. Was she worth it? Do you know what a top predator is? Carnivores eat herbivores, you dumb shit. So, now apologize, sit back down, and shut up."

"It's that bloody meat-eating testosterone. Eating meat is not only a manifestation of human hegemony, the disastrous and evil hegemony of homo sapiens over the animal kingdom, but—"

"What about the poor plants? What, no sympathy for the lowly cabbage? Does not the asparagus have feelings? A Soul?"

"You fucking nut job, you . . ."

On either side of the table, the women were struggling, with little success, to calm their men. Habib leaned in close to the German man's ear and whispered. "Shalom, brother. Salaam. This is not worth it." The man gave him a quizzical look before exhaling noisily and gently placing his steak knife on his plate.

The storm passed as quickly as it had risen, and the tip from the two couples, when they finally left, was Habib's best of the evening. As the two couples exited, chatting amiably, he laughed at the image of the two men with their steak knives, the one a committed vegan and radical defender of animal rights, threatening to kill each other. Better to slaughter a fellow human being than surrender on a point of principle. How strange our species is, he thought.

Habib, experienced in the folly of diners, quickly got back into his routine. Watching the American chef at the plating station readying the next order, he frowned. "Wait a minute. Did you plate those correctly, Paul. That one is supposed to be vegan, and this is free-range grass-fed."

"Chill, dude. It's all the same. Ersatz Bayern couldn't make an extra delivery today from the labs. We ran out of syn-trophic meat hours ago. No one can tell the difference, anyway, these days."

Habib shrugged before taking the plates. He was already plotting how best to upsell the couple at table nine on a flamboyant dessert.

Prime
Numbers

Like a sudden rainstorm on a blistering summer afternoon, with thunderheads forming from a tranquil sky to unload torrents on the overheated fields below, the cancer struck. It was not this sentence of death that Archer Halvorsen protested, but the manner and timing of its coming. It was too soon and too messy. Instead of quietly passing in his sleep after perfecting his accounting methods and putting the final perfect touches on the miniature Alpine village in his spare bedroom, he was going out amidst bloody vomit, his body twisted in pain except when the doctors upped the opioids, which then sent his thoughts into thunderstorms of euphoric chaos.

Chaos was no pleasure for Archer. He worshiped at the altar of order. His god was perfection, and its pursuit his liturgy. He knew what was said about him. He was a perfectionist and had even pursued the proper label for himself. If disorder was the Devil, ambiguity was the Devil's agent. Always best to know, he reasoned, so long as the knowing made sense and assisted in allaying uncertainty. He had shopped from clinic to clinic, psychiatrist to psychiatrist until finally awarded with an unambiguous diagnosis, the correct one, the perfect 300.3: Obsessive-Compulsive Disorder, according to DSM V, the Diagnostic and Statistical Manual of the American Psychiatric Association. The diagnostic number, 300.3, is a palindrome if you ignored the period. Symmetrical. Perfect. He did not obsess over the fact that he did not meet precisely all the DSM criteria, because he knew that DSM-V was itself imperfect. Besides, he had known, from an early age, who he was and what he was about.

¤ ¤ ¤

"And what do you want to be when you grow up?" The man in the Red Sox baseball cap worn back-to-front, the man who had been assigned to him by the agency the year after his father was killed, the grown man who nevertheless insisted on being called Billy, had already worked his way through a laundry list of opening questions. "Me, you know, I always wanted to be a firefighter."

A firefighter, an occupation dependent on disorder, feasting on the chaos of conflagration. To Archer, even the name was repulsive, composed of concatenated words, each in itself synonymous with chaos. "Are you a firefighter?" he asked his recently acquired Big Brother with deadpan politeness.

"No, I sell medical supplies. I get to travel all over the state selling things that help sick people get better." With the sales practitioner's penchant for manufacturing redemption from everything, he switched tone. "It's very interesting, getting to travel, meeting people. Every day is different, something new."

"You sound satisfied. That's good." To young Archer, it actually had sounded like a living hell, but he held up his unfailing front of apparent politeness, which he had long ago learned that adults adored when it was practiced to perfection. "I'm going to be an accountant."

"An accountant? You are the first kid I have ever known who actually wanted to be an accountant."

"I do not *want* to be an accountant. I said I am *going* to be an accountant."

Bill Polder adjusted his baseball cap and cleared his throat as he tried to remember what he had learned in the orientation sessions about affirmation and encouragement, about facilitating questions. "Well, you sound like a very determined young boy. What do you like about accounting?"

"Numbers."

"Numbers?"

"Yes, they're not people. Numbers are perfect. They always behave the same way: correctly. They are always there. I'm going to be an accountant." It was said as neither a prediction nor a promise, but a simple statement of fact.

After high school, Archer had attended Babson when it was still an Institute, interned as a bookkeeper at a Cambridge startup, graduated with a bachelor's, earned his CPA, and hung out his shingle. He had done well enough as an independent, but did not thrive. It was too unpredictable, too varied. Instead, he sought out the patterned comfort of work in a large corporation where he could become a pinion gear in a number-crunching legal machine. He eventually settled into a steady routine at Edsimon Industries, where he could rise slowly enough never to be forced to move into management.

In this way, Archer began the first leg of his journey toward perfection. His modest needs and his steadily growing compensation allowed him to indulge his one eccentric pursuit, in which the spare bedroom of his Back Bay condo gradually evolved into a room-filling N-gauge model railroad layout with every building, shrub, tree, and human figure modeled to perfect scale.

Then began the second leg of his itinerary.

¤ ¤ ¤

Archer stood in the doorway. "Mr. Edsimon, sir. Your assistant told me you would have a few minutes for me."

Hadley Edsimon, III, waved him in and gestured toward the single chair facing the oak acreage of his desk. "It's Hardiman, right? From accounting?"

"Yes, Halvorsen, Senior Corporate Accountant."

"What can I do for you?"

"I don't know if there is anything you can do for me, sir, but I do have some information I believe you could find useful to know."

Edsimon steepled his hands. "Go ahead."

"There are some irregularities in the books." Irregularities. Archer hated the very word. It seemed to imply agency that the books did not have. The irregularities were in the people, as they always were, the imperfect people who did not enter numbers correctly or debited the wrong account or misreported the figures. "There is a large sum that has gone missing and that was missed by the auditors, which seems unlikely unless . . ."

The meeting did not last long. The big boss had been simple and direct without actually saying the words. At the end, he said two words: "Fix it." He tapped the desk for emphasis. "You're the perfect man for the job. I know you can do it. Neither of us wants 'irregularities' now do we?" Archer got the message, perfectly clear.

¤ ¤ ¤

There are only two ways to fix fraudulent accounting: expose the fraud or bury it in more fraud. The implicit orders from the CEO gave Archer pause for only moments. It was not a moral dilemma for him, as only order was sacred, only perfection was holy. The sole question was whether the cover-up could be done correctly—perfect and impenetrable. Archer had a plan that rested on the coming changeover to new accounting software. It would not be easy and could not be rushed without exposing both the fraud and its concealment. Years of phony invoices siphoning off millions of dollars had to be slowly polished into the flawless appearance of perfection.

Like the sudden thunderstorm of a summer afternoon, the cancer had sent its rumbles of early warning, which Archer ignored, just as he had as a boy ignored darkening skies and distant grumbles if his delivery route as a paper boy was not quite finished. He reckoned now that he would need another three months to create all the false audit trails and trick the accounting software to make everything look right. Without getting caught, that is.

He continued to work long hours, for which Edsimon compensated him with overtime pay for which he was not, technically, eligible. He showed up on weekends even as his body began betraying him. As his energy flagged, he became furious with himself over the time he spent excusing himself to run to the bathroom. Not everyone was fooled. Peggy Barnstable, who had once been a pediatric nurse before going back to school to get an MBA in human resource management, called him out one day on her way to the cafeteria.

"You don't look like yourself, Arch. You okay?" she said, as he returned from the bathroom, wiping his lips on a monogrammed handkerchief.

He knew better than to correct her. He hated being called Arch or Archie, since his name was Archer. Archer, not Archibald. Archer. "Who do I look like, then?" It was a rare attempt at the lame humor that often passed for conversation among his colleagues.

"You look like someone sick. I'm not sure you should even be at the office. Have you seen a doctor?"

"I have," he said, knowing he had never been able to lie convincingly but also knowing it was not a lie because, on his way to work, he had passed a car driven by a man in surgical scrubs. "Just this morning, before work. It's a lot of long hours, what with the switch to the new accounting system. I've been tired, you know." More little not-lies. "I'm perfectly fine now."

The third leg on his journey started the following Monday, in an ambulance to Mercy Hospital, after they found him collapsed in the second-floor men's room at the office.

¤ ¤ ¤

"It's metastasized." The oncologist with the furry cancer of a mustache spreading across his face spoke like a radio announcer. "Do you know what that means? It's broken loose, run amok." He scanned down a list on his tablet computer. "It's literally everywhere."

Archer did not correct the misuse of 'literally', nor did he argue that he could rattle off at least a half dozen places in his body that almost certainly did not have cancer. Yet. There was also the infinite elsewhere in the universe where there was not, nor ever could be, any cancer. Literally everywhere? "What are we going to do?"

"We are going to start you on very aggressive chemo-therapy and see if we can't extinguish this wildfire. We are in for a fight, but you haven't lost your battle with cancer, not yet."

Archer winced at the references. He had never wanted to do battle, to be fighting a wildfire. He was an account-ant. "I'm a corporate accountant at Edsimon. They really need me at work. I still have some things to finish. When can I go home?"

"Not for quite a while. Between the chemo and the cancer, you are going to get even weaker. We'll give you medication to help with the pain and the muscle cramps and the nausea, but we'll have to keep you here until we complete at least the first course of chemotherapy. Trust me, it will be everything you can do just to cope."

Archer thought of the books, the accounting records that he had been forced to leave in a partially corrected state. Just a few more months, maybe only weeks if he could push himself hard enough, that was all he needed. He had to finish the corrections. He had to.

In the morning, he insisted on his rights and checked himself out voluntarily against medical advice. He made it as far as the front desk before collapsing.

¤ ¤ ¤

"We'll try to keep you as comfortable as possible." The doctor's hairy upper-lip cancer bounced. "We're upping the painkillers, and our social worker is completing ar-rangements for discharging you into hospice care."

"Hospice? No, I can't die, not yet. There are things I need to do. I need to get it right, to make it right."

¤ ¤ ¤

The fifth leg of his travels took him by ambulance to the Horace Leben Hospice Center. He had studied German in high school and would have laughed to himself at the name of the facility, but he was still heavily sedated when he arrived.

He spent his first days in a haze of rising and falling panic and euphoria: panicked whenever his medication wore off enough for him to become fully aware of his surroundings and the fact that he was dying, euphoric after the nurse tapped the button to send another squirt of happy juice down the tube and into the shunt at his wrist. Between these peaks and valleys he had visitors.

"Who are you?" he asked.

"Gavriel. I've come for you. It's time." The man at the foot of his bed wore a white coat but was no doctor. His hair was as white as his robe and glowed as if backlit by a setting sun. He hovered inches off the tile floor.

"I get it," Archer said. "I'm hallucinating."

"So you think, but only because your meds haven't fully kicked in yet. Once they do, you'll think I'm real."

"In that case, I'm not ready. I'm not going."

"Many say that, but trust me,"—Gavriel shook his head gravely—"the numbers don't look good."

"Numbers are always good."

"Your number is up."

They argued that first time until Archer yelled at him. As the nurse entered, Gavriel faded, slipping past her and out into the corridor.

"What's the matter, Mr. Halvorsen? You in pain?" She placed a hand on his shoulder. "I can't give you another dose so soon, but let me help you get comfortable."

"I don't want to get comfortable; I want to get out of

here and get to the office and finish my work."

"I don't think so, really. You should just try to rest. Save your strength."

"For what?"

"Well, to deal with what you're dealing with."

"You're new to this, aren't you, Miss . . ."

"Jenkins, Mrs. Jenkins. You can call me Bernice."

"You're new."

"Well, I've been here since August."

"Three months. New. There was a man here, in my room, pretending to be an angel. I don't want to see him again. Do you understand?"

"I think I do. I'll talk with the doctor about adjusting your medication."

"You do that. And call somebody for me."

"Who do you want me to call?"

"Somebody at my office. My boss. The CEO. Tell him we need to talk. Right away."

¤ ¤ ¤

The next morning, both Gavriel and Edsimon were there, not at the same time, but close enough to have bumped into each other at reception.

"Did you see him?" Archer asked.

"Who? The doctor?"

"No, the . . . well, the glowy guy, the glowy floaty guy."

"Look, I don't want to upset you, Halvorsen. Are you sure you want to see me. Maybe this is not a good time to talk."

"I just wanted you to know. It's not perfect yet. I still have another set of entries to redo. I'll finish them when I get back."

"Uh, when you get back. Right. But I don't think . . ."

Edsimon seemed unsure how to handle Archer.

"There's not that much left. I'll take care of it."

"Yeah, sure. Look, Deb is my direct report now. She'll wrap it up, whatever needs doing." He did not mention that he had also been banging his new financial assistant while holding out the promise of payoff in the future, a promise he had no intention of keeping.

"Deb Firestone is not a perfectionist. It needs to be perfect. I . . ." Archer's head drooped and bobbed back up. "I guess I'm a little out of it right now, but I'll be all right once I get out of here."

Edsimon nodded, then looked around awkwardly. "I should go. It's almost eight. I need to get to the office. Don't worry. After all, you're almost home free. Well, you know . . . whatever." As he left, Gavriel floated back into the room.

"Did you see him?" Archer said. "That's my boss."

"Past tense. Was your boss. Now it's time to go, time to pack it in."

"No, I'm not ready, I told you. I'll be ready when I get it right. All my life I've been striving for perfection: the perfect soft-boiled egg, the perfectly polished glass table top, the perfect set of cooked corporate books. That's all I have ever wanted. Perfection. Once I have that, then I'll be ready."

The angel Gavriel smiled indulgently. "You have had all the time you have. You have done all the things you will ever do. You have become everything it was possible for you to become in the time you had and given who you are. That, Archer, is perfection."

"But that's not fair. I mean, then, I'm no different from anyone else. In that sense, everyone achieves perfection, everyone becomes as perfect as it was possible for them to be."

"So? It's time."

"Wrong. It's not time. I'm not ready."

"Yes, you are. Whether you know it or not."

¤ ¤ ¤

Archer Halvorsen died at exactly 7:57 on a Thursday morning. He was not persuaded by the logic presented to him, but he died anyway. Ignoring the colon, 7:57 is a palindrome; it is also a prime number, perfect in itself.

Hadley Edsimon, III, died in prison after being ratted out by Deborah Firestone. When she heard the news of his death, her response was "So? Who cares. He was a perfect shit."

Keeping
the
Faith

Autumn fell on Eduardo like wet leaves in an early Nor'easter. It had always been his favorite season: Nature dying, but dying with trumpets and rockets, setting the sky on fire, once more declaring the Eternal Promise. In any other year it would have been a sure demonstration of renewal. Instead, as he drove along the Mohawk Trail toward Boston, the exuberant trees seem to whisper to him of his failure, waving damning banners of peach and burgundy, olive, tangerine, and saffron. Amidst their colors he had been moldering like compost, blanketed in a slimy self-pity.

He thought of fall as he drove. Fall. A fall. Like tumbling down a spiral staircase. He had not responded to Autumn's invitation, but merely let it blow him eastward or wherever the wind willed. There was nothing particularly waiting for him in Boston, but neither was there anything for him in his tiny apartment back in Leominster. He simply drove and brooded. He knew he was not, as his social-worker cousin would say, "at risk," but merely at low ebb. To Eduardo Ribiera, suicide would have been an act of declaration, of will, an act beyond the reach of his malaise.

Eduardo parked the truck in a corner of the shopping

center lot at Fresh Pond, saving himself a modest parking fee that was bigger than his food budget for the day, and trudged guiltily over the rusty footbridge to pick up the Red Line for Boston. Coming out from Park Street Under in time to see the lights on the Commons come on, he started walking without purpose or direction, letting the many little streets lead him around and away and back.

He was no longer in the downtown he knew, but the area had the familiar feel of one of those someplaces just around the corner from someplace else that he would recognize. He kept walking.

The crawling red dots of a cheap computer-driven display drew his attention. "Our Lady of New Beginnings," it said. Forgotten between a warehouse and a garage, with a steeple and round windows of colored glass, but only a single story high and barely a dozen feet wide, was a church. "Our Lady of New Beginnings." It sounded almost Catholic, as a parody might, stirring up vague resentment in Eduardo.

Nominally, he was Catholic, although he didn't think of himself in those terms, not even as a lapsed Catholic. His grandparents from the Azores had been both devout and observant, but the Portuguese always mixed their metaphors and their religious referents. Eduardo's father, Roberto, a boat captain and a philosopher with a mind as sharp as a fishhook, had looked upon the inconsistent chowder of his family's beliefs and heaved the whole thing into the sea. Roberto had believed in the random violence of the sea and the unpredictable benevolence of the winds as others might believe in the Savior—with a passion.

But Eduardo, who was possibly even a few points more intelligent than his father, had truly wanted to believe, had endured the ridicule of his father to study the catechism, and had failed. He could recall the precise moment of his failure, the beginning of the end of his faith. His science class had been on a field trip to the salt marshes, led by a Jesuit biologist from St. Theresa's.

Eduardo had hung back to talk with Brother Mark.

"This," he waved at the marsh, the stream, the purple loosestrife at its edge, "this makes sense. I see it and can believe. Logically, rationally, there must be a god behind it all. It's this Jesus stuff that's so hard to swallow." Had he intended to shock, or was he testing? It was never clear to him. But Brother Mark looked at him as if sharing a delicious secret.

"There are Deists among the Brothers, also, my bright young friend. There are worse fates."

Perhaps it had been meant to be reassuring, but in that moment Eduardo had felt something ominous, like a great black wave washing through his mind. He knew, with some prescient certainty, that questioning the Son was, for him, only the first step toward questioning the Father. One day he would no longer believe.

Ultimately, he had proved himself right. Yet out of his empty non-belief he had molded something solid and alive with energy, with passion for life and living, for persons and for personhood. "What do I believe in?" he would say. "I believe in you, and I believe in me. And in the power of us." He never owned another ism. Humankind had become the priesthood and the godhead of his unnamed hierarchy.

Then there were the losses.

Too many losses, he thought, as he stood watching the dotted red words crawl past, over and over. First Mona had left. Now the boys were gone. He was permitted to see Robbie on alternate weekends, but Robbie was always reminding him of things promised, and the reminders were growing too painful as the weeks between visits built into months of silence. Even in his mind, Eduardo could no longer see his son, not Robbie standing in the driveway, not an image with edges or color, only an uncertain monochrome snap: "the son I once had." But Joseph, sweet Joey, trouble-making Joe, he could see anytime. He could not call up these images by number or still-frame them at just the right moment as he could with a VCR. A memory of Joey diving into the pile of maple leaves might melt into one of him lying, unmoving, in the street, the halo of blood slowly expanding around his head. So he tried not to think of Joey, and the trying had become, in time, a part of the growing blackness in him.

At least there was his work, he had said, as the losses piled up. But Allotech Enterprises filed for Chapter II, and even in the great land of the Second Massachusetts Miracle there were specialties in which jobs were scarce. He despecialized, tried thin-film deposition, learned to like beer, switched jobs again when his probation period netted a one-percent raise. He proudly told cousins he was coping, but in a year and a half he had parlayed a CalTech degree and a quick mind to work himself all the way from a seventy-K engineering job to eighteen-five as a driver for Addaso Plastics. He drove his own pickup, drove, the pickup he had left at the shopping center, precision-machined nylon gears that should have gone to one of the robot labs in Maynard still piled in the open bed of the truck. He was past caring, almost past feeling.

He stared at the church.

The double doors stayed closed but inviting. New Beginnings. Old endings. Eduardo worked the thumb latch and pulled one door open.

The interior looked like no church he had seen. A row of desks were lined up along the left wall, each with a phone, each with an ivory or gray computer screen on it. A bank of relay racks filled with computer and communications equipment stood against the other wall. The desks were empty except for the nearest. A plastic name plate said, "Mr. Timothy."

The man behind the desk looked up expectantly at Eduardo, who answered a question that had not even been asked.

"I believed in God, once. Until it stopped making sense to me." Eduardo thought the man might say something then, but he only nodded and waited, looking somehow like a priest in shirt sleeves and a loosened paisley tie. "I mean, the odds, the odds are so enormously against it. And there's all these people, so many each claiming to have the One Truth."

Eduardo blinked. This was absurd. But the tape was running, and he couldn't stop.

"It was no loss, see, because I believed in myself. I believed in the power of the human mind and of human love and human cooperation. I was still a believer, but my faith was in what I could see and in what lay within what I could see. I believed in me."

"And now?"

"See, it's a crisis of faith. How can I believe in me any- more. I see through the thin fabric of my own altar cloth. There's no hardwood underneath. Everything I do fails. Or it's empty, pointless. I look around, view the world, and I know it's no more than a worldview, something I constructed, like a circuit on a prototyping board. I build one reality, you build another. Either of us could have construed this whole bedeviled universe some other way, and it would be no less real. That's all we know. I saw myself as a winner. Now I know better."

He stopped, blinked, and looked around. "So what is this place? What religion are you selling."

"We custom design belief on demand, religions by re- quest."

"You're shittin' me."

"The gods' truth."

Eduardo's jaw shook with the chill draft slinking under the door. "How could anyone believe in something you just invent?"

"And why not? Didn't you just now say they're all merely invented. And we do more than design reli- gions—we make converts."

"How?"

"That's not even the hard part. We get it right in the first place; the conversion just happens. We are, you might say, an engineering firm; we engineer a religion uniquely suited to you, something you can put your faith in. Believe me, I'm giving it to you straight."

Eduardo's teeth clamped and unclamped. He could leave. He should leave, he thought. The man was a nut case. Or a salesman for some nut scheme. But Eduardo stood there in front of Mr. Timothy in the Church of

New Beginnings and asked another question.

"How can you keep the faith in something like that?"

"What the hell is faith? It's an idea, right? Just a construct, really, a hypothesis. What makes faith special is that it is a vessel, the vessel that holds those hypotheses that are never truly questioned, the assumptions not tested. What we choose to believe in, we put for safekeeping in that vessel. Because, as long as it is to remain faith, we pull our punches. We may speak of someone whose faith was challenged or was tested, but against our own faith we never bring to bear the full force of intellect or experiment or rhetoric or whatever is our own best resource. Each person has limits; you gotta learn to recognize and respect yours. To keep the faith, you simply never turn all that you have against yourself. You can't win that war.

"So, I guess the answer must be: you keep faith in your custom-engineered religion as anyone else keeps the faith in theirs. You see, Mr.—"

"Ribiera, Eduardo."

"Mr. Ribiera, I respect you, so I will speak plainly. We have perfected the technology of conversion. And what believer is more zealous, more secure in their belief, than the convert? But I don't try to convert you to my way of thinking, I convert you to your own way. Where else are you going to get that? Everyone is out to make you think like them, looking for followers, new acolytes. Not me."

Eduardo thought the man sounded like a salesman again, but said, "It's that easy?"

"Oh, don't get me wrong, true faith is neither easy nor does it come cheap."

Eduardo nodded, knowing that the bottom line was coming.

"When you want the best you pay for it; we are well paid for what we do. Consider it an investment, an investment in yourself."

"How big an investment?"

The man told him, and Eduardo promised he would get it. Somehow.

¤ ¤ ¤

Eduardo found his way back to the subway station, thinking about the Church of New Beginnings and Mr. Timothy's promise. It was impossible, of course. He didn't have the kind of money they wanted, which was as much as his pickup was worth. And besides, he kept thinking, they only took my name and address, only my name and address. How are they going to know how to design a religion for me with only my name and address? They should be doing testing or something. The more he thought about it, the more it nagged at him.

That night, he fixed himself a can of stew for dinner, read the paper he'd rescued from the subway, and went to bed.

¤ ¤ ¤

It must have been after three in the morning when Eduardo gave up on trying to sleep and got up to turn on the television. A late-late talk show was on. He didn't recognize the host, one of the new breed of right-wingers specializing in abrasive sarcasm. The guest was Eduardo Ribiera.

This is how they do it. Clever. They beam their religious propaganda right to your TV. That's why they need your address. No, they couldn't do that, not technically feasible. And the tape of him: how'd they get that? No, this had to be a dream; he was still asleep.

On-screen, Eduardo turned toward the camera and said, "The answer lies in bed."

Hey, is this going to be one of those erratic dreams? Eduardo thought.

"You mean erotic. They're all erratic. You're the one who makes them mean something. Remember, Eduardo Ribiera, this is your life. The universe is random, at least to you. So what are you going to make of it?"

I'm going to look in the bed.

He looked. Eduardo Ribiera lay in bed.

¤ ¤ ¤

Weeks had passed, but he knew he had to go back the Church. He had done what he needed to do, the difficult, even quixotic, thing. Now, as he walked from the T stop, he could feel the heat trapped against his chest. He carried his truck in his shirt pocket—a cashier's check.

You don't have to be a True Believer to believe in honesty and fairness, he said to himself. They had promised and delivered; he had done neither. Now he would restore his karmic balance.

He rounded the corner and approached the church. The double doors were locked and nobody answered when he rattled them. He paced back and forth, as if pacing might change something, but the doors remained locked.

By the time Mr. Timothy finally showed up, Eduardo wasn't the only one waiting to enter. Mr. Timothy grinned at Eduardo and reached for his keys.

The next man in line said, "What's this guy babbling about? You didn't really offer to design him a religion, did you."

"Hey, listen, you always give them what they want," Mr. Timothy answered. "That's what business is about."

Eduardo stood in the doorway with the check in his hand, shame creeping into his face.

The man he knew only as Mr. Timothy shook his head and pushed away the check. "We don't take checks. Take it someplace else. Consider it an investment, an investment in yourself."

Eduardo was puzzled. "What about you."

"Me? Hey, I ain't the one who lacks faith. I believe. I believe in the moment, in the rebirth within every minute." He smirked as he spoke.

"It's hard to picture you that way."

"What? You want to see me on my knees in grateful prayer to saint P.T. Barnum? Look, son, you don't need what we're selling. You already got the answers." He swung open the doors. Inside were rows and rows of poker machines. The place, the Church, was nothing more than a hole-in-the-wall illegal gambling joint.

"I just don't get it," Eduardo said, shaking his head. "Where are all the computers? How did you do it? How did you hack into my TV? How did you send those images to me?"

"Kid, I have no fuckin' idea what you are talking about." He looked at the others in line, now impatient to get on with the pursuit of their dreams, the pursuit of redemption in hands of virtual playing cards. "Would you believe this guy? What does he think he'd find here?" They laughed as they pushed past Eduardo.

As the last of the patrons filed in to seek out their seats at their favorite machines, Mr. Timothy turned back to

Eduardo and gave him a slow wink. "Keep the faith," he said. "Keep the faith!"

Eduardo walked slowly, deliberately back toward Boston Commons. The trees in the park were just past their peak of color, and suddenly the beauty of it seemed almost too much to bear. Some lines of an old poem came to him, one of his own, an over-written work from the troubled passion of his early twenties.

> Even over the hill, the birds will cry their joy
> and fill the wind and breezes toying with the trees.
> What greens this planet has to please,
> grass and trees that pummel the eye with verdant
>   luxury.
> And fall, when Nature dies,
> But death does not come quietly.
> In one last joyful surge
> She sets the sky ablaze,
> As if to say:
> I live, I die,
> But, happy to have lived, I fly
> Once more through windswept seas of airy rapture.
> Yet, I will with bittersweet depart this world I loved
>   so much—
> And God, oh God, how deep I loved—
> long embracing hours and years,
> the burning color of fresh air,
> the aftertaste robust and clear.
> Yes, I will with bittersweet:
> the sweet for all the sweet before
> and not-sweet for the sweet no more.

I'm a convert all right, he thought, a true believer. Aloud, resolutely, but to no one in particular, he said, "It's good to be alive!" As he fumbled for his subway token, he added, in a whisper too soft to be heard by anyone else, "Keep the faith."

Death Rehearsal

More tests. Another tedious day of testing.

Day? What was a day, anyway? Taylor had no way of knowing what was day, what night. Sometimes he slept, sometimes he was awakened when he did not expect. Some periods he passed in what seemed interminable hours with nothing to do but think of what was happening to him, what happened, why he was there, paralyzed, staring at the ceiling. Thinking, thinking with some difficulty. Memories, even some words, eluded him or would come crashing in like a rogue wave, an unbidden flood of ideas, images, feelings.

He sensed that someone was in the room with him. A nurse? One of the doctors? A researcher? He assumed he was in a hospital but was unsure. Maybe a rehab facility? But why?

Now there were voices, saying something. He could hear some of it, but not well. There was something wrong with his hearing, and sounds seemed as if he had ear plugs in and could hear with only one ear.

"So, what's on the schedule today?" Siobhan Hempel had seniority and towered over her younger Project Lead, but she tried always to respect the title and sustain some semblance of deference.

Mal Shearwater looked up from his tablet. "Ramirez wants to push forward on the motor-strip analysis." Iona Ramirez, the octogenarian Research Director and one of the leading neuroscientists in the world, called the shots. "I told her that we thought analyzing vocal formant processing and the myoelectric inputs from the vocal tract would be a faster route to speech equivalent, but she said the point was to establish protocol and refine techniques, not to get the specimen verbal. She wants to optimize the signal processing strategy so it can be routinized to simplify future research."

Shearwater handed the tablet computer to Hempel without looking at her, which would have required craning his neck from his five-two perspective to her six-ten. In an era when the median height for males was six-six, he was a runt, ever conscious of his stature and always reaching and striving to compensate. Even his wife looked down on him, although she insisted it never mattered. And there were those times when his head in the middle of her chest was a match to be savored. "How does the specimen look? Holding up?"

Hempel took the tablet from him and started entering notes as she answered. "BP and O2 are good, no new losses according to last images. We've managed workarounds for the neurological deficits in the motor strip and Broca's. I'd say we're good to go. What say we push it a bit, maybe up the repetitions. We can start with the Simple Object slide deck, cut the interval between images with the same exposure time, and use the new analysis algorithm. We'll repeat images at randomized increasing intervals to maximize the learning effect." To Taylor, poised on the edge of sleep, the discussion was an articulated buzz that might as well have been a recitation of Swahili poetry.

Hempel looked up from her notes. "We'll finish the training yet. Shall I bring the specimen around?" She readjusted two sliders on the tablet and leaned over the table. "Time to open your eyes. We have work to do."

"Can't see you on that side," Mal said. "You're beyond the medial line. Come around here."

"I keep forgetting about the hemispherical blindness."

Taylor heard what was said but could not parse all of it. The brain damage that had obliterated nearly half of his left hemisphere meant he had only half a visual field and diminished awareness of the world on his right. His language abilities were also impaired. The full meaning of what was said sometimes hovered just beyond reach. At times, he even found himself thinking in the German he had learned while in the army and stationed in Europe. Somehow that seemed easier than understanding the heavily accented English used by those around him. He didn't recognize the accent.

Shearwater shrugged. "Okay, let's get the specimen over to the UFFI lab." UFFI, Ultra Fine Functional Imaging, was the technology that allowed Ramirez and her cadre of post-docs to see in real-time and fine detail what was going on inside the brain. It had revolutionized neuroscience and medicine and had been refined over a half-century of R&D into a reliable and precision tool, but it had also defied all attempts at miniaturization. Each of the four imaging machines in the UFFI lab took up an entire room and consumed as much power as the entire rest of the building.

Almost as soon as they wheeled the cart into Suite B at

the UFFI lab, the imaging technician started recitation of her standard protocol. "You will hear some loud noises; do not be alarmed. It is important the you remain still while in the machine. You—"

"This one can't move." Siobhan interrupted. "Obviously. And probably didn't hear you, since you're standing on the wrong side." She patted the left side of her head. "Mostly gone."

"Then why use the . . ."

"You never know until you bring them out. Ramirez figures half a brain is better than none, and besides, we had already gone through all the revival/recovery rigmarole. Sunk cost. You're new, right? I'm Siobhan, Siobhan Hempel."

"Adrianna Breitman. Hi."

"Well, Adrianna, you may not yet have heard what a tight ass Ramirez is when it comes to the budget. This business is expensive."

"But there's not exactly a shortage of specimens."

"True, but we're tied to the calendar. Because of the Supreme Court ruling, anything less than a hundred years back is off limits, and the odds are always better with the more recent ones, so everybody doing this work is fishing in the same pool, a hundred to a hundred ten years ago."

The technician smiled. "Yeah, ice fishing."

"Ha ha. Good one. Let's get started with this one." She leaned in close to the table and raised her voice some. "So, here's what we need you to do today." She waited to see the eyes shift first toward her, then back to a point near her left ear. "We're going to show you a series of images of common objects. As soon as you identify what the object is, we want you to pretend to say the name of the object. Don't try to say the name out loud; it will only frustrate and confuse you, since you can't speak. Just imagine saying it to yourself, subvocalize. If you don't recognize something, just say no. Well, I mean imagine yourself saying no. Got it? Okay, into the machine. It's listening to your thoughts and will let us know what you are trying to say, but it takes time and lots of practice to get it right."

The technician rolled the unit into the UFFI and tapped the icon to start the baseline reading. "Are you going to hang around?"

"No, Mal Shearwater, my Lead, wants me to rerun stats on the last series. And I'm behind on reading for my Boards. I'll be back in"—she checked the clock on her tablet—"let's call it a little shy of two hours. If there are problems with the life support, hit the Safe Shutdown button before calling in the code, okay? And only then ping our lab. We don't do medicine. That's Cryo, and we're Neuro."

¤ ¤ ¤

Taylor tried to keep track of days and weeks, but the tests dragged on beyond his mental count. Sometimes he imagined himself yelling his response, sometimes he punched the air in his mind, sometimes he retreated into sullen disregard. And there was the fury. He could become overcome with rage, red with flames of anger at himself, at the technicians, the researchers. It was not like him. Losing control like that was alien to his very makeup. He had always been Mister Even Temper, methodical and unflappable, even in the most vexing situations. He wondered if maybe personality changes might have anything to do with the left hemisphere damage he kept hearing mentioned. What had happened, he wondered.

Slowly he came to realize what was going on. They were not so much training him as training their machines to read his thoughts. It took many rounds to build up reliable pattern recognition. Despite the limitations in his hearing and vision, he was beginning to make sense of his surroundings and to puzzle out what had happened.

A lot of time had passed, and his memories returned only slowly and then unreliably and unbidden, like a badly edited music video, flashing from scene to foreshortened scene with little regard for order even as the rhythm of a drum kit in the background continued the beat.

He could talk now—or something closely approximating talking. He could not always hear himself, but when he imagined himself speaking out loud, he could hear people responding to him—or maybe it was the machines. He had learned that he had a cochlear implant and now wore a web of electrodes on his shaved head. Only his vision was unmediated by electronics, and that, too, was messed up. He saw and experienced only half a world. It was not as if he had blinders on blocking his sight, more as if there were a hole on one side of the world, one that moved with his eyes. He could move his eyes—and his tongue and lips—but nothing else.

He also remembered who he was. He was Taylor Baustein, and Baustein Building and Reno, LLC, was his, the small company he had built from scratch. He had nearly two hundred employees. Had. Once. A long time ago. He suspected that Baustein Building and Reno was long gone.

He asked questions, but mostly they went unanswered. Only Adrianna, the UFFI technician, ever had real conversations with him, and she had been reprimanded when Hempel had once returned late after a training session and heard them talking. "We don't encourage conversation with Cubes. They're just subjects of the investigation. It can inject uncontrolled factors into the experiments, and, well . . . I don't need to spell it out in too fine a detail, now do I? No."

Conversation helped. Parts of his life returned, like objects becoming visible along a fog-bound roadway. While talking with Adrianna, he had remembered his wife, although he still could not recall her name. It was frustrating. He knew they had a child named Devin, although he could not be sure whether Devin was a girl or a boy. He remembered his own fortieth birthday for no special reason. He had spent it on a tower crane substituting for an operator who had called in sick.

There was another memory of a tower crane, but it blurred into foggy unreality whenever he tried to focus on it.

"What happened?" he asked Adrianna. "The accident. I don't remember. How did I end up paralyzed?"

"You're not . . . Look, I'm just an imaging technician. I like my work and I don't want my hours cut. Working is better than not working, any day. I shouldn't even be talking with you. Frankly, it can be a little creepy at times, but I . . ." She turned away and busied herself with confirming the setup for the next imaging run.

"Am I, uh, disfigured?"

She looked up from the control panel, but he didn't notice because she was on his right side.

"You didn't answer," he said. "Or I couldn't hear you."

She walked around to his good side. "You don't get it, do you? No. I suppose not, and that's for the better. The grant on this phase runs only to October. Look, let's just accomplish what we can while we can." She looked down at her tablet and started reading out the instructions for the next experiment.

¤ ¤ ¤

Throughout the rest of August, Taylor shifted focus, spending less time trying to recall memories that defied revival and paying closer attention to what was happening around him and in him. It no longer surprised him that he had no feeling below the point where the collar of his dress shirts used to irritate his neck, but he was perturbed that he could neither hear nor feel his heartbeat. "Why is it, doc, that I can't feel my heartbeat?"

Shearwater, busy with something on the bedside console, ignored him until the question was repeated. "It's an impellor," he said, "not a reciprocating pump. Continuous flow, so no pulse."

Taylor wanted to ask more, but Shearwater was already on his way out of the room. It was mid-September before the pieces fell into place, and then it came tumbling down on him like the shell of a building in a demolition implosion. He was reviewing what he could remember about the construction business and his financial struggles when he remembered an argument with his wife, whom he could sometimes picture but still never name. It was a fight over how he spent his money, and an odd word kept playing in his mind: cryonics.

"When did I die?" he asked Hempel. They had fixed the audio feedback so that he could hear himself, and now he heard the abrupt, accusatory tone in his question.

Hempel was so taken aback that she answered without thinking. "I don't know, like, over a hundred years ago. That's the law. I suppose it . . ." She caught herself and didn't finish.

"I'm not paralyzed, am I? Something went wrong with the new body. I'm supposed to—"

"There's no new . . ." Again, she didn't finish.

"It's in the contract. I signed the contract. I couldn't afford the whole-body version, so I paid to have my head frozen, preserved. But they said that by the time I was brought back, a complete body transplant would surely be routine. It was all spelled out, in perpetuity." He could see her mouth slacken, as if shock had taken the words from her. Then she was gone.

In the morning, Shearwater was there first, briefing him on the emotion-loaded-images test scheduled for the day. "Well, are we all ready to go?"

"I don't think so, doc. Until I get some answers and some satisfaction, no more experiments, no more cooperation."

Shearwater exhaled, a long and deliberately loud sigh. "That would not be good, not for the project and most certainly not for you. Some of the data on incomplete runs would have to be discarded altogether. It takes weeks to bring another specimen fully online from cryogenic storage. Plus, a premature termination does not look good on the lab's record. Ramirez would be livid over it.

"We can always turn to pharmaceuticals to force . . .

to get what we can, but that upends the experimental design and throws our findings into a whole different category. Performance under drugs is just not baseline, and its baseline signal processing that we're trying to refine. Look, why don't you just relax and enjoy the ride while it lasts?"

"And how long is that?"

"Well, I imagine you are growing a little weary of the tests. I mean, lying in the UFFI half the day is probably not your idea of a party, but it beats the alternative, doesn't it? And it's not going to last much longer. We should be done in six weeks, seven at the tops."

"And then what?"

"Then?" Shearwater weighed his words. "We'll discuss 'then' when we get to then. Don't stress over any of this. Listen, if you want a little mood boost, that's only a push-button away. Let's get past this next round, and then I'll see if I can get Ramirez to okay some Ensoluvine at the end of each day. You'll feel ever so much better."

"I don't want happy pills, I want what I paid for."

"What you paid for? That was over and done with long, long ago. Most of the cryonic preservation companies simply faded away during the Great Retrenchment. Then the law was changed, and that was that. If it wasn't for the University and the New Federation grants, none of this would be possible. So you're lucky to—"

"Lucky to what? Be alive? Lucky to be alive? Yeah, right."

"Not exactly. You're not alive. You're dead. You died"— he checked his tablet— "just over a hundred-and-five years ago. It's a matter of record and a legal certainty. The University and the New Federation government are

very careful about such matters. Research on the de-
ceased is heavily regulated, but it's nowhere near as hard
as with live subjects."

"But I'm alive, and you have responsibilities under the
law. You—"

"Please, please. Laws change. In your day, women
could vote. In your grandfather's day neither women nor
slaves could vote."

"You make it sound as if women no longer can vote."

"Of course not. Nobody votes. That's too inefficient
and too easily manipulated, as I'm sure you were beginning to realize, even back in your day. But look, modern
politics would be too hard to explain and would make
no difference to you in any case. As I said, legally you're
dead. You've been reanimated for research purposes and
will be humanely terminated when no longer needed.

"Now, I have a meeting with Ramirez at which I will
raise the question of mood elevators. Here." He tapped
out a short sequence on the bedside console. "That
should help you nap until we're ready for the tests later
today."

"I don't want anything to help me sleep. I just . . ."

◻ ◻ ◻

Adrianna was not happy with him. "Look, you're not trying. I can see from the real-time activity map that you're
not cooperating."

"No, I'm not cooperating. I've had it. I know my rights.
This is involuntary servitude. Surely, even with the—
what do you call it?—New Federation government, you
can't enslave a person."

"But you're not a person. You are a reanimated neuro-
biological research specimen. And if I check the right

box—well, really the wrong box—on three successive days, that's it. Fini."

"Nazis! You did this to my people once before, kept some of them alive as *sonder commandos*, others as research subjects, but only as long as convenient. When they were no longer useful, that was it, off to the gas chambers."

"Oh please. I learned about all that in elementary school. Ancient history. It's hardly the same. Those were people."

"I'm a person."

"That's what you think—or say. In a sense, you're imagining you're alive, but you've been dead a very long time, and now medical science has thawed out your dead brain and tricked it into functioning again, at least partially. Even in your day, they did something like that with pigs. But it's not real."

"But I signed up to be preserved, forever. Well, until medical science could bring me back to life."

"The courts have long ruled that contracts with no termination date are invalid and unenforceable. And cryonics was first discredited and then outlawed. It did not ever really work the way it claimed. Most of the time, we get a useless organ, not even a semiconscious research specimen. Your case is a rarity, and that still gives us only half a brain to work with. But still, we got a lot this time, real progress was made. At least you have that."

"I have more than that. I have free will."

Adrianna laughed. "So you think. Don't we all. But who really knows? Now, are you going to be a good little Ice Cube and finish the experiment?"

"No."

¤ ¤ ¤

The technician with the Cryo Department patch on his jump suit rolled the unit through the double doors.

Shearwaterr looked up from his notes. "What's this?"

"New specimen. Donnelly didn't get her grant renewed in time, so we have this one as surplus and didn't want to send it over to disposal just after recovery."

"What's the inventory?"

"It's a pretty clean specimen, probably some visual scotomas, losses in prefrontal cortex and right hippo-campus, but not bad."

"Okay, you can take that one with you."

"Not without paperwork, I can't. Human remains, you know."

"Yeah, I know. Funny we still call it paperwork. Frankly, I haven't seen a piece of paper more than a dozen times since I started working at the lab."

The technician pointed to the head atop the now silent unit. "How'd this one buy it? Do we know?"

"A tower crane. You know, one of those old-style construction rigs. It collapsed with him in it."

The technician looked over Shearwater's shoulder. "Wow, he died in 2012, the year I was born. Lotta people back then took the sucker bet, didn't they."

"Yeah. 2012, huh. You thinking about retiring any time soon?"

"Naw, I figure I got a few years left. Afterwards, without work, the boredom kills ya anyway. You done with the form?"

"Just about." Under Disposition, Shearwater checked the box for "dignified disposal of human remains" and scrolled down. Under Reason, he wrote "specimen no longer functional" and pressed his thumb to the screen to authenticate his digital signature. He tapped on the Termination icon, confirmed the action by entering his passcode, and pressed his thumb to the screen again.

Taylor Baustein's long frozen brain was anesthetized almost instantly before the synth-heme flow was cut. Over a century after his death and the cryonic preservation of his head, it had been used in legally sanctioned medical experiments that advanced the state of the art in neuroscience and led directly or indirectly to dozens of scientific papers. The head was disposed of with dignity after it was no longer experimentally useful.

Equation
Fourteen

Tenra stood on the bridge, dead-center in an area the size of a small stadium, looking up and around, transfixed by the violence and the beauty outside her domed window on the universe. Swirls of color, wheels of light too intense to look at directly for more than seconds, met spires of green and violet that bloomed and arched in a desperate dance. More than aesthetic apprehension, she watched for pattern and its absence, for shape and rhythm, drawing on her training to extract meaning from the seemingly meaningless. This was her job, her profession, the task for which she had been born and to which she had devoted the centuries of her life, to be here, one of The Last, the handful of the Nineteen Peoples watching the dying universe.

Vesnio, as always a few minutes late in relieving her, entered the bridge and started an unhurried stroll to the center. As he approached, she flashed him a smile, then returned to her open-mouth staring as, overhead, super-massive black holes spiraled into each other, merging to bend farther the fabric of space-time, sending tsunamis of gravity waves outward at the speed of light. Monstrous bodies without names gorged on the last of the galaxies and belched high-energy jets everywhere.

It was an illusion, of course, a hemispherical screen that filled the dome of the bridge, a false-color display processed in real-time by supercomputers fed data from arrays of sensors and imagers, terabytes per second that were transformed by higher math into a single presentation. The universe was dying—that was no illusion, although what she saw had already happened long ago because they were still bound by ordinary physics—but the dying throes were not above her but beneath her feet, far beneath, on the other side of her planetoid chariot still accelerating at normal gravity, running away from the holocaust beneath at a large fraction of the speed of light, even as space itself would soon be rushing inward, wrapped and warped by the deepening distortion surrounding the monster of monsters behind her.

Vesnio reached her side, put his arm around her waist, and stood watching with her for several minutes. "The closer to The Time, the faster it changes. Already it seems to become more awesome with every day, doesn't it?" he said.

She nodded and stroked his head. "Vesnio, I do miss you. These alternating watches are becoming a strain."

"You're the captain. If you want to change the schedule so we share some watches you need only say the word."

"The burden of command." She laughed. "Sometimes I forget who is in charge, what I can do." She gestured to raise the work console from the floor. "Sometimes I think it is Adamah who is charge." She patted the console. "As a thoroughly modern captain, I will let the crew decide the new schedule." She turned the keyboard toward him.

Vesnio reached past her to type a few rapid strokes on the keypad. "There, the crew has decided. It was unanimous."

"Wait, you only keyed . . ."

"A new watch schedule I had already programmed at the ready. I knew, of course, that about now you would grow weary of the separation."

"And I should have known that you would have anticipated by setting something up in advance."

"Oh, you already knew. You just hadn't thought about it."

Like their quarters below, like the controls on the bridge and below, they were a matched set, inseparable since their days at the Academy. Alike and different, they were like clasped hands. She could recall the every detail of their meeting, and he could bring laughter and tears to them both with his dramatized and over-simplified synopses.

It had been at the second lecture of a mandatory course in Historical Physics, and the largest hall on campus was nearly full. Vesnio rushed in, scanned for an open seat higher up, and nearly tripped over Tenra sitting in the front row. He started to apologize but never got past, "I beg . . ."

"Here, this seat is open. I'll move my things."

"But you were saving the seat for someone. Who?"

"You."

He stood then, towering over her, studying her face, trying to recall when or how they might have met, certain that he knew her, and reveling in the familiarity that he could not explain.

"Last week," she said. "You did the same thing. Are you

always a last-minute student?"

"Always. It works for me."

"And me. Now you will have to sit here with me. I'm Tenra, Tenra Loudian Makepeace."

"Vesnio ver-Houdi." He reached out, his mocha hand wrapping around the red-brown of hers. "So, I see we are both descendants of the New Earth Diaspora."

"Far enough back, I suppose, a million years or more."

"Boring stuff, this." He flicked his fingers toward the lecture table. "Taught in the old style. For 'authenticity' I suppose." His voice dripped sarcasm. "What's your major? I'm doing Applied Hypermaths, specializing in Third Cosmology."

"Yes, I know. I looked you up in the Catalog. I'm in History, specializing in Intellectual Archeology. I love this course, the way it recapitulates the upward struggle through the millennia, the way so many of the Nineteen Peoples fell into the same intellectual traps, made the same mistakes in research and theory building, but ultimately found their way forward. That's what is so wonderful about science, that it corrects itself."

"Yes, and finally we get it right. Now we know."

"That, my cocky Mr. ver-Houdi, is precisely why this is a required course." She smiled up at him. "The lesson of history is not about what they got wrong or didn't know, but to remind us that much of what we think we know must also be wrong or incomplete or flawed. Take your cosmology, for instance."

"And a good instance that. How could the Primitives get so many things wrong? Two equally precise measures of the age of the universe off by more than a billion years, nearly a five-sigma disparity? And then the so-called standard candles to estimate cosmic distances—what a joke—wildly misunderstood. And the whole dark-matter/dark-energy debacle, endless speculations and equations about the untestable. It was laughable."

"And what about the failed New Standard Model or the discredited Big Rip/Big Bounce cosmology?" she asked.

"That was several thousand years ago, now we know better. It's more complicated, and we now have the tools. Hypermath, observations from the Remove—the list is long."

"And what will we know better in another thousand years? Which of your established truths will have proven false?"

"You, Ms. Makepeace, are infuriating." He took the seat beside her. "I entered the hall a confident man and in a few minutes you have reduced me to little more than a dung heap of doubt."

"Good. Then we will get along just fine." She squeezed his hand and looked up as the team of professors entered. "Now, listen and learn," she whispered.

¤ ¤ ¤

On the bridge, their quiet moment was interrupted by another alert from Adamah, the computer complex that accounted for nearly a third of the mass of the ship. They both read the message and studied the graph that accompanied it, then simultaneously reached to press the key to dismiss it.

"Do you ever wonder why we're here?" he said. "It's not like we are really needed. With that single exception—what was it, five years ago—all we do is confirm or acknowledge what the computers conclude or decide."

"That single exception is the answer to your question."

"A trivial correction that sooner or later would have been caught by one of the other Stations or by the linked computer systems. Or by the Remove."

"The Remove can watch, but they can't intervene, not on any scale that matters. You know that." Most of their generation had elected to enter The Remove, melding their minds with those of all who had gone before into the diffuse gossamer of the energy matrix, the universe-spanning meta-mind that had first worked out the tools of hypermath and made the observations that led to Project End Game. There were those who believed that the incorporeal multitudes of The Remove could—would—survive the End Game. The physics was ambiguous and had resisted exact solution even under the onslaught of the combined genius of The Remove and the computational juggernauts that were the supercomputers of the Nineteen Peoples.

"We are here," she said, "because we are human, because we are the universe becoming aware of itself, and because we have this in-built need to know and to have agency, however small."

"You sound like Professor Dinnailla."

"Of course I do, because I paid attention in class while you doodled hypermath equations and drew Feigelmann charts. She was right, you know, about us, about all the Nineteen Peoples and why we are doing the Project."

"I am doing the Project because of you." He kissed her and ran his hand through her ochre hair.

She gave him a quick hug, then looked once more toward the simulated sky overhead. "Enough gawking and gossiping," she said. "We have work to do, even if it is mostly make-work." A hand gesture raised the second work console from the floor, and they began their regular handoff task of checking the numbers, reading reports, responding to flags and alerts, working their way through a script of tasks as if they were administrators in some planetary bureaucracy, little more than pursers or mates on some cosmic cruise liner.

She smiled at the thought. It was at once valid and not. Alone—vast though it was, with even greater resources at its disposal—their Station could do little. But it was not alone. To the side of the console display were the scrolling messages from the others, the crews of all ninety-one of the Stations, the ships, like theirs, charged with watching, with oversight of the dying universe. Some had started on their journeys into position many millennia before; some, like hers had been propelled on station by shorter routes only centuries earlier.

She scanned the text messages. The ansibles that linked the ninety-one ships were a technology developed and bequeathed to them by a race far older than any of the Nineteen Peoples. By ansible, communication was instantaneous but limited in bandwidth, text only.

"Morning, Bleth. Hope U slept gr8 last nite?"

"Yo, Tenra. Xtra cuddl w/ Deaver helped. o from the Tactielles yet. Hope . . ."

It was chit-chat, galactic gossip abbreviated in texting-style, giving them a limited but vital sense of connection, though they were scattered across much of the universe. Most were crewed by small teams of couples, friends, and lovers. That should have been her fate, too, but just before the launch, Sadla and Yevuni had decided to join The Remove, and Tenra and Vesnio had opted to crew as a solo couple.

"You have always been single-minded," her father had said not long before his own departure to The Remove. "You have to learn everything the hard way, on your own, from your own experience. It was a miracle you and Vesnio found each other."

"It was no miracle, father, though it might have been destined. We sought each other. From the time we each entered the Academy, we were looking, and once we saw each other in that class in Historical Physics, we knew, instantly. Neither of us doubted, and there was, from that moment, no other."

"It is an old-fashioned sort of bond that few today would recognize," her father said. "Your mother and I thought we had something like that, but we were wrong. Still, I miss her and think of her, though I would not take her back any more than she would recommit to me. We are both better this way, better suited to a more fluid life, a life with the riches of many connections."

"For you, father, I am happy, but that's not who I am."

"No, and that was clear even when you were a child, even as you played in the schoolyard. You would always be on the Play Mountain, climbing alone, or swimming down the Channel while others ran laughing along the bank. You were always off in your own world."

¤ ¤ ¤

A blue warning popped up on Tenra's work console jarring her back to the present. "And now here I am, off in my own little world, captain of all I survey, master of the universe—and nothing."

"What?" Vesnio said. "You are master of me, remember, o captain, my captain." It had not surprised anyone when she was appointed captain of Station 17, and

Vesnio had never been bothered by the choice. She was the one who was grounded; he was the thinker always off in the clouds of his equations. She was decisive but deliberate; he could be at once both indecisive and impulsive. Together, they were a team that bettered the others and moved them to the front of the queue awaiting assignment on the Project.

Vesnio, glancing at the screen, anticipated her and dismissed the warning, flagging it for sharing with the entire fleet. It would be easy to dismiss their work as little more than nodding assent to the computer and the ninety others like it to which it was linked by its own ansible. Like the flight deck crew of any spacecraft, any airship, they were there for the unanticipated, the exception that might warrant human judgement, human action. "Eons of boredom punctuated by rare moments of sheer terror." So it had been said at the Academy, a saying descended from similar formulae in all the languages of the Nineteen Peoples.

"Are you prepared?" the computer asked? It was the same question she and the others of The Last had been asked on graduation from the Academy. She looked at Vesnio. "It's yours. You're relieving me."

"I took it last time. And besides, with the new watch schedule, we are on together for the next four hours. So, as senior officer, it's you, my love."

"Yes, I am fully prepared," she said to the computer. It was the same answer she and the others had given that day in the small theater. "Activate manual override on bridge control console."

She turned to face the rising control console with its matching sets of twin four-axis joystick controllers, its array of buttons and levers and rotary controls, and its own curving display screen. Her heart pounded, as it did every time at the controls, but she knew it for what it was, a primitive biological reaction evolved to propel her to a hyper-alert state. She wrapped her hands around the left pair of joysticks. "This is Captain Tenra Loudian Makepeace of the New Earth Diaspora," she said. "Ready for handoff to manual on board Adamah."

"Handoff ready, verification mode, activate on code sequence input."

Tenra tapped the sequence through the finger keys on her controllers, then thumbed the master buttons atop both at the same time. The countdown arc on the display blinked, until a faint thud beneath her feet and the blooming of a dozen signals on the display told her she was in charge.

She relished this daily exercise, her proof to the system that she was alive and well and fully capable of making decisions independently. Vesnio hated it. For fifteen minutes, she flew the ship and directly monitored the hundreds of effectors under her control. A handful of effectors were idle, standing by for eventualities that could be anticipated but not predicted with precision. She concluded from the display that one effector would need a tiny increment in acceleration for the mass it steered to thread its way through an appointed narrow window at the end of the year. She tapped a command on the keyboard, the effector confirmed, and the computer flashed approval.

"Thank you, oh, Adamah," she said, addressing the computer by the same name as her ship. "Nice to know I'm not slipping." She tried not to think about the fact that what she was doing was somewhere in the ambiguous territory between real-world action and playing a video game or flying in a simulator. She was controlling the ship and its armada of effectors, but the computer was looking over her shoulder, second-guessing and double-checking her moves, standing ready to jump back in to take over should she ever do something stupid or bizarre. That was unlikely. Aside from the mind-boggling calculations of the many-body problem, what she and others of The Last were doing was a variant of meteor defense, just on a far grander scale, not only of space but of time. Some of the manipulations had actually been initiated millions of years before.

In school, Introduction to Meteor Defense had been one of her favorite early classes. Meteor defense had developed into an elaborate but well-worn specialty protecting inhabited planets throughout the galaxy. The assumption was that the same technology would evolve in any sufficiently advanced civilizations in any galaxy. Rarely did one try to explode a large object on a collision course with one's home planet. It was far more effective to plan far enough ahead so that an almost infinitesimal pull over a very long time could deflect the object onto a completely different path. Position the right size mass to one side of the offending object and use the small tug of its gravity to slowly pull the object onto a new path. In principle, such a gravity tractor could be carried out on any scale, and effects could be cascaded, deflecting smaller objects to intersect or avoid larger ones, which would change the course of still others and . . .

Tenra loved the concept and the hubris of applying such basic ideas on the grandest, cosmic scale, and

Vesnio loved the advanced mathematics that was required to actually make it work.

"Good job," he said. "Now that we have a joint watch, want to do breakfast? We can switch to the crew quarters console or have something sent up here, a picnic under the open sky."

"I like the latter. Let's do it."

¤ ¤ ¤

Vesnio sat looking at her as she lay back on the spread comforter, staring at the sky display. "Over there," she pointed to a dot near the artificial horizon. "That. I swear it's been in that same position for some time. I don't remember when I noticed it, but it is definitely more noticeable now."

"If it was anything, the computer would have warned us."

"Maybe it did. We deal with hundreds of alerts a day. Maybe we dismissed it, since it is unlikely to relate to our mission." She reached in her pocket for a laser pointer. "What's that, Adamah?" She positioned the beam on the spot.

There was a brief but noticeable delay. "Rocky fragment, asteroid, diameter 907 meters, closing. Calculated distance at nearest approach four kilometers."

"That's as good as a collision. If the calculation is even a tad off, we're cooked. When is nearest approach?"

"Thirty-one hours."

"Thirty-one hours? There's no time. Why weren't we warned?"

"You were alerted when the collision path was calculated, but the minimum distance at the time of the alert was estimated at over one hundred kilometers. A close encounter with a wandering planet has reduced that to four kilometers. As it nears, the precision and reliability of the estimate improves. It will not strike the station, confidence level 99.9."

Vesnio scrunched his eyes closed and shook his head. "One-in-a-thousand that it does hit us is too high. What are we going to do? How do we shift the odds? It's not like we can take evasive maneuvers in this thing. And there's no time to set up a gravity tractor. What are we going to do?"

Tenra's fingers fluttered in the air as she typed on an imaginary keyboard. "We're going to go the old-fashioned route." She stood and trotted to the control console at the center. "You plot us a torpedo intercept with the fragment. I'll also get one from Adamah to cross check. We're going to blow that thing into a billion bits, many of which will hit us, but they'll be too small to do any real damage."

"We could lose sensors, imagers."

"They're all triple redundant. We'll be fine."

Vesnio tapped away at his work console, while she worked the keyboard on the control console. "They agree," she said. "Your plot and the computer solution are within a tenth of a percent."

"One part in a thousand, same as the odds. Of course, my solution is still really a computer solution. It's not like I could do those calculations in my head."

"Okay, I'm arming the missile with your firing solution anyway. I want the explosion to take place as far away as possible, so I'm launching now."

"How big a warhead are you using?"

"Big enough, big enough."

◻ ◻ ◻

They were in the crew quarters nearest the exact center of the Station when the pieces started hitting. Damage reports scrolled in on the auxiliary console, pieces of the image on the wall screen flickered and repainted, and the lights blinked out once. There was a shudder of a small quake as one large fragment struck, but then the artificial meteor shower was over.

"Well, how about that?" he said. "An anticlimactic finish. Good shooting, Captain."

"Good computing, Lieutenant. Let's head back to the bridge."

Vesnio was first up the stairway and nearly to the top when the wall beside him cracked and the section of stairs pulled loose from its anchors, twisted free, and collapsed, sending Vesnio and pieces of cement and steel plunging twenty meters to the floor.

Tenra ran down the surviving lower staircase, but it was already too late when she reached him. Vesnio was dead, the Station was damaged, and she was alone.

◻ ◻ ◻

"How I wish you were standing here with me, Vesnio, or at least experiencing this from the Remove." She now captained a constant reminder that there had been another. She had renamed her craft for the partner who should have been at her side but had died in an accident that could not happen, but did. That was already decades ago, too many to count. She had learned to live in the emptiness, to survive on rations of abbreviated words on the ansible links with the other stations. The interstellar gossip continued, despite the handicap of time that passed at different rates for each Station, all continuing their outward rush at differing fractions of the speed of light. Geanna and Taff had decided, against protocol and defying their contract, to have a baby, a boy who was by now already full grown and learning hypermath.

What was it like to be born knowing you were going to die so soon? She laughed at her own question. It was the fate of all and everyone. The only difference was in the definition of 'soon.' It was more than a matter of semantics. For some of the oldest Stations that had been accelerating far longer and were closer to the speed of light, time had slowed to a crawl, meaning the events outside were whizzing by ever faster.

To Tenra, it was both tedious and a rush. One day the Remove started talking with her. "We've learned how to do it more easily, though we don't all know how we are doing it."

"I thought you were one mind, a single thinking entity."

"We are and we are not. When we speak to you, the living, we are one. When we speak to ourselves, we are many."

"And now? Why? Why me?"

"We are speaking with all of The Last, about that which we have learned."

That which we have learned. It was clumsy and archaic language, but instantly recognizable as the opening words of the text that had first appeared on an ansible millions of years earlier. And she knew at once that she was imagining the voices from the Remove, that she had conjured the voices and the text out of her loneliness.

That original text, which had taken a long time to write itself, was a monologue—there could be no reply, as there was no ansible on the other end. The monologue was about what came to be known among the Nineteen People as the Third Cosmology, a treatise about what the Remove had learned, thought, sensed since its creation.

There were others. That had always been assumed, but the Nineteen Peoples were all from one galaxy, the survivors of intelligent life from the billions of natural experiments of a single island universe in a universe of billions of galaxies. The ansibles that provided instantaneous communication had to be delivered by ordinary travel, spaceflight that took thousands or millions of years. In the histories of the Nineteen Peoples, only one ansible had ever reached a civilization in another galaxy, the Terts, who had poisoned themselves out of existence not long after contact had been established. Something of that sort seemed to be a common fate of far too many advanced civilizations.

But the Remove spanned the universe, everywhere and nowhere, and it learned of and from the others. And what it learned was that one people, in one galaxy, had solved the so-called Sutcliff-Rami-Brenslo Equations of the Third Cosmology and had begun, more than a million years earlier, to play god.

¤ ¤ ¤

The Academy taught science as history, beginning with simple mechanics and chemistry based on orbits and bonds, moving onto relativity and quantum theory, to electron clouds, uncertainty and complementarity, the Big Bang theory, string theory, and a string of other historical burps and boggles, each one taught as real, complete, and correct, only to then be challenged, corrected, or discarded altogether, all the way up to the New Standard Model, and finally the Third Cosmology. It was a luxury afforded by very long lives. Tenra remembered the long anticipated unit when the full implications of the Third Cosmology were introduced and dissected.

"And so, from equation twelve, it is easy to see how it would appear that the universe was poised on the narrow point of flatness, to mix a metaphor, neither positively or negatively curved. But, in reality, something else altogether was the case. The Movers, the only name by which we know them, had already begun to take action on the basis of an alternative solution to equation thirteen, which I will now derive."

There followed nearly forty minutes of polynomial pyrotechnics on the projected screen that brought tears to the eyes of Vesnio and his kin and gasps to the mouths of those like Tenra, who thought in the sweep of cosmic history but could barely keep up with the hypermaths being spread like a spatchcocked bird before them. It was not that she could not think through the hypermath—she had scored a perfect on the last examination—it was rather that she was more interested in what it meant.

She raised her hand. Professor Dinnailla, who could not miss her sitting there in the front row, ignored her. "And so, if we substitute the tensoritic gradient here, we get"—a fresh spray of symbols peppered the screen, which auto-scrolled to make room— "this. Plugging in the Leonitz Constant and simplifying reveals—"

Applause filled the room, even from those who had done the reading and were anticipating the results.

Tenra's hand was still in the air but had now been joined by dozens of others. Professor Dinnailla stepped to the side of her podium and nodded toward Tenra.

"Yes, Ms. Makepeace. You have a question?"

"So what you are saying—well, the equations are saying—is that the universe could have expanded at an accelerating pace ending in the fabric of space-time ripped to shreds, as it were, except that somebody or something at some time began a process that started, well, tugging at the fabric and pulling mass, whole galaxies with super-black holes at their centers, into a region that further warped space-time to create an ever deepening and spreading gravity well that may have changed the fate of the universe."

There were shouts of "Duh!" and "Obvious!" from around the hall, and dozens of conversations broke out within small groups.

Professor Dinnailla raised her hand, signaling the students to settle down. She waited for full silence.

"Not exactly obvious. There are other solutions to these equations that lead to other conclusions, but given the data that accompanied the Third Cosmology, this is the one in which we have the greatest confidence. And that is why the Nineteen Peoples decided to join with our unknown and unknowable compatriots, to launch Project End Game, and finally, this final class at the Academy. It is why you are here, to become part of this. The universe is dying. So are you, so are we. We do not have any say in that one, undeniable truth, although there are some few who still believe in some afterlife—alongside those who consider entering the Remove to be a route.

"For the rest of us, the only choice we may have is how to die. The universe will end. The Sutcliff-Rami-Brenslo equations of the Third Cosmology suggest, only suggest, that we may have some say in how the universe dies. Perhaps we do not. But, collectively, the Nineteen Peoples and, apparently, some others before us, have decided to try. Those of you who graduate and choose to join the final Fleet, will be the observers and the hospice workers of the dying universe, seeing it on its way to a good death, a death with meaning."

The class rose in a standing ovation, the only one Tenra remembered. Even the stirring commencement speech by the Speaker of the Combined Parliaments drew no more than enthusiastic applause. When the ovation had finished, Professor Dinnailla gestured for them to sit, cleared the screen, and started working out equation fourteen.

¤ ¤ ¤

Tenra stood on the bridge. "How long have I been here?"

"Nineteen hours," Adamah answered. Years earlier she had reconfigured it for spontaneous conversation. She did not want to lose the power of speech as her own end approached, and she needed more than the exchange of text messages to keep a tight hold on sanity. She needed somebody to talk with.

"No, I mean, onboard. How long?" She was aware that the clock kept slowing as they crept up further on the speed of light, the ultimate speed limit. Outside, the universe was now racing toward its ultimate fate. For her, it would happen in mere days, so extreme was the difference in relative clocks.

"You have been aboard nearly three-hundred years, after the hundreds of your younger years, a good long life."

"Where'd you get that? 'A good long life.'"

"From you, you've said it on a number of occasions.

You should think about getting some sleep. You have some busy days ahead."

"In the end, which wins out? Our relative velocity or the steepening gravity well sucking everything in."

"It's all the same. Time slows. At the speed of light, which we will not and cannot reach, time stands still. The same is true in the gravity well of a singularity. At least that's what the mathematics says. I guess we will find out. Or not. You might know better, and perhaps have some thoughts about the subjective experience of time stopping."

"No time, no such thing as time. Without time there is no experience. It's like the question about what happened before the universe came into being, but time started with that instant. There was no before. It's like asking about before inflation, before the Big Bang. Meaningless. Unless." She stared off into the distance that was painted on the dome then continued. "Vesnio once said the real mindblower was in equation fourteen. I was always captivated by equation thirteen and its implications. If. If the universe were to collapse. If it were to collapse in just the right way, with sufficient symmetry, it would ultimately warp all of space-time around it to such an extreme that the continuum itself would wrap around and collapse in on itself into a singularity that would, at that instant, become a new universe propelled into being by inflation. But our universe, absent some change in the data or new parameters, would not, could not collapse or collapse in the right way, into a single region of sufficient symmetry."

The response came back in the baritone voice of Adamah but the inflection of the long dead Vesnio. "That's what it says in my databases. Go to bed, get some sleep."

¤ ¤ ¤

Tenra awoke in a panic. How long had she slept. She looked at the wall clock. She had slept the better part of the day. She was already into what for her would be the last day. She showered and dressed as if chased by demons and ran up to the bridge. Above her, the violence seemed oddly less violent, less chaotic, and the bright center, at least as the computer presented it, was slowly growing even as she watched. She turned in a circle, looking for anything along the false horizon that might hint at a problem. She pulled up her work console and checked every report, every screen, every chart and graph. They were all nominal. She sent an all-hands call to the other ninety Stations but got only eighty-nine messages back. One of them explained. "The Dunloff group are gone. Caught early. Their effectors were all nominal, so we should be all right."

"What happened?" she texted back.

"Just a little off on the timeline. With these extremes, even the Extended New Physics can only do close approximations. Exciting times. We are entering the unknown."

"Scary."

"Not really. What a way to go! We can't save the universe, but at least we can make a new one."

"How much time?"

"Depends on who you are and where you are. Any one of us might be caught by incoming, but, if not, in the end, we'll all be in the same place in the same gravity well, so time will stop at the same time for everyone." The txt was unusually long. "Kinda cool, if you ask me.

175

Right now we are scattered across the universe and aging at different rates, but soon, we will be together." If ansibles had allowed for sound, the remaining Stations would have heard singing.

At the end of her shift, Tenra decided she would not take a break. She could have food brought to her, maybe a tall glass of *tigg* to keep her mood and alertness up. She set Adamah to synthesizing the mild euphoric she had once sampled while on vacation with her parents.

It was sometime in the last hours, as she watched the remaining few thousand years of the universe rush by overhead, that she understood what Vesnio had been trying to tell her about equation fourteen.

The monster of monsters was now growing visibly in her field of vision. Even as she raced outward, space-time was beginning its inward rush. In the last moments she would be going nowhere fast.

In the final analysis, equation fourteen meant that, if the Extended New Physics and the Third Cosmology were correct, no universe arising from a singularity and born in inflation could ever, of its own, collapse in on itself to form a singularity and birth a new universe. Of its own. No universe.

She suddenly had a vision of others, like her or unimaginably unlike her, who had to have been standing, like her, watching, helping to orchestrate the death of their own universe in order to be midwives to a new one—her universe, the one in which she had been born and raised to this end.

"In the end, time stops, there is no time, all time is the same, everyone and everything that ever was or will be is in one place, a single point, perfect synchrony," she said, speaking into the emptiness.

◻ ◻ ◻

A flashing red warning on her screen caught her attention. She read the message but struggled to make sense of the graphic. "What is it, Adamah? I can't . . ."

"It's still too asymmetric, according to my computations."

"Is it too late? Are there any effectors still online? Any that might be deployed? How much time do we have?"

"Time, impossible to say: too many variables, unknowns. Thousands of years, perhaps, but not millions. Subjective, maybe mere hours. I just queried the fleet by ansible and we are the only one in position. We still have forty-six effectors online, two that might make a difference. There is a planet that—"

"Skip the details." She looked down, as if she could see through all that stood between her and the maelstrom behind, then up, as if she could see past the illusion of the display to the bending space above. "Use both, maximum effect. I'd rather risk overkill than undershoot. It's hard to imagine that anything we do now could possibly make a difference."

"The anomaly is tiny. We only need to tweak. Then again, the calculations may be wrong. The computed probabilities are—"

"Shut up and do it!"

"I need authorization."

Tenra took hold of the twin controllers, keyed her code, and pressed both buttons on top at the same time. "You got it."

"The commands have been sent, and the Fleet has been notified. Oh, we lost other Stations. We're down to eighty in all."

"Really, so many years out?"

"As I stated, the calculations are only approximate from here on in, and they do not converge as we get closer."

She launched a follower app to keep tabs on the results of deploying the two effectors. Then she waited. And watched.

Time passed, but it was no longer time as she knew it.

"You know, this happened before, all of this," she said at last to Adamah and to no one.

"Yes, we know." It was the Remove, the imaginary voice in her head again.

Adamah spoke. "What was that you said? Hard radiation, interference across the spectrum, all becoming a real problem."

"I said this has happened before. Somebody did this to bring our universe into being, otherwise there would have been one shot and then . . . nothing. Equation fourteen. I can almost sense their presence, as if it were all happening at once: the beginning, the end, this universe, another universe."

She looked around again, but something was wrong. I think I am hallucinating, she thought. She surveyed the bridge. Surrounding her were men and women and beings who were neither, a growing crowd filling the bridge. She thought she saw Vesnio, and her heart skipped. She thought of the others of The Last. "They're here, with me." There was Brauniff and Zella and Ktahners from Station Eleven, and the group from Station Eight and . . .

The display above flickered and returned, a simplified,

posterized version of itself.

Must be trouble with all the sensors, she thought. Overloaded. "Adamah, switch cores and do a display restore." There was no reply. Adamah was no longer functioning at a level that could sustain conversation.

"I should say something," she said. "There I did. I'm getting a little giddy, discombobulated. Wow, what a word. We should all say something. We . . ."

And there it was, whether in her head or in the Remove or in some other dimension: a chorus, a chord, a synchrony of beings and being, a stadium crowd all speaking at once, saying many things. We who are the last to die. Good luck and godspeed. Go, go, go. Good to go, good to go. One small step. Another chance. We are gods. Yes! Now! I am. I was. Be. And a thousand million words she had never heard before, all at once. She blinked, a long slow blink, and . . .

Time stopped; time started.

After 10^{-36} seconds, inflation began.

Somewhere Else

My name is Istvan. That is not the name I was given, but it has been my name since that day in the woods. I was born Yizhak Froeman in a small village near the border between Lithuania and Latvia. If I told you the name of the village, you would know on which side of the border it lay, but I will call it, instead, Nearthere, which, for those into codes and clues, might point the way to its real identity. I will not tell the name of the village because there are still people there who knew: people who lived nearby in Nearthere, the neighbors who hid me and those who betrayed me. Or their descendants. In any case, my family was not from there originally. Whose family is? We are all from somewhere else, save for those whose people never left Africa. They are technically the only truly indigenous on the planet. All others, whatever their story, are immigrants.

Today, my surname is Foreman, a simple transposition, the most common typographical error, but in my case not an error but a typographic trick, a transformation from one ethnic identity to another, at least on my Swedish passport, where I am Isaac Foreman. But things have only worsened there in recent years, and that is why I am now here, asking for admission, to be once again from somewhere else.

However, my name will always be Istvan, ever since that day.

I was twelve, nearly ready to become Bar Mitzvah, when the Germans arrived. To be politically correct, I should say the Nazis, but it was nationality not party affiliation by which we knew them. With them came new rules and restrictions that transformed neighbors into nemeses—or rescuers. Suddenly there was no work for the Froemans nor their kinsmen nor their kith, so it was a surprise on that spring day after a brutal winter in which there was neither food nor work and the firewood came from abandoned buildings and furniture that had passed from functional to frivolous. It was a surprise that the German's started recruiting us for work. "Come with us. It is hard work in the woods, but we will pay in hard currency. You can buy bread for your families. Bring them along. Anyone who can handle a shovel or pickaxe or wheel a barrow or carry a rock, we will feed and pay."

What could account for such a change of heart from the very ones who denied us work and stole food and tools from us? Nothing. Nothing could account for it. Even my young friends, just boys, could smell the trickery whether or not they could name it. But we had no choice. The German soldiers beat the ones who declined and threatened the men who would not bring their families along. And they had guns, which they waved and pointed and even sometimes fired into the air or at the ground and once used to shoot in the back a young boy who had run from them after grabbing a crust of bread from a plate on the ground.

The forest around Nearthere is a mix of birch and co-
nifers, which may also be a clue to those who are com-
pelled to be detectives about such things. That day we
marched for more than an hour into those trees until we
reached a clearing—not a natural one, but an area where
the trees had been felled some years before and had not
grown back. We were told to dig two trenches, from this
point to that and so deep. We were told to work, all of
us, girls and women, too.

The clearing was quite large and the sun soon quite
hot. The ground was the soft humus of forest floors, but
it was also a shepherd's stew of rocks and tangled roots.
We slaved well into the afternoon with rising thirst and
growing unease. We asked for water. "When the truck
arrives you will have water," we were told. "The water
and your lunch are on the truck. Trust us."

It must have been nearly two when a truck finally arrived, backing down the narrow track by which we had
marched there in the morning. It was followed by another truck that maneuvered around tree stumps to
align itself alongside. Out of the back of the second truck
spilled men, police and townspeople armed with rifles,
plus a few members of the militia, also armed. Last,
emerging from the cab of the truck, was the officer in
charge, a German lieutenant, with slick blond hair and
polished black boots.

We were ordered to line up for inspection standing in
front of our diggings. We were such an odd and scruffy
brigade that I almost laughed, but ours was hardly a
laughable situation. I glanced over my shoulder at the
deep trench we had spent the day digging and suddenly
my stomach lurched. I looked back toward the men now

arrayed in an undisciplined line opposite us, hunting rifles shouldered or pointed earthwards from a crook in an arm, glancing at each other nervously. They were only a handful to our many, but they had the weapons. I recognized some of them. The head of police and a butcher, the sexton who opened our small synagogue on Saturdays, and Istvan, our neighbor from just down the street, who was also someone from somewhere else. Istvan and another man leaned on the gate of the first truck and talked in low voices. I was close enough to hear phrases and fragments of sentences. The other man was talking about the younger children, who now clung to their mother skirts or were held to a father's shoulder. Something about sparing them, saving them from suffocation under the bodies by aiming straight for their hearts. I weighed my options.

When the German officer in charge ordered the men to raise their weapons, there was a moment of disbelief and confusion among those standing by the trenches, leaning on their shovels and picks, or slumped on the ground in near exhaustion. And then I heard it clearly, Istvan swearing as he worked the bolt on his rifle. "The goddamn thing has jammed. Give me yours," he said, as he climbed into the back of the far truck, just as two soldiers pulled aside the canvas that covered the back. Inside, a gunner sat at the ready with a machine gun on a tripod between his legs.

"Goddamn you bastard," Istvan said, "let me do that. I can't do anything with this piece of crap." He threw his rifle at the gunner, catching him in the face. As the soldier raised his arms in defense, Istvan shoved him away from the machine gun and took his place. "Stop!" the gunner yelled, as Istvan swung the barrel around to catch him on the cheek and knock him over the gate of the truck. Just then, the German officer lowered his hand and snapped, "Fire."

At the first shot, I took a backward dive into the pit, scrambled up the far bank, and started a crouched run toward the tree line. The rifles fired in erratic waves. A boy behind me, a year or two younger than me, struggled up the bank and tried to run after me. The machine gun began its rapid crack-a-crack-a-crack. Just as I reached the trees, I stupidly turned to see what was happening. Behind me, people were running everywhere, some toward me. They fell as shots caught them in the back or a leg, and one man was gunned down just feet before he reached me. And then there was only the sound of the machine gun, still firing non-stop, and I realized that Istvan had not been shooting at us, but was gunning down the other soldiers and the policemen and the militia. One of the soldiers, nearly out of sight beyond the second truck, knelt, took careful aim with his rifle and put a bullet into Istvan. As Istvan slumped, he fell on the back of the machine gun, tilting its barrel skyward. Somehow he kept his finger on the trigger until the belt had run through, using up the last of its ammunition.

He chose. Istvan chose to die giving his life meaning and purpose beyond what he had been ordered to do. He found a choice in the face of no choice, and from that moment, I vowed always to do the same.

As I broke again into a run, behind me, I heard the sharp thud of a rifle butt against someone's head and a few shots from an officer's Luger delivering the coup de grâce to some of the still-living victims in the trenches. One bullet whizzed past me as I ran through the trees, but I was by then too far and too fast for them to get me. Then I felt it, the sharp pinch in my thigh that was too sharp and too deep to be a pinch. I ran despite the pain and the bleeding. I ran until I could hear neither shouts nor shots, and I hid for days before finding a boat and starting the journey that ultimately took me to Sweden.

And now I am here. Once again asking to become someone from somewhere else.

¤ ¤ ¤

"And you are Jewish? You can prove that?"

"Of course." Istvan undid his belt buckle and started to unzip his trousers.

"That won't be necessary. Nor enough. Many who are not Jewish are circumcised. You know, don't you, that Muslims also are circumcised. And most Americans."

Istvan laughed. "No, I was going to show you the scar on my thigh. The bullet is still in there. I was told it was too close to an artery for them to extract it, but medicine has improved so much since the war years. Perhaps it can be removed, and you can check the caliber and markings to verify its age and that it was fired from a war-era Luger. Then you will know that my story is true. Of course, I will still walk with a limp afterwards, but at least I will be walking in the Land of Israel."

"I'm sorry, but . . ."

"I'm sorry. Those words, which so seldom are sincere and so often mean quite the opposite. And, that particular form of 'I'm sorry,' the kind followed by a word that negates everything before and reveals the truth so starkly. But. I heard that word said so many times from the

Germans and the neighbors who helped them. I accept neither your apology nor its negation. I am here and I intend to stay."

He started toward the exit. Behind him he heard the sharp thud of a handstamp on his papers, sealing his fate. It reminded him of the sharp thud sealing the fate of the boy in the trench so many years before in a woods now so many leagues behind him. Istvan kept limping toward the door, ignoring the shouts behind him as he struggled not to break into a run.

Forever
Christmas

No one knows. Not this, this now. And no one knows the long loop of despair that led to this now— neither the shallows of quiet desperation through which I have doggedly paddled over the years nor the benthic depressions into which I have plunged in recent times. This time, this now, is not one of those, only the end product of all that accumulated silent suffering condensed, synopsized, synthesized into a single now.

I am here, on the highway, but I got here by another route known only to me.

¤ ¤ ¤

Nina turns to me. "Merry Christmas," she says. "I . . ."

I nod and keep driving, tuning out the rest of her monologue. The traffic is heavy, but at least it's moving. Merry Christmas. Yes, Merry Fucking Christmas.

I hate Christmas, and it has nothing to do with being Jewish. Jews are past masters of borrowed holidays. We cribbed from the Romans and the Canaanites with enthusiasm and denial, and Christmas itself is a remake of pagan winter solstice tradition. In fact, the trees and wreaths, the holly and the lights are all good with me. What I hate about Christmas is the frenetic buying and boxing, the omnipresent onslaught of carols dripping with schmaltz and piety or with excess exuberance. I hate the frenzy of wrapping and the orgy of ripping, with its exhausted climax of crumpled colored paper stuffed into those green-black trash bags, jumbo size, that will take centuries to degrade in a landfill. All that for just those few hours before magic moments fade and new presents are set aside to join a long parade of forgotten gifts, the perennial detritus, the true Ghosts of Christmas Past.

I hate the pressure of presents, the implicit competition to come up with something, always something more. Year after year it goes, until one would think there would be nothing left to get or give, all things having once rested, however briefly, in that overflowing cornucopia spread beneath a gaudy tree, a tree that is always "the best tree ever" even as the ritual annual cellphone photos prove them to be indistinguishable reincarnations of the same ancestral spruce or Douglas fir.

I have tried without success to introduce the family to the less frantic pace and less commercial rituals of Hanukkah, but it is no contest. Heaps of new clothes and toys under a tree bright with LEDs will win every time over a row of candles that grows by one flame each night. Contemplation and rededication—what the word Hanukkah means—are no match for instant gratification.

But it's okay. This is a bargain I struck at the beginning and have been making the annual payments on ever since. Nina is Roman Catholic, though she goes to Mass only a few times a year, the midnight Mass on Christmas Eve being among them. In all fairness, it actually would have been more complicated to raise the kids Jewish, even if Nina had been willing, which she was not. My older brother took the traditional route, the preferred route, and married a good Jewish girl. Bar mitzvahs for both their boys and four proud grandparents looking on with approval and sizable checks waiting in envelopes. I was the family rebel who married a stubborn shiksa.

¤ ¤ ¤

The trip to Grammy Winthrop's is an hour-and-twenty minutes each way if the traffic on the Interstate cooperates. There is only enough time there for the kids to shred through the presents from her and Granddaddy plus a long hour of painfully pointless small talk and the perennial promises to get together more often. We have to get back home because Nina has promised, as she does every year, to cover for the afternoon shift at the clinic.

It's no problem; the kids dispatched the gifts with practiced efficiency. The tags on the packages all read, "Merry Christmas, from Grammy and Granddaddy," but Nina's father played no role in either shopping or wrapping. He has been stretching out the last years of his life in the incontinent ignorance of Alzheimer's. His wife is convinced he'll outlive us all in serene senility. We all try to do the right thing by visiting him now and then, but he has no idea who we are, and it always strikes me as meaningless.

On the return trip, the kids argue in the backseat, reprising the bickering fugue from the outbound leg. Belinda is a pre-teen bully who can reduce her overly sensitive little brother to tears of desperation with mere words—or even nonsense. "Marrakesh!" she shouts, making a karate chop that stops millimeters short of his face. "Stop it," he whines.

"Marrakesh!" Chop.

"Don't! Stop it."

"Marrakesh!" Slice.

"Stop it. Make her stop it." Each round notches up a few decibels.

"Are you going to let that continue?" Nina asks me in a voice that is less loud but every bit as penetrating.

"What do you want me to do? I'm driving."

"Discipline them."

Right. Discipline the kids at seventy miles-an-hour. The speed limit here is sixty-five, but cars are whizzing past us nonetheless. That won't last. By the time we reach the interchange with Interstate 93, we could be crawling in stop-and-go traffic. "Cut it out kids!" I snap at them, and Nina gives me a look of disapproval.

In the back seat: "Marrakesh!" Whack.

"I told her, stop it," Travis says, the plaint more resonant and more desperate. "She won't stop. Make her stop." Louder sobs.

"I mean it, kids, settle down or . . ."

There is no 'or'. I have nothing to follow up with. The kids know it, I know it, and Nina knows. Sometimes I can finally reach a point where a single syllable escapes at full volume, a verbal thunderclap. "Stop!"

"What the hell was that about?" Nina would say, as if everything leading up to then were my imagination. This time, though, the winter storm in the rear soon passes and merges into the next backseat crisis.

Travis wants to play with his new Bluetooth-Enabled Transformer Truck that can be controlled by an app on his Android phone. Today, I finally get my answer to the longstanding question of why a nine-year-old boy would ever need a smartphone. He needs it to control his Blue-tooth-Enabled Transformer Truck.

"It's in the trunk," I tell him, stating the obvious, which is increasingly my special but limited role in family conversations.

He whines with a pulse of isolated words interspersed between sobs and sniffles: I, sob, want, sniffle, it, sob; why, sob, can't I, sniffle, have it, sob, now.

Nina turns and puts her arm over the back of her seat. "Daddy can't just stop here on the highway." It's the same lecture-voice rhythm as she uses with her student nurses. I know that voice well. "You know Daddy can't stop here."

That is the moment. I say it to myself. Yes, I can.

¤ ¤ ¤

Time. Flowing like a tide that only ebbs, each wave lifting and falling but always outgoing, time carries us seaward, bobbing in fluid inexorability, ever seaward toward a deeper ocean. But. There are also discontinuities, those rare occasions when there was the before and then there is the after, with only a slice of the abyss between, a point where mathematicians would say the slope goes to infinity.

Then. Now. A total, absolute, and qualitative difference of such magnitude that the universe is altered fundamentally. Like the birth of a first child. Before: there were two of you—she, bulging and off-balance, five days overdue and exhausted; you, on the cusp of a career with potential but struggling to be what she needs at the moment. After: you are three. "It's a girl." The midwife hands you a tiny, pasty creature, still attached by a ropy cord. The baby's blue-black eyes are open. You look down into them and the universe fractures.

Before. After. A discontinuity. Like the moment you tell the assembled senior partners at Sandberg, Whittle and Soames that you are quitting. There is no going back. They make a show of trying to persuade you to stay, but everyone in the room knows: it's over.

Discontinuity. Before: rising star, lawyer on a fast track to make full partner. After: writer wannabe, journalist with a box of business cards pursuing an impossible dream. Impossible.

No one knows. The deadline for *The Atlantic* passed a week ago. The family celebration for that first big sale was a face-saving sham. The editor only said she'd take a look at it when the story is finished. I didn't finish.

No one knows. Hours can pass typing sentences and backspacing over them. Pages pour onto the screen only to be scrapped with a simple Select All and a tap on the Delete key. Days can fill with depressing "expressions of interest" and emails that start: "I really liked your story, but . . ." Holiday parties are punctuated with, "A writer? You too? My cousin says he's a writer. And my neighbor is working on a memoir . . ."

No one knows. Blank screens. Failure. An end-of-day ritual: "Did you remember to call the plumber?"

"Oh, no. I'm sorry. I was busy writing, caught up in it." Fail.

Or: "How was your day?"

"Well, I cranked out another three thousand words on that novel." Words. Three. Three thousand. Worthless. No one knows. Sinking, word by word, into abyssal deeps.

¤ ¤ ¤

Discontinuity. Like the moment I realize it. Yes, I can.

I signal to shift into the right-hand lane.

"What are you doing?"

"Shifting lanes."

"Watch out for that car."

"I'm watching."

"Careful."

Nina is a nurse. Actually, she's now a Nurse Practitioner. She makes more money, can see patients on her own, and can be in charge of an entire team at the clinic. It's a portable profession. So is writing, but demand outstrips supply for her chosen field. We could move almost anywhere, and she'd have a job within days. Not only that, but we can get by on what she makes. And she likes being in charge.

My signal is still flashing. Click-a-click-a-click-a-click.

"Your turn signal is still on." I know. "Why do you want to get over? This lane is better."

My roommate warned me when I started dating Nina. "Watch out. Nurses are all control freaks." I guess I liked it. Did. She takes charge, makes most of the important decisions and all of the unimportant ones. She tells me when I'm wrong.

"Not now," she says. "Wait until we're past the interchange onramp."

I know. I'm driving. But I'm redundant, an appendage, vestigial. No one knows. It is quite possible no one cares.

¤ ¤ ¤

Actually, I figured this business out long ago. I didn't know the when, but I did know the how.

Merry Fucking Christmas. The timing resonates in

some perverse way, like one of those plangent medieval carols, filled with strangely sad minor-key dissonance that can sometimes seem almost like more honest reflections of the season. I don't know which is worse this time of year, the faked and forced merriment or the genuine joy. Both are abundant, both are reminders that I am not there.

Travis is singing an off-key Christmas carol, and Belinda is correcting him. She'll do all right, probably become a nurse—or a doctor—and marry a devoted nebbish. Travis is on track to becoming someone else's devoted nebbish. He adores his big sister even as she is abusing him. And I adore Nina.

◻ ◻ ◻

I finally spot an opening and shift lanes. I take advantage of the break in traffic to slow and pull off into the breakdown lane. We crawl to a proper AAA-approved stop with the passenger-side tires just off the paved shoulder onto the narrow strip of dead grass spattered with clumps of dirty, salt-infused snow.

"What are you doing? Why are you stopping? You can't stop here. Don't be silly. Travis doesn't need his truck."

"I'm not getting his truck." I open the door just wide enough to slip out. "I need to check something." I slam the car door before she can protest or interrogate me further, but she is undeterred. Through the metal, glass, and plastic box of our beat-up car, I can hear her rant, though not every word. It doesn't matter, I can fill in the blanks.

I stay close to the car and look both ways as if I were checking for traffic. Suddenly inspired, I kneel as though I were checking the left-rear tire. With the noise of heavy traffic, I can barely make out the muffled voices of Belinda teasing, Travis whining, and Nina continuing with her tirade, her targets now alternating between the kids and me.

The traffic is still zooming by, a seventy-five-mile-an-hour succession of semis and vans, pickups and sedans. Pulling back out into such a stream takes precision. My father, a delivery truck driver himself, taught me to anticipate, to time the acceleration to mesh with the traffic like gears in a clockwork. It takes an intimate and intuitive sense of the physics of motion to pull off the exquisite timing that puts you precisely in that gap moving at the right speed at the right moment. I was always good at it, another finely honed skill valued too little in the real world.

I see a big refrigerated rig approaching over the rise just a few car-lengths behind a Jeep Grand Cherokee. The eighteen wheeler is letting the gap grow as it crests the hill. I mentally calculate, picturing big gears and little gears meshing.

Five steps. I stand. Nina is texting. She is probably telling her mother about me. Belinda is now reading. Travis is playing a video game on his phone.

Discontinuity. I can do this, no need even to face the traffic. Five steps. One. Two. Three. Four. . . .

The driver of the Mack truck does not even have time to hit the brakes. I am slammed against the flat, massive chrome grill, my head is snapped around, and I am looking into the bulldog logo. It's like a movie freeze-frame, except the tide of time is still flowing. Most of the bones in my left side are crushed. I am flying in a screaming rush of wind, pinned against the front of the truck for that fraction of a second before the driver's foot can leave the accelerator and reach the brake, which he slams with full force. He is good, though. As fast as he hits the brakes, his muscles spasm and he is already easing off, avoiding a lockup. The trailer swings toward the shoulder and back as he wrestles to keep from jackknifing or skidding out of control.

Time shudders and sputters as the truck skids and slows. As it brakes, I am thrown ahead of it. A car in the next lane swerves. I hear a crash from somewhere farther back, then I strike the pavement with such force that I hear the crack, feel it in my neck and head. I tumble. My neck snaps and something in my back is wrenched. I am rolling, somersaulting. The truck catches up, strikes me again, and is on top of me. The driver is fighting to keep from sliding off the road. He's a pro, pumping the brakes, double-clutching to downshift, tapping the gas to straighten the cab again, checking his mirrors, all within seconds. My father would have approved.

I am caught and dragged by something on the undercarriage. I know I am dead, and I am angry that I am not dead. I am thinking about the news accounts that say "killed instantly." No one knows. I am engulfed in a ball of searing white-hot pain. Or is it red-cold pain? No one knows. It is total. There is nothing else in the universe: only the bright strobe of pain—and me.

Then I am loose and there is a tire above me, a huge truck tire and the weight of a fully-loaded semi-trailer.

That's it. An instant. I am dead. The truck tire is rolling over me. Still. It is not frozen in time and it is not in some kind of loop, but somehow it is still atop me. There is no sound and no movement, yet nothing has stopped, only time itself. My time. It's over.

No one knows. Nina and the kids will be all right. They didn't even see it happen. It will be—is already, was already—a tragedy, terrible, but they will get over it. Did. She took charge, put her life back together again, found somebody, remarried. They had a bonus baby together, an accident but no accident, and another contingency for her two teenagers to cope with as they struggle to find their own meaning and direction.

No one knows what led me here, to this, this now.

And it's Christmas. Forever Christmas.

Gym
Rats

Blake waved his key tag under the scanner and pushed through the turnstile at the Grant Street YMCA. It was mid-morning, the changing of the guard at the Y. A gaggle of fidgeting preschoolers in the day camp were lining up single file, one hand dutifully clinging to a red-and-blue polypropylene guide rope, ready for an expedition to the pocket park two blocks away. By now the jocks and gym rats were thinning out while the stay-at-homes—mostly moms—were showing up for yoga and Zumba sessions. The big wall fans were beginning to fall behind in their struggle to clear the air of the acid of sweat and the medicinal tang of antibacterial spray. "Please remember to wipe down your machine when finished," the signs nagged members, with nary a word about contributing to the evolution of the next generation of superbugs.

The Y was an urban commons where races and strata mixed, where working-class single parents dropping off their little ones for daycare did the morning hello dance with young professionals arriving to slip in a few quick laps in the pool before heading to the office on the eighteenth floor of some skyscraper. Here the pudgy middle-aged and paunchy oldsters pumped stationary cycles next to the achingly slim who were determined to stay that way. Everyone was there for a reason. Take it off. Keep it off. Tone up for bikini season. Show off the pecs. Or stay alive.

Blake was there on doctor's orders, a six-day-a-week prescription following his heart-attack three years earlier: warm-up, twenty-five minutes with his heart rate in the prescribed zone, and a five-minute cool-down. Blake headed straight for his favorite treadmill, third from the end, and launched into his cardio workout, a routine that varied little. Others might find it boring, but Blake used the time to people-watch and make up stories, holdovers from his pre-retirement years as a clinical social worker treating couples and families.

Today, the woman was already there, working her elliptical in the row just ahead of the treadmills. She was another creature of habit, nearly always putting in her solid, even-paced forty minutes before heading for the water cooler—four days a week.

Blake didn't know her name. In his head, she was Dee, after the letter decaled on her preferred elliptical. He guessed her to be a youthful forty-something. She was athletic and slim, on the near edge of skinny, with frizzy brown hair that sprayed out from beneath her Red Sox cap worn backwards. She favored colorful stretch leggings and crop tops that showed off her figure, though she seemed indifferent to the attention she sometimes drew. The one exception was Jim—Blake had heard her use the name once— the gym rat who usually arrived about this time. Blake scanned the room as he started ramping up his routine to the four-minute miles that kept him in the zone.

A good clinical social worker was both a listener and a watcher. People wanted to tell their stories, to be heard and understood, but Blake knew that keeping your eyes open to little things could often clue you in to the untold story. A ten-year-old boy might invariably squeeze between his parents sitting on the couch while his teenage sister paced in the corner, as far away from her father as possible.

"What do you think is going on?" his training supervisor would ask him.

"I don't know, that's why I'm bringing the case to you."

"Okay, make up a story."

Blake had learned early that the stories he made up in his head were working hypotheses springing from intuition and insight, a piece of the picture that could lead to deeper understanding, connection with the core of the problem, the backstory to the clients' own stories.

Blake had been building a backstory for Dee and Jim ever since he had switched from afternoon workouts to mornings in a bid to get away from the after-school teen crowd. Although both Jim and Dee were regulars, their styles could not be more different. Jim looked to be at least ten years her junior. A body-building blond who worked out in shorts and sleeveless tee-shirts that showed off his tats, he favored classic exercises: free weights, the punching bag, and an impressive mix of pull-ups, push-ups, and sit-ups. On his high-speed jump-rope routine, the plastic-coated wire rope spun into invisibility, and his feet seemed to hover a mere fraction of an inch above the floor.

The dance between them had started simply enough and had elaborated slowly. Jim, who usually arrived after her, would nod and smile before turning to the hand weights. The nod and smile progressed to a few words as he walked past her. Then, one Wednesday, came the touch. It was fleeting and subtle. His hand brushed hers as he slipped between machines to stand and chat with her. She did not pull away but kept her left hand on the same spot on the handrail, making possible another passing touch as he threaded his way back out to the exercise floor. At the time, Blake had noted the wedding band on her hand. An affair? They seemed to be an unlikely couple, but he'd seen stranger pairings over his years of clinical practice.

This morning, Jim arrived late, hand towel draped over his shoulder, and made a beeline toward Dee on her elliptical just as Blake was cranking up the angle on his treadmill to its steepest setting. Jim leaned on the frame of her machine and smiled up at her as she continued her routine. With each cycle, her hip would make the briefest contact with his fingers. As they chatted about the news, he lifted his hand and touched her bare arm to make a point. After a few minutes, he placed his hand on her back before heading toward the exercise floor. It was the sort of move that these days could get you ejected with accusations of unwanted advances or outright sexual harassment.

When Dee wrapped up her time on the elliptical, Blake punched the stop button on his treadmill, did a perfunctory spray-and-wipe, and race-walked to catch up with her at the water cooler. He filled a paper cup, chug-a-lugged, then smiled at her as he tossed the crumpled cup into the recycle bin. "Well, back to the rat race," he said.

She grunted in agreement as she kept sipping from her

just-refilled stainless water bottle.

"Yeah, well, see you next time," he added.

It was lame small talk that he hoped would not be taken as a pass. At sixty-six, he had learned that one of the benefits of being his age was that he at last could chat with younger women without their automatic assumption that he was hitting on them. With Dee and Jim, he had entertained fantasies of sitting down over coffee to draw out their stories, but he knew he would never act on the impulse. Hello and a grunt by the cooler looked like the limit of that fantasy.

¤ ¤ ¤

As a sullen spring finally brightened into the warmth of early summer, the crowd at the Y gradually shifted. With school out, older groups of day campers took over the pool or lined up for games in the park. A bevy of new exercise classes were on offer, and workout attire began to show more skin.

Blake watched as Jim and Dee progressed from stolen touches to a hand squeeze out in the open whenever they separated. And he noted her watching Jim in the free-weights area off to one side, following him with her eyes as he did his curls and vertical rowing with hand weights.

Because even the regulars varied their schedules and days of the week somewhat, Blake did not at first notice she had not shown up for more than a week. He was waiting outside the workout room, feigning interest in the various classes and competitions posted on the bulletin board, when Jim arrived. As the man passed, Blake asked him, "You a runner? What do you think of this race, the Pond Run 10K coming up?"

"Not a runner. You?"

Blake laughed. "At my age, I'm a walker, and just glad I don't have to use a walker. Yet."

"You do all right. I've seen you sweating away on the treads. You oughta cross train, though, vary the routine."

"It's post-cardio purgatory. My doc says I have to do that five or six days a week if I want to keep seeing next year."

"Really? I guess you do what you gotta do. And I better go do it."

"Yeah. Funny, I haven't seen that friend of yours lately. She's usually someone you could set your watch by. You know, the one with the Red Sox cap and the frizzy mop."

Jim's eyes narrowed in disapproval. "She'll be back. And she's . . . she's not my friend."

"Sorry, I thought you and—"

Jim just shook his head and walked away. Blake watched him cross to the punching dummy and start pounding away in a fierce left, left, right-cross syncopation.

¤ ¤ ¤

Jim proved right in his forecast. In another week, Dee was back, doing the ellipticals again and flirting with Jim as if nothing had intervened, except that maybe she had lost some weight and now crossed over into the genuinely skinny. At one point, as she pedaled away on the elliptical, Jim leaned in close to her, said something softly, then glanced toward Blake, who pretended to be staring off into space.

By the following week she was gone again, and Jim continued his regular workouts as if he were a semi-pro welter weight in perpetual training for the next match.

At the end of the week, Blake dragged out his stay on the treadmill until Jim headed into the weight room. After wiping down his machine, Blake walked over to the long, low rack to pick up a pair of five-pound hand weights. "I decided to take your advice."

"What?" Jim looked up from the bench where he looked to be pressing more than Blake weighed.

"You said I should vary the routine, cross-train. Thought I'd try it."

"Sure, that's always a good idea."

"She's gone again," Blake said, "that woman, the one with all the hair."

Jim started laughing so hard that he struggled to lower the barbell. "All the hair? Are you talking about Eagle?"

"Eagle? Is that her name?"

"No, just her nickname. And what is your thing with her, anyway?"

"Not a thing. Just curious. I thought . . . well, I thought you two, well, knew each other."

"Well, you could say that, I suppose, although she certainly knew me better than the other way around. Why are you so curious?"

"I'm just the curious sort, a people watcher by nature. I noticed her hair and . . ."

Jim slid out from under the weight and sat up. "You know how funny that is? You know why we called her Eagle? It was a wig, the hat and hair. Get it? Eagle? Bald Eagle? She was balder than . . . balder than you."

"Well, your friend seemed . . ."

"I told you, not my friend. She . . ."—he licked his lips— "She's my wife . . . ex."

"You two . . . oh, now I see. Here I thought maybe you

two were, like, more than friends."

"We were. And less than friends, too."

"I think I understand. I'm sorry. I'll leave you to your weights."

"Naw, that's all right. I've probably been over-training lately anyway. You drink coffee? Or are you one of those health nuts like Eve-Lynn?"

"Eve-Lynn?"

"Eagle. Eve-Lynn."

"Ah, I see. No, I'm no health nut, which may be part of what bought me a heart attack a few years back. What they call a widow-maker, but I'm not married and I guess it wasn't my time."

"You end up with one of those, like, triple-bypass operations?"

"No, I got lucky. They put in a couple of stents, told me to start working out and stop drinking, and sent me on my way."

"And here you are, a gym rat."

"Hardly. I do my treadmill run fleeing the Grim Reaper, but I still having a glass or two—or three—with dinner. There's only so much I'm willing to give up, and good wine is not on the list. Good drugs are what get us through the night."

"Amen, bro, so let's knock off early and knock back a couple of espressos. I mean, it's morning, too early for alcohol, and there's a nice little coffee bar around the corner."

"You don't have to do this, you know. I really didn't mean to intrude."

"Sure you did, but it's okay. You're easy to talk with."

"Thanks. I'm buying."

"No you're not. I invited you."

¤ ¤ ¤

Zarah's, a friendly local hold-out against the Starbucking of the world, was only a little over a block away but new to Blake, whose world was limited to a handful of preset pathways. Both men ordered a double espresso before staking out a table-for-two toward the back. After a stir of the crema and a couple of airy sips, Blake opened. "So, is Eagle . . . er, Eve-Lynn coming back."

"No."

"You say that with such certainty."

"Yeah. She died last week."

"Oh, I'm so sorry."

"Me, too. But it was a long time coming. Cancer. The chemo took her hair, pubes and all. She pinned this wig she picked up to the baseball cap. It was her thing. Four rounds of chemo that went nowhere, but, in the end, she got to go the way she wanted."

"The way she wanted?"

"Watching the sunset with me . . . ,"—his voice cracked— "with me holding her hand."

Blake took his time with another sip. "I thought . . . didn't you say you were divorced?"

"We were. What difference does it make? You love somebody. Doesn't stop because you split."

"You left her? With her dying of cancer? You walked out on your dying wife?"

"No, she left me. I couldn't handle it. I was so angry at her. I beat her up with words. You know what I'm saying? There she's the one dying, and I was so fucking pissed that I couldn't keep from yelling at her because she was leaving me. So she did."

"She did it to get away from . . . from your anger, your resentment?"

"No, she did it for me, a parting gift. She knew I couldn't handle it, so she walked out to spare me."

Blake nodded. There was nothing more to say. He understood. He'd lost Sue when they were barely more than kids. She was pregnant, young, and invincible—no seatbelt. She flew through the windshield when the car struck the bridge abutment, but Roberta, a toddler responsibly strapped into her approved car seat, was spared. Sixteen years later—sixteen years of fighting and recrimination and single-parent schedule-juggling later, Roberta hopped a train for Seattle and disappeared into the Pacific Northwest. There was no anger left in him by then. He had been so angry at Sue for . . . for what? For hitting a patch of black ice on I95 heading south from Portland, a patch no one could see until they were on top of it? For not wearing a seatbelt? For dying? Yes, for dying, for leaving him. He had been livid with anger and overcome with remorse and embarrassment for it. And his anger poisoned his relationship with his daughter, who came to look more like her mother with every year. Her last words as she boarded the train for Washington struck him like an RPG: "Fuck you. Fuck you both. I love you." The train growled the rest of her anger for her as it pulled out of the station.

One didn't need to be a dispassionate observer to know what had been going on. The diagnosis was easy, even from the beginning, but recovery remained always just beyond Blake's ability. Now he worked out on a treadmill, fittingly running while standing in place, watching. Watching.

He nodded.

Jim sipped a milliliter or two from his coffee and nodded back.

They sat for several minutes, wordless in a way men could be when wrestling with the overwhelming, slowly sipping their bittersweet coffee as if they needed to make it last for a lifetime.

Death's
Children

1

Fiery Meltaa pursued her tangerine companion across the sky. Earlier, in the ruddy morning light of lone Melduu, people had strolled the streets and broad avenues of the Orange City in comfort, but with the Great Twins together in the sky, there was no escape from the heat. Delaware Jackson began to sweat as he puffed toward the central plaza, his anxiety growing with the rising temperature. The i-Mel were all around him, yet somehow, even in the double glare of full daylight they seemed to elude him, giving him everything and telling him nothing. He knew he needed to act soon, yet he feared that either his own self-doubt or the festering distrust between him and the i-Mel would stop his plans. Del scanned the crowds for his partner, unsure whether he really hoped to see Joanna Ent or wished more to avoid an uncertain encounter with her.

Ahead of him, the cubist bulk of the Science Complex loomed, topped by a bronze casting of the i-Mel emblem: the Unclosed Square. Del raised the cowl of his cloak to protect his dark head from the suns and began the climb up the broad stone steps, their finely pitted orange faces made almost smooth, almost amber by the harsh, doubled light. Concentrating, watching his feet, he made a careful diagonal ascent of the mountain of blocks. Even after months of experiment and practice in the almost daily pilgrimage, Del still arrived at the top humbled by the stairway. At the correct angle, he could manage a steady, though strenuous pace—long push up, short step, short step, long push, short step—but the early crowds prevented him from climbing more than a half dozen of the stones on the same tack.

As he neared the square-pillared summit, Del's concentration was broken by the rasp of a hoarse voice.

"Why do you walk the steps so?"

Seated in Del's path was an i-Mel, bony arms crossed over her thighs, long fingers idly exploring the texture of the zei-stone. Her bright yellow eyes studied him with the intensity of Meltaa.

"You walk this," she waved one bare arm upward and out. "Then this," she added, gesturing with the other, "like a stone-lizard prey-stalking."

Del said nothing. It surprised him to be addressed in English by a stranger on the street. As if impatient for an answer, the i-Mel rose and stood, towering over Del from the step above. Her voice lacked the trombone-like sonority of an adult, and Del realized she was not yet full-grown. After one last spurt of growth she would stand a graceful two-and-a-half meters tall, but now, her high knees made her seem almost unbearably awkward, a stilt-walker in danger of being toppled, as though a modest gust could send her tumbling down the steps of the Complex in a flurry of blue-brown limbs.

She reached down and touched his cheek, turning his

face to one side then the other with her delicate fingers. At this familiarity, Del involuntarily stepped back, stumbling on the edge of the stone. He writhed to regain his balance. With one unsteady foot on the step below, he looked up just as she began to laugh.

"Your nose is not so long as the hmerbot, as they tell," she said between husky hoots, "but your odd-bent legs make you as clumsy as the tales say."

Del struggled to keep a grim face, unwilling to accept mockery at the hands of a youngster. Sensing victory nearing, she continued, "But it is so. You do not move with ease, no fault to you, but to your legs. Your legs are wrong, so you walk wrong. So," she said, swinging her long, lower limbs in a goose-stepping parody. Through his quivering grimaces, Del began to laugh, and the girl hooted again.

"I speak well," she said. "See, I know this because you understand enough to laugh. You even laugh strange. So." She started to imitate his raggedly suppressed snigger but broke into loud, uncontrollable hoots. Del laughed, too, and soon both were helpless to stop. Each time they would regain composure, one would look at the other and begin to laugh, the sound so funny to the other that soon both were victims once more.

"How are you called?" the i-Mel asked, at last catching her breath.

"Delaware E. Jackson, cultural exchange representative from Earth."

"Delawareejackson, yes, you are the one who studies us, while the other studies what we make."

"Well put."

"And I," she said, placing her hand on her head in the

i-Mel equivalent of pointing to herself, "am called Dinaillaabrolgdth." The name tumbled out, each consonant distinct, each vowel a definite pulse.

"Well, Dinaillaa . . ."

"Dinaillaabrolgdth."

"Yes, well, it has been good talking with you, but I have business in the Science Complex. Very important things, hard to explain even if they are 'soft' science. Ha, ha." He started up the last dozen steps.

"But wait," she said, following after him, "we do not hand-press yet. I plan catching you or the other here every day when you come. Ahbainevvfer, she is mother to Sirssenduula, well, Sirssenduula is a friend, see. She does the loops and bars with me after," she paused, frowning, "after schooling, yes? Well, Sirssenduula does the bars better than the loops, but Ahbainevvfer said we should not annoy the ones from other worlds. Even for hand-press. The others ran. I do not know the fear they feel, even on the highest loop." She stopped talking just as they neared the top. "On one foot!" she declared in an afterthought.

"I am not quite sure I understood all that or who every-body is. The words were fine, though, and we can handpress if you wish." He extended his hand, palm outward, in the i-Mel form of greeting, but hers remained at her side.

"No, it is not enough. This," she said, as she placed the back of her hand to his cheek and held it there for a second. "Because we laughed together."

Suddenly she croaked with delight and turned to run effortlessly, full-tilt down the stairs, crying in u-Mel to several other youngsters who suddenly appeared from behind the pillars of the nearest building. Their rapid, high screeches and hooting laughter echoed through the stone colonnade.

Del mounted the last few steps and entered the Complex, for a moment wishing he, too, could run away, down the steps, to join the young i-Mel in their easy games.

2

Once inside the gloomy entrance, Del threw back his cowl. He surveyed the crowd but recognized no one among the dancing blue-brown faces. Acutely conscious that he was recognized by everyone, he hurried toward the stairway, hoping to be spared the embarrassment of having to ask the name of someone with whom he might have worked for weeks or months. He could sympathize with those who daily suffered his confusion. As a young man he had so often heard that "all you blacks look alike." Still, he could not tell the i-Mel apart, and his difficulties with the everyday discriminations of life on Melem had become legend.

He thought back to the encounter with the girl. She had been, like most i-Mel, so artlessly open. He felt almost embarrassed by his own scheming. With little direct evidence, he had convinced himself that he was being misled, that significant information was being withheld. Now, his i-Mel counterparts were beginning to recognize his distrust and suspected him of stalling. He knew they wanted him out in the field, away from the Complex and the Orange City. It galled him that he could not draw on his partner's expertise, but the rift between him and Joanna kept widening. He would have to find a way himself.

He tightened his robe around him as he made the final turn leading to the Form Room. Here, the massive stone kept the temperature cooler than on the sun-parched streets, but Del recognized the chill he felt as a sign of his own unease.

On the heels of two specialists, Del stepped into the huge room. It was crowded with geometric blocks in various regular and irregular shapes, mostly waist high or shoulder high, but here and there towering over Del. Among them, only twisting, single-file aisles remained. Nowhere could more than two people gather to converse except around one of the many forms.

Beside one irregular block near the center, he spotted Dortaal and Martezth. Perhaps he counted them among his first i-Mel friends largely because he could so readily distinguish them: Dortaal, whose ears sported the small incisions popular in Eastsands, and Martezth, who had lost a thumb in childhood. The others were mostly "the others" to him.

Martezth spread her arms, beckoning to him as he picked his way through the maze.

"You walk with your face in shadow today," she said, implying that she found him somewhat remote.

"And you are tall in the suns," he answered in greeting. "I have thoughts on the directions of our exploring together."

"Ah, good!" another trumpeted quickly. It was Alseq-qinhh, elder social scientist of the group, Del surmised, although he was not certain. "Enough time has elapsed on this armchair anthropology we do," she continued. "You have shown us that you can handle yourself with the constructs of our culture, and we have given you what we could of the abstractions. The concrete and the stone of our world await." She slipped into the rhythmic u-Mel language and added, "I admit to impatience to try our teamed abilities, to see Melem through your eyes and to offer mine. Though I have studied many of our cultures, yet have I to represent one. The chance, at last, to be the informant in a field study and to confound elaborate scientific theories with casual comment is," she hooted with delight, "more delicious than winter love."

"Alseqqinhh," Del responded, continuing in u-Mel, "I, too, am as impatient as the Great Twins in winter, but this is no small matter, the first social congress of two races, and I am chased by doubts as a sand-bird by a stone-lizard. I sense there are important things still darkened to me, like the void within a zei-stone, unseen, known only by the ring of the stone-worker's hammer on its hollowness. I am not ready to meet all of Melem."

Alseqqinhh held her mouth open in the broad oval of an i-Mel smile. "Aside from your excessive use of the ex-emplative form, you will do quite well among the scorched peasants."

The assembled group all hooted softly as Del blushed, grateful that his skin disguised his embarrassment. As the rest discussed his social acclimation, he wondered whether the i-Mel representatives back on Earth would get the same encouragement to mix and mingle. Fat chance, he thought. The four-stars and the politicos would keep them politely sequestered, incommunicado as long as possible. You would need a press pass and six initials after your name just to get into the same building as the i-Mel. Why, then, were the i-Mel here so eager to get him into the field? Did they want him away from the Complex and its vast files, its computers? They offered sound and ingenuous arguments, which Del instinctively distrusted. His childhood had taught him to trust only his own ability to decipher hype and double-talk. He was all but helpless before anything that sounded straightforward, as the i-Mel usually did.

Del spread his hands to gesture for silence. "I have an idea by which we may all be satisfied." They grinned down at him, gaping-mouthed, for he had chosen one of their favorite opening lines. "What we will do is use the function-forms to aid us in searching out areas of deficiency in my knowledge of the language, the morés, and the basic facts of life here on Melem. We will look for potentially significant matters on which I am still ignorant."

"But is that not precisely the purpose of field study?" asked Martezth.

"And what," continued Dortaalgnuwaar, "do you propose to use as search keys? Perhaps 'not-in-the-mind-of-Delawareejackson' and 'probability-of-gaff-exceeds-twenty-percent.'" Again, easy laughter. "You have taken our Principle of the Absent too seriously, work-friend, too simplistically."

Dortaal was both the warmest and the most remote of the i-Mel. He was not merely customarily open, but actually friendly to Del and to Joanna, yet his immense intellect and his mastery of information technology made him a distant and formidable figure to Del.

"Dortaal, I think it can be done; I cannot be certain. From our discussions and from my experience here in the Orange City, I have a conception of life on Melem, but I do not trust it. I don't know why I do not, nor even if I should not, only that I have a sense of, of non-fit."

Martezth offered an u-Mel word. "The shape that touches irregularly," she translated.

"Exactly. But my conception can be modeled, its shape made visible and matched against what you know. I believe we can computerize the model using the conformal mapping techniques you have described to me."

"Delawareejackson, you know not the words you speak," Dortaal said. "Heuristic modeling of symbolic processes is our greatest skill in information science, but you are proposing no less than a complete and comprehensive world model, not merely economics, but complete in socio-cultural terms as well. It is theoretically possible to define the conformal contours and to game with the two models were we to build them, but the effort is beyond our resources.

"Why do it? Why study a model of the world when the world is there, just beyond these walls?"

Del studied him, trying to decipher or guess the true nature of Dortaal's objections. To him they seemed valid but beside the point, perhaps just another obstacle to keep Del from the truth. Still, they could be used to help him spring his trap.

"It is overly ambitious, then," he said. "You should humor me and test the feasibility of the modeling with more limited subject matter." Slowly, he told himself.

"Certainly, if the domain of discourse were modest enough," began one of the specialists, "the model could be programmed. But if the map were so small, would not the results be predictable? Would you not already be confident of your knowledge? What would you model, anyway?"

"Something well-defined, but with broad socio-cultural implications. Let's say, i-Mel biology."

"Still too broad."

Almost, Del thought. "Okay. Look, we know how pervasive is the influence of human development, birth to death, on the shape of human culture and history. The trauma of birth, the protracted dependency—it all impacts our socio-cultural structures, if not directly, then through personality. The focus could be on the biology of i-Mel development, its manifestation in i-Mel culture." Del waited.

"I suppose, but I doubt much will be proved."

"Then it can be done? So, let's start." Careful, Del told himself, don't shake the trap and frighten the quarry. He sensed, though, that he was at last getting someplace. If his finger was not on the key to unlock the mystery, it was at least in the right pocket.

But the i-Mel temporized much of the day, debating the approach, even returning to the question of feasibility. With intense seriousness, they turned to one or another of the forms in the room. Each form had some function, or many, identified by its shape and position. Most gave access to the intricate network of computers that served the facility or, as it sometimes seemed to Del, were served by it. A question would arise in their discussions, and one of the i-Mel would stride purposefully to a particular but undistinguished block, touch it carefully on a spot completely unmarked, and its formerly stone-like exterior would flicker with pictures and graphs or glow with the outline of a keypad or open to reveal a slit from which emerged stiff, narrow sheets imprinted with u-Mel text. It was part of their aesthetic, Del knew: nothing becoming something, the nondescript emerging as distinct. There were also forms that were never visited, at least not that Del had noticed, and these he suspected did nothing—the ultimate enshrinement of the i-Mel riddle.

By the end of the day, neither the function-forms nor the i-Mel had produced much of interest to Del. One by one the i-Mel left, quitting, as always, as each saw fit. Finally, only Martezth remained.

"I think," she said, placing her thumbless hand atop her tight, black curls, "you need to get into the field. Even your partner has had to work in our laboratories to understand our science. Have you not, Joannakarenent?"

Del turned to see Joanna threading her way through the maze.

"Of course I have, Martezthyeddil. But what is this about?" she asked, picking up the pile of imprints in front of Del as casually as if they were hers, a manner in which she dealt with much of Del's world. "I see they haven't loosened you up enough yet, Jackson." She riffled the imprints. "More stuff on biology? Does this have anything to do with me?"

"No, I just needed an area to model, something precise, easily defined." Joanna had made him feel defensive, as she often did. "It's no accident that I picked the one overlap in our assignments."

They left the Form Room, and as they walked the nearly deserted hallways, Del told Joanna of his suspicions that the i-Mel were withholding important information.

"What do you think it is?" she asked.

In tones mockingly conspiratorial he offered, "Who knows? I have a hunch it has something to do with death. Maybe they're immortal."

"You have to be joking!"

"Why?"

"Because immortals don't laugh," she said, laughing. With a quick flip of her head she bounced away like the young basketball star she was.

"But what if they were?" he mumbled as he stepped into the peach and mauve of the double winter sunset.

<h1 style="text-align:center">3</h1>

The girl sat on the end of the bottom step, bare feet shuffling in the yellow-leafed planting that bordered the plaza.

"You stand stooped in the waning suns," she said in u-Mel.

Del, still several steps away, looked down at her and marveled, not only at the i-Mel practice of interpreting one another's moods on meeting, but also at their unerring perceptiveness. How did they read him so easily, when he had to work so hard to understand them?

"I am puzzled, Dinaillaabrolgdth," he said, stammering out the string of final consonants. "And I surprise myself that I recall your naming."

"Is it hard, this remembering how each of us is different?"

"Yes. Very hard for me. I admit it. To me, you all look so much alike." He was surprised by his own confession, his candor. He started to apologize.

"No, it is good you say this. Before this suns' risings I thought you had a nose like the hmerbot." She gave one hoot, short and high.

Del laughed. "You must tell me about this hmerbot. How does it look?"

"Like this," she said, wetting a finger in her mouth. She traced on the zei-stone a squat quadruped with a trunk-like proboscis, then, with finger re-wet, added a field of grass. With a fingernail she meticulously worried at some minute feature amidst the grass.

"It is hard doing it this way," she said, licking her finger again to retrace the already evaporating outline of the hmerbot.

"You do very well. I think I would recognize it if I saw one. In fact," he said, sitting down beside her, "we have a creature much like it. An anteater, it is called."

"Yes, well this one eats the hmer, see, there in the el-grass. They are dark blue, like the el-grass, and very small. But this hmer is not well drawn. With ink, though, are there many sketches under my name.

"You should call me Earth-style, by small name. Then you will always remember. All my friends are taking Earth names. Sirssenduula is calling herself 'Sarah.' I could call myself 'Daniel,' no?"

"No."

"It is not an Earth name?"

"It is, but a name for males; you would have to use a feminine form. We have this strange custom that men may only have certain names, women others. You could shorten your name in u-Mel to Dinail."

"If you like it, then I shall be Dinail. Does your naming have a meaning, Delawareejackson?"

Del smiled, remembering to open his mouth wide. "I have three names, as most of us do. My first name was my grandmother's choice. Delaware. It is the name of a river and, before that, the name of a people. The 'E' is just a letter from our alphabet. It stands for my middle name, which I hate, and which I tell no one. My last name is Jackson. There are many with that name on Earth. It says the family to whom I belong."

"I do not belong to anyone," she said emphatically.

"No, I imagine not! But you are of a house, yes? What house is it?"

"The House Deruudth: I am daughter to Dortaalgnu-waar and Graillinevf."

"You're Dortaal's daughter? That explains it, why you speak English so well. How do you keep straight who is of what house with everyone having a different name?" he asked, shifting the focus to professional interests.

"But why? Does it matter from what house I come? What I do is written under my name, not my father's, not my mother's. I am not a suckling within my mother's belly. I am already nearly eight and a fine artist. But the naming cycle is not hard. In the cycle of the house Deruudth, after Dortaal comes Debv, then Dinaillaa, after Evf comes Vfer and Brolgdth in the cycle of four fours. There are many cycles, but one need learn only those of interest. My slow-name, which is Brolgdth, is of my mother's cycle, my fast-name of my father's. With my brother, of course, his slow-name is of my father's cycle. See?" She stopped, holding her breath.

Del was unsure, but he said, "Yes, well, I must get back to my room, Dinail. I have much to think upon."

"Then I will walk with you," she announced, taking his arm.

Del started to protest, but succumbed to her jostling

insistence. Only the palest of afterglows lit the sky as they walked. Concealed gas-tubes lighted automatically to mark the walkways, and faces became dramatically modeled by the suffused neon glow reflecting off the streets. I-mel, many in the crepe capes of current evening fashion, moved hurriedly to their destinations.

Del found himself chatting with quiet, unexpected ease. He felt free to talk in this way to her, a young alien, as others might disclose themselves to a bartender or unburden themselves in prayer or speak foolishly and with emotion to a stuffed bear, the status of "non-person" being the catalyst for deeply personal revelation. Truly an i-Mel, Dinail matched him disclosure for disclosure with the artless authenticity of youth, which i-Mel of all ages seemed to practice.

"It scares me to show anyone my sketches," she said. "They will approve, I know. I do not fear their scorn." She wheezed a sharp sigh. "They will be honest, maybe. Then maybe I will learn that I am no better and no worse than any others who draw in the school. But probably they will just approve, and I will know nothing, which is worse. I want to show my work to the whole of Melem, but I want no one to see. That is the fear I know, not on the loops and bars or speaking the exemplative in front of the entire school."

"It is the same for me," Del whispered.

"Do you also sketch?"

"Only in a manner of speaking. I write poetry, rhyming words. I have written quite a few since reaching Melem. There has been much silence and solitude for me in the Orange City."

She stopped walking and pivoted on his arm to face

him. "I would hear this poetry. And I would show you my sketches. Some."

"No, Dinail, it's all in English. I haven't learned enough u-Mel to write poems in it."

"Ah, but your u-Mel is good, and my English is even more. I would understand," she pleaded.

Del felt awkward. He blushed, but even as he hesitated, he began mentally sorting through pieces he had committed to memory, searching for one suitable.

"There is one, a poem about Meltaa and Melduu I wrote in the plane from the Slowlands, shortly after I arrived here. It goes:

> The wearied, arid Twins descend.
> As one, Melduu and Meltaa bend
> To take
> Small sips, a day-long thirst to slake.
> Then deeper from the placid lake
> Of sand,
> Of crimson runnels fanned
> In waves that flood and flare and break
> Upon the drinkers. Drenched
> In orange fluorescent spray,
> And still unquenched,
> They drown to end
> The day."

Neither spoke. Del studied her face, desperate for some decipherable reaction. Her eyes, set wide astride her small nose, held his as she reached to place the back of her hand once more on his cheek. Then she turned and ran.

"Damn," he said, without emotion.

4

The frequent restdays were a treasure. Del spent his in his room going over notes and a small stack of imprints carried from the Complex. He had that industrious habit, built out of the cheerless rise from blue-collar origins, of filling leisure time and odd moments with extra work. As a schoolboy he had learned that the difference between a successful WASP and the black kid who wore a better jacket or beat him out for the last place on the debating team was often in how they spent their Sundays. So, by the light of his treasured tungsten lamp, Del agonized.

He thought of the strange, non-violent birth of the i-Mel. It seemed reasonable that societies would be shaped by patterns of birthing and child-rearing. Death was another story, and Del understood little about its place in i-Mel culture. What had he and Joanna missed? A secret cult of death, a complex of powerful taboos, a fear of death so deeply enculturated that it had become endemic repression? No, no, and no. None fit. Perhaps they could arrest aging but wanted to keep the technology from humans. It seemed unthinkable to Del that anyone who possessed the knowledge would forego its use. The imprints yielded little, though he read and reread the difficult technical terms and phrases that peppered the texts.

Finally, the confinement of his studio overcame both his work ethic and his preference for the room's temperate comfort. Del grabbed his cloak, hesitating briefly as if trying to recall a purpose, then opened the massive olive door. His apartment was a roomy ell a few steps off the lobby of the modest in-town inn: cool, accessible, and therefore choice by i-Mel standards. To Del, who had known his share of efficiencies and had walked down to an apartment more often than he had ridden up to one, it felt familiar from the first. Joanna and many of the dignitaries drawn to the Orange City by its outworld visitors preferred the luxury hotels in the newer sections at the Perimeter. But here, near the city's hub, yet not truly at the center of things, Del treasured the closest thing to a private life that he would know until many years after his return to Earth.

He crossed the quiet, foam-floored lobby to leave his tubular door key with the innkeeper, a pleasant, talkative man who knew Del well enough merely to nod. Del had become another odd but accepted fixture in a small inner-city neighborhood. At the Perimeter he would have remained a celebrity, like Joanna, who relished it.

He was on the street before remembering to don his cloak. It still felt unnatural to him to cover up in the heat of the day, but Melem's blazing Twins had reminded him that not even black people were immune to sunburn.

On Earth he would have been a striking figure, his towering cocoa head set off by lemon robes. To the i-Mel he looked like a short and homely adolescent, with sallow skin and overly dark eyes. He and Joanna had often discussed the wisdom of sending two tall African-Americans on the exchange mission. Perhaps squat Mongolians would have been more readily seen as alien, more easily accepted as truly different. Instead, he and Joanna were often seen as misshapen i-Mel. Of course, even had he anticipated this problem, Del was certain he would not have protested, because the superficial racial similarities had paid his ticket to the head of the line.

Race alone had not been the whole story, of course. For once, Del's obstinate refusal to specialize in one discipline had been valued, and he ended up paired with a woman as eclectic as he was, one of three pairs of young scientists competing for the joyride of the generation. As he saw it, Joanna's quicker wit and more visible energy had carried the day, compensating for his inadequacies. He envied her talents but never resented them; they were simply givens, to be accepted and taken into account, like his self-assessed limitations, like the color of his skin.

Meltaa was setting just ahead of her twin, leaving Del to walk in the russet light of lonely Melduu. He pulled back his cowl and turned onto the Avenue of Waters, heading nearly into the low sun as it played with the diamond waterfalls of many fountains. The Melduu-slow sunset was perhaps the loveliest, drenching the world in red wine, fading gradually into deep maroon. As he marched sunward, Del's mind blanked out everything except the deep ruby orb settling patiently into the misting waters.

Slowly returning from a thought-free reverie, Del realized the sky had blackened and filled with stars, though a faint glow persisted ahead. Disoriented, he whirled to get his bearings and discovered the neon of the city proper already well behind him. The glow ahead, he figured, must belong to the Perimeter, the ring of commerce and communications that buffered between the city and the far continents. Joanna's hotel, he knew, fell midway between the Avenue of Waters and the next thoroughfare connecting the rim to its hub. He could be there in half an hour. His stroll took on purpose as he tightened his waist-belt against the chill air and quickened his stride toward the multi-hued sky-glow.

As he approached, the glow gradually resolved into the distinct sources of the Perimeter's gay shops and bright avenues. Here, the gas tubes shone in the myriad colors of a carnival midway. Small, turtle-like taxis wove in and out of traffic that was mostly pedestrian. Joanna's hotel erupted from a phosphorescent garden of spotlighted fountains. Its windows, like those of the low-lying offices scattered in its shadow, searched the night with their orange-yellow beams, the tint to which the i-Mel eyes were most sensitive.

In the gaudy lobby, Del waited for an elevator with the studied impatience of someone absorbed in business to come, thus avoiding conversation with curious i-Mel. At last he was rescued by the irising gate of the elevator.

He got off on the sixteenth floor, a number so auspicious that it had its own special ideograph in u-Mel. At the end of a hall, he found the simple placard: "Joanna Karen Ent, Terrestrial Representative." Only after repeated knocks did the door crack open to him, revealing Joanna's shocked face.

"Del, what a surprise! What brings you to the decadent rim of the world?"

Behind her, Del could see another figure, taller. "I'll see you at the Complex tomorrow," he said quickly. "You have company." He started to tighten the sash of his cloak, wanting neither to interrupt anything nor to spend an evening with a stranger.

"Nonsense, Del! It's just George. Certainly you can join us. George wouldn't mind." She tugged Del's elbow and drew him into the large sitting room of her suite. Its walls, finished in slick plastic with the sheen of wet leather, were patched with news photos of their arrival on Melem. "Del, this is Jurshaabrolgdth who insists on being called George. George, Delaware Jackson, my younger brother and expert on the mushy sciences." She giggled and reached for a slender budvase of a glass.

George rose to proffer his hand in an Earth-style handshake. Del's, however, met with palm reversed, and the i-Mel hooted. Scowling slightly, Del turned his hand around.

"I write copy for the Eastsands Network," the i-Mel began, "You certainly have seen my nameprint on stories." Del started to say that he had, but George continued without notice. "Your house-sister has been of great service in bringing me to the current of the exchange." It was Del's turn to laugh.

"We're not of the same house," Joanna explained. "Del, can I get you some tigg? You have tried it, surely." She refilled her glass with a muddy brown liquid.

"I find its effects too much like lunch on a roller coaster. I'll take water, thank you. Interesting issue the tigg raises," he said, seeming to address George. "We were warned against experimenting with the native psychotropics. Considering what we know of the differences in cytochemistry between i-Mel and humans, isn't it surprising that the alcohols should have such similar effects on the two species?"

Joanna looked annoyed. "Not surprising at all, Del. They are all simple neuro-depressants. And look, we were expected to make discretionary departures from guidelines. Tigg is rather essential to social intercourse on Melem. But then, you might not know much of that."

George, wishing not to become ensnared in their disagreement, quickly took his leave. As the door closed behind him, Joanna attacked Del for driving him away.

"Wait just a minute," Del interrupted. "Your protest broadcasts more than casual interest, Joanna." She avoided his eyes. "Wait. You? You and the i-Mel?"

She faced him defiantly. "Why not? We are adults."

"Adult whats? Joanna, really, it is simply not the same. We may think in anthropomorphic terms, but they are not humans. There are many impolite names that come to me now. I'd hate to think of you in those terms."

Joanna pursed her lips and leaned toward him, studying the pores of his face with exaggerated interest. "I don't think you're concerned with either sexual ethics or the paraphilias. Know what I think? I think your male ego is threatened. Just like all those closet racists back in training who were fearful that your black schlong might be bigger and more satisfying than their little white bananas." She waited, but he said nothing. Then, very softly: "It didn't work with you and me, Del. Sometimes the best of friends and partners don't hit it off in bed.

"Whatever you think, Del, George is a person: intelligent, ambitious, determined, exciting. I like him. We make love, Del, simple, affectionate, easy love. I know you know about that kind of sex, Del. You're a good lover. So am I. We just weren't good together."

Del looked around helplessly. "But what can you do? I mean . . ."

"You mean physically? It works pretty well, frankly. You've seen the slides. That's anatomy, that's all. It works, and I admit the physical novelty was part of it at first. But novelty doesn't last six months; George and I have."

"That means you two started making it shortly after we arrived, even before you and I stopped getting it on." He smiled. "You're pretty fast for an old lady," he said, teasing her about her prematurely gray hair.

"Watch who you call old, brother!"

They both laughed, relaxing the bristles finally, and began to bring each other up to date.

"I'm afraid I have little to relate," Del put in when there was a lull in Joanna's recitation. "There isn't a lot that's not in the reports already. Except this thing about death. Oh, I know it may seem chimerical, but by anthropological and ethnographic standards, the evidence is beginning to feel heavyweight."

"Maybe you better fill me in, then, if you can tolerate my ethnographic ignorance."

So Del began to assemble for her the puzzle pieces he had been saving, pieces that did not appear in his reports because they were the things not there or almost seen, the outline of a void.

"Del, maybe you're onto something. I'm just not comfortable with either the kinds of inferences you have to make or the data from which they must be drawn. I have to trust your skills and intuition, up to the point where you infer that the i-Mel are withholding some great secret from us. What I have just doesn't support it. But this adds even more weight in favor of you doing field work. Surely an entire planet cannot keep a secret from a nosey behavioral scientist, even if a building full of bureaucrats can."

Del got up to leave. "I have one more angle to try for

out-maneuvering the bureaucrats in their home camp before I give up and try for a bivouac. G'night." He kissed the white margin of hair at her forehead, then left.

Back in his room after a brief taxi ride, Del lay awake, brooding over Joanna's involvement with the i-Mel. It seemed so human a thing, but condoning her involvement implied granting humanness to the i-Mel, who, for Del, remained an ambiguous borderline case.

Their anatomy simply clouded categories. The apparent physical similarities were misleading, of course, and were based in very distinct cell chemistries. Both species metabolized carbohydrates and lipids, but there the physiological overlap ended. Del knew that on Earth, though not on Melem, were plausible precedents in the evolution of placental and marsupial mammals. Millions of years of independent evolution had often led to startling superficial similarities for marsupials and placentals in comparable ecological niches.

The i-Mel were something different altogether, as Del had learned back in training. As the details of i-Mel anatomy had become known, speculation had quickly gone beyond mere biology. Although few would have admitted it except to closest friends, most of the trainees harbored erotic fantasies about the i-Mel, with their gentle, gold eyes, their tiny, up-turned noses, and their lean, uncomfortably familiar bodies.

Del still preferred to stay clear of uncomfortable ideation. Before falling asleep he turned his thoughts from sex and birth to the issues of age and dying that seemed to be his real problem.

5

Rounding the blackened needle of the Odus to the Stars just east of the central plaza, Del spotted a group of children at a makeshift stall that had appeared, as they did from time to time, at the foot of the Science Complex. Suddenly, he discovered a craving to top his light breakfast with the chewy sweetness of gum-root. It was still Early Light. The children and the wrinkled skeleton of a stall-keeper were the only others in the square. As he self-consciously paid for his confection, Del looked for Dinail among the customers, their round faces blackened by the predawn glow. But none seemed familiar as they studied him with innocent gold eyes.

"Stand to the East Light," he said in u-Mel, waving his rolled gum-root to them as he mounted the steps. They hooted and waved back, then broke, like a startled flock of ravens, into a pell-mell dash across the plaza, the cacophony of their laughter reverberating in the empty square.

Del was finishing the last bits of sweet when Dortaal and Martezth strode toward him, blue satchels swinging.

"You are faster than the Great Twins this work-day, Delawareejackson. And have you rediscovered your childhood from the function-forms of the Complex of Science?" Martezth asked, pointing to the yellow gum still clinging to his fingers.

Del started to lick the sticky mess from his fingers and mumbled an excuse. Dortaal gestured for him to stop, then opened the satchel he carried to reveal a paper-wrapped parcel. Unfolding it with precise, dramatic movements, Dortaal produced a pair of the gummy confections. One he whipped out with a flourish to place in the corner of his mouth, where it hung and bobbed like a limp yellow cigar, the other he refolded meticulously in its white wrapping and returned to the satchel.

"We are," he said, gum-root waving rhythmically, "both children today."

"As always," Martezth added, bowing. "Perhaps we should, as good school children do, begin our lessons early." She nodded toward the first hallway and the three of them started toward the Form Room.

But the early start came to nothing for Del's ends. Impatience and irritation wore through the layers of his professional manners as, one after the other, technical obstacles were placed in his way. Finally he slammed down a sheaf of imprints. The room fell silent; scattered knots of i-Mel stared over at the group.

"I do not like the way you are handling this, Dortaal. And damn it, Martezth, you are too good a linguist to be this impervious. Alseqqinhh!" He turned imploringly to the elder scientist, who lifted her elbows in a gesture to show her own dismay.

Martezth lowered herself heavily to the edge of the rectangular form at which they worked. She spoke sadly, "I had thought, perhaps, just this morning, that you were young enough to understand us. I must conclude that we understand each other far less than we believed. Alseqqinhh is right. To know more about us you must live among us, know the growing of the i-Mel by growing with us. The answers will not come from the function-forms. Only inside." She put her hand to her head and walked away.

Del wavered between anger and puzzlement. "Look, we

are going to have to turn elsewhere to resolve this. I want to talk with someone higher up, someone who can authorize release of any information."

"Higher up? What does that mean?" asked one of the information specialists.

"I mean the manager, the boss, someone who oversees not just the Relations Team but the whole Complex of Science." Del's request was met with uncomprehending stares.

"What is this 'overseer' function, Alseqqinhh?" Dortaal asked.

"Martezthyeddil would know for certain. Maybe he refers to the Nexus."

"I want to deal with whomever coordinates the entire Complex, one who knows the complete operation."

"That would be the Nexus, wouldn't it, Alseqqinhh?"

"Yes, but why would he wish to deal with the Nexus?"

Once again Del felt the irritation that, to him, identified disguised resistance. He pressed modestly but steadily against it. "Can it be arranged?"

"Not this workday, certainly. The Nexus is a demanding function to fill." Alseqqinhh paused for an eye-blink, then offered, "But I would take you to her workday next. Together we may learn more of why our communication remains so limited."

Perhaps, thought Del.

The real work ended with that and soon the i-Mel commenced their customary, irregular drift from the Complex. As Del made for the door, Dortaal caught up with him, gently placing a hand on his back in one of the few gestures shared by i-Mel and humans. "It is so like you, Del-friend, to want to drive for what you sense to be the heart of the matter. How often it is that the heart lies where we do not look. One can best see into the deep shadows left by the late suns merely by waiting until dawn."

"Philosophy, Dortaal, clever homily."

"Do not sell philosophy for less than its weight. You find us to be paradoxical, therefore you reject your findings. But we are paradoxical. In the Principal of the Absent, what is not, is, and what is, is not. It is paradox, certainly, as we see all important matters in life to be.

"Which brings me to a small matter which is, therefore, one of considerable moment. Dinaillaabrolgdth has told me of your talkings and of the rhyming words. Do not be distressed by this disclosure. She wishes you no embarrassment, nor do I. We are close, as daughter and father are on Melem, so she confides in me her wishes and her discoveries. She wishes you to spend the restday in our house. I would find that thought filled with warmth, too, provided you are not too clouded by the darkness between us here. She will come for you at third hour, if you desire to brighten our house."

Del almost declined automatically, but, sensing another path opened to the information he sought, he said, "It would lighten the day like the Great Twins lifting a summer fog."

6

Del cracked open the heavy door, not knowing what he expected to see, but impatient for Dinail's arrival. There she sat, cross-legged on the thick foam, her lemony eyes fixated on the door but focused far beyond it. She dressed in the style of a young adult: a sash of bright cloth looped around her neck, stretching over her chest and tucked into a belted skirt, thus baring and accentuating her breasts. The fluorescent pink she wore seemed both a cheerful and daring contrast to the bluish iridescence of her deep cocoa skin. He could not remember how she had dressed on their other meetings and by that knew this to be a holiday or occasion.

A fleeting image passed before Del's eyes: himself seated in front of Dinail, the two adrift in the meditative sea of each other's eyes. Somehow the simple vision shocked him, but before he could analyze his reaction or the thought, Dinail looked up at him.

"Sweet brother Delawareejackson, I contemplated the uurd-wood of your door, and my mind took me on a journey to a high place of trees and mist where I once spent a year of my girlhood. I am sorry you caught me in flight."

Del, awkward and unsure whether she expressed regret or apology, said nothing, but reached for his cloak.

"You may not need your cloak, though Meltaa is already high. I will take you by the second-ways, which are shaded and uncrowded at third hour."

Del's cautiousness won out, though, and he pulled the wrap over his shoulders as they left the inn. In the street, the sharp shadows and the dazzling capes of the milling i-Mel danced like a bee swarm before his eyes. He was grateful when Dinail turned immediately from the avenue, leading them down a narrow alleyway between the inn and the low, concrete row of shops to its side. Instantly, the thin air cooled and, almost as fast, grew noticeably damp. Small patches of morning-frost still clung to darkened spots on the sunward wall. Del had avoided all such passageways out of conditioned wariness, but now he saw that this was no mere alley, such as he might have turned into back home. Bright tiles in colors of high contrast—chartreuse and maroon, Prussian blue and peach, lemon and dark olive—adorned the walls. Windows, some with patterned curtains, some displaying small goods, peeked from amidst the tiles.

Dinail led them past shops filled with rock candy and gum-root and the other confections already familiar to Del; others were stacked with unfamiliar cakes and breads. In one window pane, he looked past his own reflection into a small workshop where the shelves were lined with filigreed sculptures and lacy figurines carved from uurd-wood and magenta paccah. That shop was deserted, but in another, young i-Mel with flying fingers wove fine reeds into knotted baskets.

Dinail turned corners at odd angles too many times for Del to keep his orientation. Each street, despite the spontaneity of color and diversity of shops and dwellings, nonetheless had a noticeable character. In one, tiles of diamond shape and earthen hue made the signature instantly visible. In others, one recognized the feature only upon passing out of the street, having encountered no shops at all or only those in which craftsmen worked the bark of the leather-tree.

This was a city unknown to Del. As they crossed over the Avenue of Waters to enter another cool side street, he wondered what else of Melem lay undiscovered right beneath his fabled, but insensitive nose. Had he, in his single-mindedness, passed over his responsibilities— and the opportunities—to truly know the people and the culture?

They entered a small square where five narrow streets converged on a modest fountain of grainy, gray stone. I-Mel, from young toddlers to several wrinkled ancients, sat on the edge and splashed their feet in the frothy water.

Snatches of conversation trailed off, and the hoots and croaks of youngsters died as Del and Dinail crossed the square. Just as they reached the slightly wider street on the far side, Del heard a high, fluttering shout in u-Mel, too fast, too screeched for him to understand, but with a desperation in it that transcended language. Dinail wheeled, pulling Del to her side and planting her feet wide apart. A toga-clad boy, arms flailing, caught Del full in the stomach with his headlong charge. Del stopped his own savage, instinctive chop in mid-swing, changing tactics to fit the young age of his assailant. He grabbed at bony arms, expecting to hear them crack as he closed them in the vise-grip of his huge hands. Using his bulk as a counterbalance, Del swung the boy off his feet and flung him back into the square.

Dinail was on her back beneath another i-Mel of indeterminate sex, struggling to raise her knee and lever him from her. Like a hammer thrower following through on his swing, Del scooped the i-Mel from atop Dinail. Her shout caught him just before he would have slammed the frail body into the rough stone wall.

"Don't hurt him!"

Off balance from his interrupted turn, Del staggered and toppled into a heap with his victim.

Dinail stood over them with arms held wide in threat. "You are a slug from the Dark Pit of the Under Lands, Dortaalsaggthe!" she cursed. "Your house never knows the sun! Your brothers are of hollow zei-stone!"

"Dinaillaabrolgdth, you lie with stone-lizards and brown dwarves," the boy spat, freeing himself from Del. The other boy finished: "You have no house, neither a proper naming." They backed off, continuing the u-Mel cursing as they did. Dinail pulled Del after her.

"The House Deruudth is in the next street but one," she said. "We can clean up there."

"What was that all about?" Del asked as he rubbed his hip.

"I do not know with sureness, but that you accompany me on my Naming Day is looked upon darkly by some. Dortaalgnuwaar may have more to say."

Del walked in puzzled silence down the last street, a narrow alleyway walled by blue-green vines clinging to the orange stone. It ended in a doorway held open by Dortaal. The oval smile on his face quickly flattened in concern as they approached.

They were ushered into an open courtyard, then brushed, groomed, and fussed over by Dortaal and others of the house. In a rush of colloquial u-Mel, Dinail described their encounter. From what he could follow, Del learned that he and Joanna were sometimes called "brown dwarves." This revelation of prejudice on Melem unnerved him, and he remarked on it and the unexpected violence of the attack.

"We are not," Dortaal spoke, "the perfect society, Delawareejackson. No doubt we share with humans a drive toward that perfection, but on Melem we still have cities of poverty and islands of ignorant prejudice, though both are on the wane. For the most part you travel among us unmolested and, I gather from what little I

244

know of your private life, often unnoticed. It would not be likewise for the i-Mel on your planet. But for some among our young, especially those of houses recently moved from Eastsands, the sense of loss and of threat to their culture is most keen. There are many such in this district. Here the seeds of racial anger lie in shallow soil and germinate easily. That you would walk with Dinail-laabrolgdth on her Naming Day is to those seeds like the sudden showers of spring.

"I can see that you remain puzzled. Is not the same horror strong among some humans? Martezthyeddil told me the word: miscegenation."

"But wait." Del spread both hands in a gesture of inno-cence. "Your daughter is barely more than a child. What could be wrong with visiting her house on her birthday? I would never . . ."

"This is not the mere day of her birth we celebrate, but her Naming Day, her second. On the first, eight days from birth, her name was given to a child; now, eight years later, the name is given again to a young woman. That your motives were not libidinous does not ensure that hers were necessarily without that element."

Del felt a rush of blood to his face.

"I will explain to him, Dortaalgnuwaar," said Dinail. She looked at Del eagerly. "Today I no longer wear the clothes of children, as my body is ready to bear them. I wanted you to share this day with me, but I have heard how easily embarrassed are the men of Earth, so I did not tell you all that it meant to me." She tugged at his coat sleeve. "Please stay."

"Perhaps, but first you must tell me why you call your father by his name?"

"I do not call Dortaalgnuwaar by other than his name because neither of us wishes to be more distant than we are with friends. I do not have his name, nor that of Graillinevf, who is mother to me, but my own."

"We have no separate word for children, either," Dortaal added, "but only use shtaa i-Mel, which means simply 'short person.' We sometimes speak the same of you."

"Better that than 'brown dwarf.'" Del said. "I'll stay." At that, Dinail fairly bounced, and the smile on her face turned into a full circle.

Throughout the festive afternoon, the family and guests played games. They chased each other around the central court and laughed from behind the columns that ringed it. They rolled small cylinders along the ground according to complex rules and hid behind the wooden doors that opened to the wedge-shaped dining hall and to other rooms of the house. Del understood little of the games, but joined in imitation as best he could.

Dinner, elaborate by i-Mel standards, was prepared in courses over a ceramic urn of glowing coals and was marked by frequent pauses to toast the celebrant with tall glasses of tigg passed from hand to hand. Even Yeddilerrn, youngest son, little past his own first Naming Day, drank of the heavy liqueur. Each member took his turn at serving, Yeddilerrn balancing in both hands the small cups of an icy infusion of herbs, which he served in his turn following the long meal.

After dark, the entire household warmed themselves around the glowing urn. At a lull in the quick-turning conversation, Del remarked on the occasion and on the importance of rites of passage for conferring status on people. Dinail objected.

"Perhaps, if a people find it necessary to give status to some and withhold it from others, then public ceremonies to announce this status would be important." She said it with all the earnest investment Del remembered from his graduate students in Comparative Cultural Analysis. "But we need no status to know our own worth, so then we need no ceremony to acquire it."

When Del turned to Dortaal for clarification of the Naming Day, a boy, not much older than Dinail, answered instead. "We do not give Dinaillaabrolgdth a place she did not have. We are only happy that her body grows beautiful and soon will urge her into sharing the joys of the sleeping room with us." He hooted in sharp bursts and Dinail joined him.

"Look," Del said, hoping to move back onto safer, more intellectual ground, "every society depends on the acquisition of respect obtained with age and experience. Some—the older, the wiser, the more competent—must have authority over others, or there would be chaos."

"Delawareejackson, how unlearned you can be for one who has studied so much and traveled so far," Dinail reproached him. "Wisdom needs no authority to be recognized, nor competence any status to succeed. I respect Dortaalgnuwaar no less nor more than little Yeddilerrn. As i-Mel do they not deserve respect? I would freely borrow the wisdom of either—that is my wisdom. Does not the blind person also dry a dew-soaked coat in the Great Twin's light?"

Del sighed. "Sometimes I have difficulty understanding the exemplative mode. Surely, though, you do not mean to accord the same status to Yeddilerrn, who cannot yet speak of his own interests and barely toddles with the teacups, as you would to your father?"

"Surely I do, Delawareejackson. Pick him up, this lowly person of whom you speak." Reluctantly, Del reached toward the boy, who turned aside and watched him warily through eyes half obscured by fat cheeks. "Do you not hear his message? Is it more right to ignore it and force upon him your intention merely because he is small enough to be picked up bodily?"

Del felt trapped. "I suppose not. Still, some manner of hierarchy is necessary to maintain an efficient and ordered social machine."

"Those words—efficient, ordered, machine—are such revealing choices," Dortaal commented. "Are these your priorities? They are not ours. Because we value other things more highly, ours is seldom a well-ordered life. It is efficient enough, no more. A machine? Emphatically not! But, you will deal with the Nexus tomorrow."

The talk ranged freely for hours. No topic seemed beneath any adult and the youngest child was listened to on the deepest subject. Del wasn't used to it. He grew restless waiting for the children to be off to bed so he could turn the talk to death and age, but the matter entered of its own accord.

"Sometimes I think of death when I fall asleep at night," said one of Dinail's younger sisters.

"We do call it the Great Sunless Night, do we not," said Graillinevf, passing on the communal glass of tigg. "But it is not the same meaning for 'night.' We all know what the night is, the peace and the joys it holds, the promise of morning suns, but we know nothing of death, only that it is the end of all these things. Still, we shall know, we shall." All but Del laughed.

Emboldened, Del followed her lead and asked, "Are you not afraid of dying?" Again the laughter, this time waved to silence by Dortaal's eldest son.

"I think he does not understand what gifts death gives us." The coals snapped in the quiet as the boy turned to face Del squarely. "Each of us, some time, wishes death away from the door of the house, even as we may curse the coming night when there is still savor-grass to be harvested from the field. I am now with love to Suudaqqinhh. I would not want the Great Night to come now, but knowing that it could reminds me to savor the days of warmth and nights of joy she brings me. We have a saying: against the velvet night is painted the splendor of the setting suns." This time no laughter, only solemn, nodding affirmation.

With that, the talk ceased for another round of toasting. There seemed neither planning nor pattern, but suddenly a small parcel was thrust into each pair of hands. Del found in his a rolled packet bound by a bright speckled reed. Unrolling it, he looked upon his own face rendered in finely feathered, brown brush strokes. He glanced at Dinail.

"You did this?" She smiled hesitantly. Del reached over and brushed her cheek with the back of his hand. The family hushed, but when he scanned their faces for disapproval, he was met only by smiles.

It was near first hour when he took his leave, still unsatisfied in his search for understanding of the i-Mel, but growing in the uneasy conviction that he had somehow misread the evidence.

7

Immediately on entering the office, Del was thrown off stride. Where he had anticipated the sumptuous furnishing of a directors' suite, the office of the Nexus looked more like the control room of a television studio or a station on the Northeast Power Grid. Function-forms cluttered the room, and the walls were decorated by displays and graphs, by cork-like panels peeking from beneath a papering of small notes, and by a matrix of video images. Amidst a small mountain of loose paper and narrow tablets sat the only i-Mel Del had ever seen who looked wizened. When she stood to greet her visitors, she remained slightly bent and did not tower over Del as did the others. Alseqqinhh introduced her as Sirssenvfeduula.

Beneath Alseqqinhh's interested gaze, Del told of his investigations. To his delight, the Nexus spoke with authority on every matter raised, and he began to marvel at an executive who could retain mastery over so great a range of scientific fields while running such a large organization. The conversation meandered through a mine-field of interruptions, as though everyone in the Complex felt free to barge in and prevail upon the Nexus for information or assistance. She was unfailingly personable and authoritative in her responses, and Del grew more impressed by the minute. Consciously avoiding his prime interest while still being studied by Alseqqinhh, Del nevertheless gleaned much useful data to fill small gaps in his understanding of Melem's science and culture.

He was certain that Alseqqinhh had been following this

deliberate skirting of his central concern. When, as they separated for the afternoon meal, Del still had not raised the subject of death and aging, Alseqqinhh took the initiative from him, saying, "The Earth-friend suspects us of withholding information from him. Speak of that with him over your roasted savor-grass root."

Del deftly took up the theme. "Yes, Nexus, perhaps you could tell me of the possible reasons why some files would remain closed to me or would reach me only highly transformed. And how might I obtain from you a ruling that would grant me free access to the data I seek?"

"Perhaps I do not understand the English with ease," she answered. "A ruling is not something I could grant. I do not rule, but only serve the Complex. Still, should you tell me of what you seek, I would learn what I can of it or why you have been so troubled in obtaining it." She turned around, heading back to her office.

"It is of death or of the end to death that I wish to know," Del explained as he followed. Again she turned, resuming her route to the cafeteria.

"I shall not need the function-forms to assist with that. All that we know is there for you to read if you will. We do not research death, not for over a hundred years."

Del fought down his sudden excitement. She had confirmed for him a date, or at least a period, and opened another plausible lead. His search had focused on contemporary science and current documents. He let the topic drop and stood in the double line in silence as they waited to be served the tart cuts of brown root.

Only on the next workday did he reopen the inquiry, this time in idle exploration of history. Her knowledge seemed to weaken there, as it did for many i-Mel, and she had to make extensive use of the function-forms to identify periods of intense social change during the previous several centuries. Nothing concerning death nor occurring in the neighborhood of a century earlier showed up in the imprints. The analyses did suggest an explanation for the relative disinterest in history shown by the i-Mel. Theirs was a near-stable society that evolved very slowly, exhibiting a remarkable capacity to absorb the agents of change without noticeable effect. First contact with Earth some decades earlier had seemed to cause little more than a ripple on the placid surface of a contented culture.

Del's reactions to the many dead ends was atypical for him. His determination was not re-fired, but blanketed. He continued to work with the Nexus because he enjoyed her company and found her often to be the most efficient route to small bits of information he sought. But as the number of intriguing questions dwindled, he lost interest and began to absent himself from the Complex.

Some days he spent in solitary exploration of the city, ranging wider and wider still until he could no longer find new areas on foot alone, but first had to hail one of the turtle taxis to take him to a farther district. When at last he reached the open sands of the countryside, Del realized that his fieldwork had already begun. On the following workday he announced to an ecstatic assemblage of i-Mel that he would start operations in Eastsands within a fortnight.

And some days he spent with Dinail, who was becoming not only a friend, but a partner in his search for understanding of the i-Mel.

8

The Orange City spread magnificently below them, its cubic buildings of sienna, umber, tangerine, and peach wavering in the heat pressing down on the Plain of Hharjj. The breeze, drawn steady as a trade wind by the Plain's updraft, and the shimmering shade of the silver-leaf tree made the top of the hill comfortable, even so soon after midday. Pouring the last astringent juice from the vacuum bottle, Del washed down the remaining crust of black bread. Dinail looked at him eagerly, her mouth set square in a questioning expression. Del kept his own lips noncommittally pursed, pleased with his facile mastery of the i-Mel nonverbals. With calculated sluggishness, he slowly opened his mouth, rounding it into the broad oval of a silent laugh. It now felt natural to express pleasure in this way, and he wondered how long it would take to become comfortable again with the bared-fang smile of his fellow creatures.

"It was good, yes?" she asked, checking with him as she refolded the eyelet-edged spread on which their picnic had been laid. Del answered with a quick flick of his chin, then spontaneously put his hand on her head to tousle her hair. It was unexpectedly cool, incredibly fine, yet wiry, like glass wool. Startled by the brush of grass blown against his leg, Del realized he had been stroking her hair for many seconds. He returned his hands to his lap.

"How is it that we are so alike?" she asked, interrupting the silence.

"Are we so alike?"

"Yes, well, I mean it is the legs we have, and knees, even if yours are too near the ground. We have all the same, even if shaped different, yet never has there been contact before."

"There is this kangaroo rat," he answered. "Lives in the American desert. Looks like this." He sketched a crude outline in a sandy patch between tufts of el-grass. "Small, hops around very quickly on those strong hind legs, well adapted to the hot, dry desert. Living in the same way in the Australian outback, the desert of another continent, is the smallest of the kangaroos, the rat kangaroo. Looks like that." He pointed to the same drawing. "Separated by half a world, these evolved independently for millions of years to fit nearly identical conditions. We think it may be like that for humans and i-Mel."

She tugged on a tuft of el-grass. "Can these two, the rat kangaroo and the kangaroo rat, can they have young together?"

"No," he answered. "Perhaps they could mate, but they bear young in completely different ways." He started to explain the technicalities of marsupial and placental reproduction, sketching in the sand as he did, but Dinail did not appear to be listening. It was, he realized, as though he were answering the wrong question.

She interrupted him to tell of her plans for higher study, then continued to pepper him with tales of her friends, fragments of the songs she liked, and musings on the tremendous trifles of her life. The sky grew dark.

"I cannot bear them," she said, looking up toward the awakening stars. "They mock me, for I know them not and never will." She sprang suddenly to her feet with careless energy. "Let's go," she added. In silence they gathered their gear and started down the hill toward the lights of the city.

¤ ¤ ¤

It was past thirteenth hour when they gently closed the gate from the vine-draped alleyway. Remnants of a fire glimmered in the large urn, but the courtyard was otherwise dark and the household silent. Del felt Dinaill's hand on his wrist. She guided him through one of the ring of doors. The dark deepened as she closed it behind them. For a moment Del felt the night close in upon him, constricting his throat, then a neon coil sparked overhead and the pressure eased.

Dinail bent to the lowest of five panels set into the wall. It swung to one side on well-oiled hinges, exposing a cache of scrolls like the one he had been given on her Naming Day.

The first scroll she handed him held the sharp-lined image of a great bird frozen at the instant of taking flight. The second, a study in stippling, became, at arm's length, a finely shaded portrait of Dinail's mother breaking into laughter. There was a baby, waddling erect but reaching with one too-long arm to break an imminent fall. There was a young man, naked and beaded with bright water, leaping from a shallow pool. The subjects varied as much as the technique, but always a single object in studied dynamic sprang from the center of the sheet.

"These are . . ." Del searched for words to convey the impact he felt. Finding none, he said at last, lamely, "They're good."

She held his eyes with a slightly pouting expression of

seriousness, and Del struggled not to see more than her face as she walked toward him. The overhead light sent sharp shadows down her body, emphasizing her small breasts. As she neared, she was transformed with each shift of lighting and each fresh attempt by Del's mind to fit his experience into some category. She was a young girl, lovely and untouchable; she was a woman, as tall as he and an arm's reach away; she was an exotic, feline succubus, waiting to be stroked and petted; she was totally alien and frightening.

Then she was in his arms.

Del's awareness seem to split in two, as if a part of him were outside, watching, aloof from his inner torment. Only in this detached self could he allow himself to simply see the unfolding of events that denied categories. He watched himself as they undressed, slowly and seriously, then touched with tender tentativeness and explosive releases of hushed laughter.

Del brushed his lips down her cool, slim body, sliding down to the dark, cottony dampness of her belly. A smell like nutmeg engulfed him as he held still, afraid to move on and discover her response. She tickled his ears, shattering his indecision, then pulled him up to press her cheek to his.

As they touched and played, Del's inner war raged on over ever-shifting fronts. She was barely more than a child, she was grown. She was human, she was not. He loved her, he could never.

In the end there was no penetration, no climax for either, only passion dissolving into tenderness, anxiety resolved into peace. As, at last, he drifted into sleep, armistice came to Del's inner battlefield, and the creature he embraced became for him merely Dinail, i-Mel, person.

¤ ¤ ¤

The heat of late morning tugged him from his turbid dreams of dancing with a lanky Masai maiden and of pursuit by orange-maned lions across the Tanzanian savanna. Dinail was gone, but hoots and shouts carried through the light wood of the door. Outside, Del watched from behind a boxy pillar as Dinail and several other young i-Mel feinted and dodged in a game of fetching small figures from circles drawn upon the ground.

"It is a light and still morning, is it not, friend of the House Deruudth."

Del jumped at Dortaal's voice. Shame, remorse, and fright flooded through his veins, searing his face as the blood flashed to it. He upended mental files in a desperate search for a plausible lie with which to escape. He was stopped by Dortaal, who offered truth as an exit.

"Dinaillaabrolgdth tells me with joy of her first night with you."

Del stammered, "You approve?"

"It is for me neither to approve nor to condemn my children, but to celebrate their laughter and sorrow for their tears. It was she who shared her bed with you, not I; it is her choosing, not mine."

"Wait! Nothing happened," Del pleaded, answering not Dortaal, but his own inner prosecutor.

"I do not speak of a consummation, Delawareejackson, but of a meeting, of becoming known and accepted by another."

The hooting in the courtyard reached a crescendo as two small boys collided with Dinail. Dortaal swept wide his arm and said, "Would you give up that music for any-thing, Earth-friend? No? Perhaps? There! Life's greatest gift, Death's greatest gift: they are one and the same."

Del regarded him blankly.

"With all you have learned from the daughter of our house, how can you not see?" He took his hand from Del's sleeve and backed away a few solemn steps before turning to stride into the sunlit yard where he joined his children in their game.

Del left the courtyard. He could make no sense of the exchange, no sense of a people who did not keep sepa-rate their children or their childhood.

9

The small turbofan plane crouched on the airfield, its sleek impatience matching Del's own. His pilot ap-proached in bare-headed comfort. The mornings now were almost cool with the approach of the soft-days, as Meltaa distanced herself and began to hide behind Melduu in their circling dance. Pilot and passenger ex-changed pleasantries as they awaited Del's co-investigator.

Alseqqinhh, tall even by Melem's towering standards, crossed the field with stately grace. After greeting Del warmly, she hunched in beside the pilot, bristly hair scratching on the smoke-tint cockpit canopy as she squirmed to get comfortable. As they exchanged rapid u-Mel chatter on flying techniques in Melem's dramatic thermals and melodramatic shifts in weather, Del climbed over the bulging belt of the air intake for the high-bypass jet and lowered himself in the rear seat.

The turbine's cry at his back rose to a scream, and they

were airborne almost immediately, climbing in steep surges through the uneven winds of morning, sending the wings flexing and shivering. The sensuous leap of the small plane and the awesome sweep of the Orange City falling away below them brought back for Del memories of early flights before the monotony of countless commercial trips had taken the thrill away. As the engine cut back to a breathy drone, he settled into a reverie of boyhood dreams, of pretended voyages and fantasy flights to distant stars, while a world that was not his crept by below.

As many hours as dreams had passed before he reopened his eyes. Melduu was already nearly skimming the corrugated crest of a vast escarpment. The pilot throttled back, turned in his seat, and said, "The Scar!"

Del asked how far this put them from the Scarlet City of Eastsands, then translated the answer into kilometers: several hundred. Would they be arriving after dark? "Perhaps," the pilot said, "especially if we get into the head winds of the great counter-current from the Southern Continent."

Del idly watched the approaching ragged edge of the world. So it must have seemed to early inhabitants on either side, for along the Scar, the world dropped from plain to plain a shear kilometer. As if in response to his unspoken wish for a closer look, the plane's nose dipped, and they glided downward to settle into a level, low altitude approach.

"I have left our flight of plan to share with you a special thrill, man-friend," the pilot said. "Watch!"

The engine slowed still further as they slid toward the edge, so low that the entire lower plain lay hidden from view. Then, like the flash of a strobe, the bottom of the world dropped away as they shot over the cliff. The pilot shoved the throttle forward and started to bank to give his passengers a better view of the escarpment face.

A powerful and unexpected gust in mid-maneuver sent the world twisting sharply while Del's stomach lunged skyward. The engine, still winding up for the climb out, now rammed them downward. To the pilot's credit, he flattened their approach and nearly leveled the wings before they slammed into the gravelly sand. The left wing tip sheared off on the first bounce. They skidded and spun until the stump of the wing dug in, whipping the plane over, hammering the nose into the ground. Del was wrenched from his seat and shoved into the pilot's back.

Del was wet. He couldn't figure it out as he struggled to clear his head. Jet fuel? He panicked as he wriggled his arm free. The sticky wetness covered everything. He opened his eyes and managed to swivel his head a few degrees to survey the cabin. Green fire-control foam still dripped from a nozzle to his right. That explained the stickiness. Not all of it. Del saw spatters of blood: some red, his, some deep brown from the i-Mel. The pilot was buried where his body had cushioned Del's. Del reached gingerly beneath and touched bloody flesh. There was no pulse or movement.

Del worked free of the wreckage, then turned to see what had become of Alseqqinhh. She was not in the plane, but he spotted her gaunt form sprawled on the sand a few meters away. Del hobbled to her, gently turned her over, and brushed coarse grit from her face. The frail i-Mel scientist strained to smile roundly as brown blood bubbled from her mouth.

"Look, I'll take care of you," Del reassured her, unaware that he had slipped into English. He realized that he was whistling in the dark. He knew little enough of i-Mel medicine, not even the rudiments of appropriate first aid. It did not look as if Alseqqinhh would be in position to correct his ignorance. He wondered if shock were a possibility. In the plane he found some foam-soaked coverlets, which he tucked around her long body.

The remnants of sunlight drew long shadows from the wreckage and made the Scar a bright, banded curtain. Del could not free the pilot's body, but, from what he could see of the cockpit, he was reasonably certain that none of the electronics beneath still functioned to broadcast their location. He cursed his lack of knowledge of mechanics, his inadequate first aid, his shortcomings in all that suddenly seemed to matter. He did not know what he faced on the desert at night. Even common sense, Earth sense, might be useless. Or worse.

He figured a fire was a sure bet: a beacon visible at great distance on the dark plateau, an antidote to frigid desert nights, and possible insurance against a host of unknowns. Del remembered pictures of carnivores on Melem but could not recall exactly where they had been taken.

He ripped out one of the cushions from the rear seat. It was more of the ubiquitous foam, an i-Mel specialty: foam to walk on, sit on, to ignite, or to extinguish. The cushion had been missed by the fire-retardant spray and ignited easily when doused with aviation fuel. Del huddled as near to the acrid fire as he dared, trying to avoid the smoke, waiting for the cold and the creatures of the night. Neither came. When Del awoke with a jerk and whirled to face the animal whose breath had warmed his neck, he faced only the wind. It blew steadily from the southeast, hot and steady through the night, invading Del's uneasy sleep of puzzling dreams.

In the harsh shadows of early morning, his situation looked even worse. He could find nothing in the plane that still functioned and little that might have survival value in an alien desert. The first aid kit that he assumed must be stowed aboard eluded him, though he found a metal vacuum bottle of cool water, which he rationed, drop by drop, between himself and Alseqqinhh. The i-Mel stared without focusing and grunted with pain. Her chest was bloated, and large blotches on her skin were darkening from blue-brown to black. Were these bruises? Edema? Del could only guess.

He passed the slow day in the shadow of a blanket lean-to, listening helplessly to the occasional groans and hisses of his friend. Once, for more than an hour, he cradled the i-Mel's huge head in his lap, stroking her wiry hair in rhythm with a tuneless song. Del could not leave her, nor could he carry her. He could wait, only that, and wonder at their chances, designing contingency plans against a miraculous recovery on her part that would leave them both mobile.

The plans went out on the second night when Alseqqinhh laughed suddenly, briefly, in the fireless dark. Del felt his way to her side and found her dead.

Freed of an impossible burden, left only with his guilt to carry, Del rekindled his drive to survive. He surveyed the wreck again and found several items missed in his apathetic search of the day before: a small, file-like tool, a cowled naftaa to protect him from the sun, and a map. By the pilot's last report and Del's rough reading of the map, they were some fifty or sixty kilometers north of their flight plan, still some 300 kilometers and a range of hills from the Scarlet City. Between escarpment and the hills on the city's outskirts, only the Scar and a tiny, kidney shaped lake interrupted the blank of the map's center. The lake, almost due south, would be less than seventy kilometers away and just beyond their planned route. No symbols indicated any settlement there, and Del wondered if it might be a salt lake, a common feature of Melem's deserts. Were it certain that he find people there, it would still be an enormous gamble. Without a compass and with only strange constellations overhead, it would be far too easy to miss the target, overshoot, and perish in the desert. The suns' arrow was an uncertain compass to Del, who did not know how to allow for the season and the irregular motion of the double star. A degree or two would spell failure, and he could not see how to cut the margin of error.

The jagged gash of the escarpment's image on the pliafilm suddenly stood out in relief. The lake, which waited so far from the wreck's imprecisely known position, was only a dozen kilometers from the nearest point on the escarpment, a point where a distinctive double notch would give Del a precise point of reference. Tracing two legs of such a thin triangle would add about the distance of the lake to the Scar, but would almost guarantee finding the lake. How long to hike more than eighty kilometers across the desert? Three, four days? A liter-and-half of water remained in the large vacuum bottle. Not enough, but better odds than the remote chance of the wreck being spotted by a search that would begin with their original line of flight.

Melduu would be the enemy. Only the blessing of Meltaa's eclipse by her larger, cooler companion gave him a chance. He assayed the option of traveling by night, but Melem had never spawned a moon and the nights were pitch. He rested, instead.

With the first, faint phosphorescence in the east, Del was up, ladling fuel over the wreckage and on a line of debris arranged to point southward. The i-Mel bodies were solemnly anointed with the vaporous oil, and the whole set ablaze with Del's pipe lighter. He shed no tears for his colleague nor for the brave stranger, though he felt Alseqqinhh's loss painfully as he trudged away alone.

As he angled toward the dark wall of the Scar, he recognized the escarpment as a double blessing, for he would be able to walk half the day in its shadow. Nearing the rock curtain, he could see mounds of talus at its base and among them sparse vegetation: a few like winter-barren trees and many shrub like gray-green coral. Motion caught his eye, as a stone-lizard zigzagged in front him, the knobby leather of its salmony skin blending in with the stony desert floor. If it was stalking prey, Del knew he had nothing to fear from the small creature, but whatever it might flee was a complete unknown. Del's eyes followed it where it darted from sight, beyond a cluster of coral bushes forming a dense, two-tiered ring. Curious, Del walked over to them and found a thin carpeting of brittle el-grass in a central depression. It made Del think of an oasis and buried water.

He dug eagerly with his hands, then, screaming, jerked them from the sand, blood oozing from a hundred tiny cuts. He cursed his lack of caution and over-eagerness for a resource he did not yet need. He wiped his hands on his shirt, unscrewed the cap of the vacuum bottle, and gingerly began to scoop a hollow in the pink sand. A few centimeters down, the earth writhed with animated macaroni, eager mouths lined with tiny razor blades. Deciding he did not really need the water that might be recoverable by digging more, Del returned to his trek.

Approaching noon drove Del closer and closer to the cliff as the shadows shortened. He raised his cowl against the midday sun, thankful that Meltaa did not also glare down upon him. An hour passed, maybe two, before he could bear the heat no longer. To wait out the height of the day, he would have to find shade. The escarpment was no longer of any use; bright sun filled even under small overhangs. A slim shadow forming on the east side of a boulder was the best that Del could do, and he huddled against its slightly cooler surface to catnap through the hottest hours.

He stiffened, suddenly awake at the touch of something against his left boot. Pressure on his leg increased as he slowly raised his head to see his guest, a hmerbot. It shivered in short tremors as it nestled against the back of his knees. A harmless insectivore? Del was unsure, but the assumptions were forced, since it was too late to get away from the animal even if it were dangerous.

They napped longer into the afternoon shadows than Del had planned. At last he chose to risk stirring the hmerbot by sliding away from it. The spiny sphere uncoiled to become an ocher sausage half a meter long, then raised itself on short legs and casually waddled over to Del. It probed his boot and the hem of his naftaa with its wrinkled proboscis. Del, remembering a faraway meeting, could see no resemblance.

"I must be on my way. I've tarried too long with the likes of you," Del said. He laughed, gathered his things, and walked off. He'd been walking only a few minutes when he heard a soft crunching in the sand at his back. Glancing over his shoulder, he saw the hmerbot padding after him. He welcomed the companionship. Over the hours of late afternoon walking, he grew used to hearing the soft pad, pad, pad whenever he halted and to glimpsing the bristling gold spines whenever he looked back.

It was near sunset when Del noticed he could no longer hear his companion. The hmerbot was nowhere in sight. Del could think of no justification for backtracking on its behalf, but curiosity nagged him, and he resolved to retrace a short distance to see whether it had veered off only recently. He quickly found its tracks toward the cliff and impulsively followed. The splay-footed prints led toward another circle of coral bushes where Del found the hmerbot slurping up the little worms that plied the sand. Having stirred up an area an arm's length across, it began pawing in the sand, soon gouging a hole as deep as half its body length. Del peered in. A mat of root-like tubes criss-crossed the bottom. Where the hmerbot scratched with its stubby claws, drops of clear fluid formed and were quickly sucked up by the animal. Gingerly, Del reached down beside it and got a drop of fluid on his finger, then touched it to his tongue and spat.

The thin, musty liquor left a sweetish aftertaste that hinted of carbohydrates, almost as important as the water itself. If it were potable, Del thought, it might furnish a needed safety margin. Having scrambled awkwardly from its own pit, the hmerbot lounged at the rim. Del pulled the file from his bundle and made fresh incisions in the roots. Several bright drops he gathered and licked from his fingers. Meanwhile, the hmerbot, protecting the roots against future need, brushed the scattered dirt back into the hole with its hind legs.

It came as no surprise when Del discovered the hmerbot still tailing him in the late afternoon. By dusk it was at his side and looking about nervously. In anticipation of the lightless night, Del cast about for a sleeping spot, settling on a hollow near a talus mound. The hmerbot would have nothing of it, however, and settled down on the open sand some ten meters away. Having seen good reason to trust his small friend before, Del left his sheltered spot to lie down beside the hmerbot.

In the predawn glow he awoke, aware that he had slept well. He had been foolish, he told himself, to worry about predators in the night, for moonless Melem had no true nocturnals. But crepuscular animals were another matter. Of the half-night before dawn and after the Twins set, there were many travelers. This worried Del, for the hmerbot was gone again. However, the press to continue before the heat forced him to stop once more was stronger than the newly formed bond with the hmerbot, and Del set out alone. Within minutes the bristling animal was at his side.

Once again they stopped in the late afternoon at one of the tiny oases. This time, reassured by the lack of effects on the day before, Del drank his fill of the musty liquid.

The second night of his trek Del spent in sleepless pain, racked by stomach cramps. By noon of the third day, his thirst a nagging companion, he finished the last of the water from the vacuum bottle. His stomach recoiled, and he watched, wide-eyed, as the thin vomit sank into the thirsty sand. By late afternoon the cramps were constant and walking had become difficult. As he slowed, so did the hmerbot, until it spotted another gray circle of the coral bushes and trotted off toward it. Del caught up slowly, then lowered himself to the sand to sit and watch.

Dehydration now seemed an even greater danger, so Del decided to risk the sap water again. As he reached with the metal file to incise the exposed lattice of roots, he saw his hand, puffy with a network of pussy white ridges. Still, there was no discomfort in his hands, only pain in his belly. He drank sparingly of the sap, fighting down the reflex to vomit it back to the earth that gave it.

On the fourth day Del's arms began to swell, but he pressed on. Late in the afternoon, about the time he had come to expect his companion to lead them to another circle of bushes, Del heard behind him a screeching hiss of air followed by a sharp squeal. The hmerbot scrambled toward him, pursued by two rapidly closing jackal-like animals, thick saliva dripping from the blue fur of their muzzles.

Del ran as the jackals fell on the defenseless hmerbot. For a moment, one of the pair hesitated, assessing Del as another victim, then returned to complete the kill with its partner. Grateful for the distraction created by the hmerbot, Del kept moving until, with the passing of the last dim, yellow glow of sunset, he collapsed. His shoulders were swollen and he burned with cool fire as he lay in the sand.

Del ambled through the fifth day, stopping often to catch his breath. The distinct double jag in the Scar loomed ahead, marking the turning point where he would have to leave the rugged security of the cliff for the bland uncertainty of open desert. Desperate with thirst, he searched for another circle of bushes. They had seemed so common that there had been no obvious need to fill the vacuum bottle earlier.

He almost tripped over the circle of low plants. Digging gingerly with his cup, he encountered none of the cutting worms but neither were there any of the matted roots with their store of water. Something differentiated the oases, something recognized by the hmerbot but unknown to Del. He fell asleep on the sparse, spiky grass within the circle of leafless shrub.

The sun burned hotly on his face before he awakened. With luck and an accurate bearing, Del thought he might make it to the lake in a day. But his head throbbed, a pungent smell exuded from the cuts on his hands, and he spent the day in delirium, sometimes digging at the hole in the sand, sometimes tossing in the not-sleep of fever. When at last he awoke without the pounding at his temples, darkness blanketed him. His right arm hung over the edge of a hole nearly as deep as he could reach; his hand was cool and wet. Del flexed the hand cautiously, creating a gentle splash. Fumbling in the dark, Del located the abandoned cup from the vacuum bottle and scooped liquid from the bottom of the pit. It was water, cool and tasting of minerals. In the morning, he vowed, he would fill the bottle and start out again for the lake.

But in the morning Del had visitors and did not awaken to greet them.

10

"We can see the toxins of the smer devouring his body. Why then do you not give him the antibiotes?" the Administrative Coordinator asked impatiently.

Kesellaadebv nibbled his lip as he looked down at the unmoving body, deformed and made more alien by the tiny parasites ravaging it. He had never felt more helpless as a doctor.

"The vectors are not safe with this one. They destroy his blood along with the smer. Both here and in the Orange City we are testing other treatments, using his blood and that of Joannakarenent," he gestured toward her image on the video screen. She nodded in recognition. "But what is toxic enough to stop the smer is too toxic for his cells."

"What of the medicines of Earth?"

Karen answered. "There are few that we have carried. Those have been tried without success."

"His blood, is it as important to him as ours to us?" The Coordinator raised his hand. "No, do not regard this as a stupid question. We must think in new channels for a new problem."

Kesellaadebv and Karen exchanged looks, waiting for the other to reply. "As important," he answered.

"New blood, then, transfusion. It is done easily. Kill the smer, kill the blood, then start over."

"There is not enough. Ours is of no use and there are only four units in storage from the Joannakarenent and the Delawareejackson. We can take only a unit or two at a time from her and then must wait eight or more rest-days. We do not have the time; he will die long before the store is large enough."

Joanna spoke, her slow-scan image moving jerkily. "There might be a path in this administrator's musings. There is a difference in temperature, i-Mel and human. What happens if the smer become too cold?"

"They do not die, if that is your hope. In the cold of the desert they are stilled but do not die."

"Then we will slow them and buy time. There are some simple chemicals that block our ability to keep the body warm. I will tell you what to make and administer to Delaware. Then you will cool his body until the smer are stopped."

"He will not die?"

"He will not, but his life will be slowed. We will have the time to build a supply of whole blood and to prepare for a complete transfusion."

There was not enough time, however, and Joanna ended up giving permission to end the hypothermia early. They were still short two units of blood and had to make it up with saline solution. Del remained in a coma.

11

The blinding sunlight leapt from the white mirror of the salt flat. Kesellaadebv averted his eyes as he hurried between buildings of the station. Though he had slept nearly through the restday, his limbs still ached from the long vigil. He passed the crowded biotechnics lab without a glance, but at the school building slowed for a peek in the low windows, hoping to catch a glimpse of his son. He passed without success, then turned the corner down the narrow passageway toward the infirmary.

He wheezed loudly to make his presence known as he

entered the room. Del turned from the window.

"You unbend like the el-grass to the double sun," the i-Mel said to Del. "I have heard of your awakening and come to examine you." He swung out a tray concealed in the wall, selected a device from it, and approached Del. Del started to speak, but finding his tongue and lips numb, merely nodded dumbly.

"It stops the tongue for a while, the smer. It was your fortune to be found, for it stops other things, too, in time. Here." He pressed the instrument to Del's chest, then studied its tiny lights blinking in a rhythm Del recognized as his own heartbeat. "We check by radio with Joannakarenent to know what is good, what bad. This, I know, is good and means you will not have to stay here many more restdays."

Del looked at him imploringly and tried to speak.

"No, we will answer your questions when you can ask them. Tomorrow, perhaps." With that, the doctor left.

It was not until the second day following that Del could ask, in thick, slurred u-Mel, about what had happened to him and where he was. The "where" was a scientific research encampment on the edge of a dead lake. As Del had feared, the lake was dry, but there were people, nonetheless. A team of botanists checking on an uncommon variety of the ringbush had found him. Neither wit nor wile nor stamina had saved him, but ignorance and chance. Had Del known the kind of plant he sought, he would have passed the one being monitored by the scientists. As he heard the rest of the complex story, he realized again how much he owed to Joanna.

Under the ministrations of the camp's medical officer, Del continued to recuperate, although a sluggishness reminded him of what he had been through. Kesellaadebv would not let him leave for the Orange City until this partial paralysis was gone, so Del decided to settle into the routine of the small community.

For the first time since the early weeks on Melem he was again a celebrity. What he had freely withheld from mere hosts, he could not deny to ones who had saved his life. He became accessible. The scientists and their families—educated, enthusiastic, isolated—involved him in their every affair, watching carefully his reaction to the staff chorus ("Best tuba choir I've ever heard!"), to braised salt-worm ("Not too bad with plenty of ringbush ash to cover the taste!"), and to the sport of "salting," which he never figured out. All this he called diversion, for he had also begun his field work.

Of the baker's dozen community buildings, he spent the most time in the one-room school. Perhaps his friendship with Dinail had been a useful apprenticeship, for he found himself at ease with the children and young people of the community, and they were proving to be eager informants. He discovered in the stories and lessons of the schoolroom clear crystallizations of the i-Mel culture. Alseqqinhh, whom he missed more with each passing workday, would have been proud of him.

He thought of her as he sat quietly on the blue-cushioned window seat, taking notes on the behavior of the assortment of short and shorter i-Mel as they attended to a mop-haired Guide who was responsible for the day's lesson. Suddenly something the Guide had been saying intruded on his thoughts. Del recognized the slim volume of children's tales from which she read, having seen it in the House Deruudth, though he could not recall it from among those given to him to read. The Guide had asked, "Must life end?"

Deference was not easy to express in u-Mel, but Del approximated it with the most extended forms of speech he knew, asking the Guide if it would be possible to hear the first part of the story once more. Short honks of muffled laughter sprang from the class, but the Guide assented with a quick flick of her chin and began again.

12

The Valley Ssarrdanth was much as today in the days when names were short. Walonn, as are many of the Valley people still, was a farmer of the paper-trees. He was not young. His arms were gnarled with small knots of muscle, for he had unwound the skin of uncounted trees and hefted the heavy parchment rolls on either shoulder since his boyhood. His ptaneevaa, the Unclosed Square that hung from the necks of all i-Mel of those times, recorded by its rounded corners the years of gentle abrasion from his worrying fingers.

In his age, his daughter had presented him a grandson, and he would play quietly with Devfer whenever he returned from the forests at suns' setting. He no longer carried the paper rolls, but rode in the long wagon and kept account of the work. He loved little Devfer and would talk patiently with him of many things, of small hmer and great kaajjel, of wagons groaning with the weight of many tree skins, of growing up and growing old. And, of course, he told the tales of the Unclosed Square, recounting the four ages of the i-Mel as his thin fingers caressed his ptaneevaa. He spoke of Meltaa and her sister Melduu, of Melem, their brother, and of The

Fourth, which was gone. Devfer, who had seen only two winters, struggled to understand how it was always the thing which was not that defined what was. By the sunless shadow, the brightness was defined; against the nothingness before and after was life known. Without its one absent point, the ptaneevaa would be but an ordinary square.

And from Devfer's understandable confusion, in Walonn grew doubt. Must there be night to know day? He was no longer certain. Must life end? He began to wish otherwise, to make known his wishes, and to speak his doubt to others. But of his village, neither the old, who were certain, nor the young, who knew not the slowing of age, could understand him. One alone listened patiently: Brolgdth, woman of the somber eyes. As a girl she had hated her distinction, and, longing for the amber eyes of all her friends, had journeyed to the top of Mount Taavf to seek out the Woman of the Mountain, who, legend said, could grant all wishes. Brolgdth returned with eyes still deep brown, but with laughter in her voice. Of her journey she would say nothing, save that the Lady of Taavf had granted her wish.

Now, older still than Walonn, she listened to him speak of unfilled longing, of wanting to see Devfer as a man, sinewy and tall, of wishing to see the uurd-wood seedlings, planted only a winter past, grown higher than the village hall. Before the hot fire of uurd nuts, she told him of her girlhood pain, of her desire to bring into being that which was not. She told him of the end of her long quest and spoke, for the first time, of the gentle crone who had asked her which she would choose of two wishes: a life with eyes of gold or one of joy.

Hearing of power but not of wisdom, Walonn packed cheese and nuts and dried fruits into his leatherwood pack, donned his thickest naftaa, and began the climb up, out of the Valley Ssarrdanth, toward the freezing crest of Mount Taavf. It measured his desire that a grandfather would attempt what had nearly been the end of a wiry young girl. The path steepened and disappeared; still he continued his climb. Great boulders blocked the way, freezing rain turned his naftaa to ice, and thorn-apples ripped the wrinkled flesh from his legs, yet he continued, seemingly unaware that he risked death in search of an alternative. The last of the nuts in his pack were three days gone when he struggled to the door of a black stone hut near the summit. The aged woman who answered his feeble knock was met by a wraith, brown blood frozen in the cracks of his skin, protruding bones visible even through his ragged naftaa. She marveled that he lived at all and took him in to warm and bathe and feed him before he collapsed into a stupor that held him for days.

On a crisp morning he awoke and spoke. He called her Lady of Taavf, and she did not correct him. He told her of Brolgdth's tale, and the woman nodded. He wept, saying that he wanted to live, and she smiled. He cried that he did not want to die, and she laughed.

"What do you seek, truly?" she asked, at last.

"The point missing from my ptaneevaa. I wish to fill the nothingness. I want my life to go on until my years number as the days I have known."

"But if your years are as days, will not you still have lived only the days of your life?" There was genuine puzzlement in her voice. He was not swayed. "Would you not rather spend five final days in gentle laughter or in contented contemplation than a year in misery?" But he was undeterred.

"How, Great Lady, how do I close the gap in my ptaneevaa?"

"I would think," she said, tilting her head from side to side in solemn dismay, "that a small drop of solder, of the melted Metal of Life, would be drawn into the crack and would join the ends. Yet," she began to explain just as the heavy uurd-wood door closed. Her words were heard only by the cold stone.

At pass-end Walonn stood in the village foundry, fanning a tiny crucible into incandescence. He studied the minute fracture in the corner of his ptaneevaa, the tiny crack that was the great abyss and that was merely nothing, which is the same. It drank of the Metal of Life when he touched it to the bright pool. When it cooled, the square was closed.

Whether for this, or for the wisdom and power of the aged woman, or whether for his will alone, which had certainly proved great, Walonn lived on. Perhaps the journey hardened him, perhaps it was his constitution and destiny from the start, but the years passed and he did not die. Devfer grew tall and joined the women and men in the forests. Brolgdth, dark eyes clouded and blind, died in the heat of summer. Walonn was saddened, but he did not die. His loving wife he buried in a gentle winter rain, and he ached for her. Still he did not die. He lived long enough to see the broken bodies of Devfer and a young woman brought back on one of the long wagons. He hated the tree that felled them and hurt for the loss of his beautiful grandson, but still he lived.

So many winters passed that he became legend, and the people of far villages made pilgrimages to the Valley Ssarrdanth, but he did not know them and paid them little heed. His daughter died and then his son, both old and knowing many joys and losses, and he buried them beside his wife.

And there came a day when he watched the flames take young Mmarstuul, who was not young when he died and who was the last person to die of those known to Walonn before his journey up Mount Taavf. Walonn cried to the fire, "Why! There is no one left. I live and yet I know only death. When death was mine, so, too, was life. Now I have neither, and there is no joy, only emptiness unending."

The paradox was thus made clear to him, and he resolved a plan. Once more he prepared for a journey, and as he packed small, tart cheeses and green nuts, the young strangers around him marveled, for he sang and laughed and smiled roundly as he worked. Few alive could remember his smile.

Again he started the climb toward the summit of Mount Taavf, this time accompanied by laughing, dancing children, for he was the Old One, the Timeless One, the Changeless One, and now he had changed. What he did was mystery to them, but mystery that did not matter, for they were young and played happily, without care.

He did not climb to the summit, but stopped at a massive zei-stone outcropping that guarded the range of mountains. Alone, for the children had turned back far below, he surveyed the fog-spotted, turquoise valley. With undimmed memory, he thought happily of the easy joy of his own birth so many lifetimes earlier, and, with a laugh of triumph that echoed from mountain to mountain down the length of the valley, he threw himself from the rock.

13

In the whitewashed classroom, Delaware Jackson made his own leap, realizing that what he had rejected as impossible was very likely the truth. What could not be found in adult science or official history was waiting in the folktales of childhood. The hint had been on public buildings and in personal jewelry everywhere on Melem. In their treasured symbol, the Unclosed Square, birth and death were represented by a single point that, missing, gave both beginning and end to an otherwise closed figure. Here, perhaps, was an intelligent race that not only did not hate and fear death, but believed that death was advantageous, the grounds of renewal and the source of collective joy. Given the keys to immortality, would they throw them away?

Del shivered. There were things more alien than the monsters of his imagination. How could he expose them? He could feel the uncomfortable contours edging into his mind. He would begin with his field work in Eastsands. Knowing the picture makes the puzzle easier to assemble; knowing the gap into which they must fit makes the pieces easier to find. Del knew he could now dig the pieces out of the deepest rooms of the Science Complex or wrench them from the top of Mount Taavf, if needed.

14

In slow, even arcs, Joanna swiveled the foam-padded chair that engulfed her, flipping up the narrow pages of the tablet as she read. Del could not decipher her reaction, though her face twisted and bent, her tongue dipped and darted as she neared the end of the draft. He wondered if the knack would ever return or if the demands of his work required him to unlearn forever the kinesic cues of human communication. Certainly the months of field work in Eastsands had confirmed his ability to see across the cultural gap separating him from the i-Mel. He turned to Dortaal. It had become easier to follow his reactions than Joanna's.

"You lied to us, Dortaal, didn't you?"

"It is true," Dortaal answered, sliding a tablet back across the table to Del. "We are not good at it. In the decades from our first knowledge of humans to your arrival, we destroyed the truth as best we could. The tools of modern information science are sharp along both edges. How easy it is to store and recall the know-how of a world, how readily it may be erased. But we could not erase it from our culture, nor would we choose to."

Del pursed his lips in grim concentration, waiting for Dortaal to continue.

"I am hardly an old-one, yet I have been rich. I would die tonight wanting little. What if I were to live ten score more? It would be possible, I assure you. Would my last decade be blessed with the laughter of children or with my own as I delighted in their endless re-invention of life? Where would there be room for the yearling or bright youth if the earth were crowded with those whose life stretched on for ten or thirty score?"

"But why, Dortaal? Why did Melem try to hide this from us?"

"We did not know what you would do with it? To us it was the most dangerous knowledge we ever developed." Dortaal's face twitched in discomfort. "We did not know what handicaps of culture you might bring to its study."

"Is it all gone, irretrievable, then?"

"Nothing of such elemental importance can be truly destroyed; it is tied to so many things. We only wanted to make it difficult. We succeeded. Perhaps you learned enough to make sense of it."

"What do you think?" he asked Joanna, his nervousness obvious.

She laid the tablet across her knees. "You're the boss."

"Why the sarcasm?"

"Sarcasm? I just can't fathom why your report has no direct mention of the i-Mel findings on retarding the aging process. Considering the evidence for their potential applicability to human physiology, this is the only real scientific headliner we have."

Del walked slowly over to the narrow window and stared out across the bright city as he thought. He had agonized for months over the report, the agony increasing as he drafted the final section without reporting his confirmed suspicions. The i-Mel had unlocked fundamental biological secrets. They understood the immuno-catabolic clock that governed the decay of all living organisms, assuring that each, within its appointed hours, repaid its debt to entropy.

"I haven't put it in yet," he said, speaking to the window. "I just don't know how or how much to tell the rest of my fellow creatures about something that may not be within their abilities to master."

She stood, letting the report slide onto the chair. "I can't . . . I won't delete mention of the biochemical bases, so far as I understand them, from my report. I will defer, under protest, to your judgment on your end of things, but, as a scientist, I cannot be remiss on the very thing that justifies my plane fare. What will it look like when you say nothing?"

Del looked perplexed. "I just don't know. Even you admit you might not have recognized the significance of the pieces of theory had you not known what you were looking for. It requires some unexpected links between cell chemistry, information theory, and non-equilibrium thermodynamics."

"Damn it, Del, that's not what it's about. It's about ethics: our ethics as scientists and as employees of the whole damn human race. We were sent here at prodigious cost for one end—learn what we can, establish the basis for the next hundred years of exchange between us and the i-Mel."

Del cut her off. "What will be the response on Earth when it's learned that the i-Mel may have the basis of a technology that could eventually extend the life of every living human being to somewhere in the neighborhood of three centuries? Does the Andaman Islander calmly consider the long-term consequences when the bright baubles of advanced technology are dangled before him? No, he grabs—as we will—never knowing what is being discarded in reaching for that brazen ring. Back on Earth, we're just now entering the downslide onto a safe and sustainable population plateau. We are not out of the woods on that yet.

"Joanna, the i-Mel have no across-the-board scientific edge on us; in some corners—propulsion, solid state physics, for example—we have a big jump on them. Yet, over a hundred years ago, acting as one people, this world decided against any applications or further research on the immuno-catabolic clock. They were not worried about the kind of population pressure we have had bearing down on us. They were concerned with social ethics, with the quality of life, and they were nearly unanimous. It was no big deal to them, no enormous social watershed, just a matter-of-fact expression of their inbred cultural wisdom."

Joanna frowned. "Their notion of wisdom, remember."

"Yes, theirs, because they love their children without fearing or idealizing them. The arithmetic of population means that children would have become rare. That was only a piece of it. Alseqqinhh, who was as much psychiatrist as anthropologist, once remarked to me that anyone who believed in an afterlife or who held out for some elixir of longevity had simply not come to terms with his own death. In her view, making that peace at the deepest level was necessary to the fullest enjoyment of life. The i-Mel do not fear death, nor do they need fairy tales to deny the fear."

Joanna's impatience edged over into annoyance. "Del, stop preaching in u-Mel. You sound like Dortaal. No offence, Dortaal, but none of this is a valid argument for us not using the means if we can develop them."

"Except that we humans will not consider these or any other arguments," Del said. "We will simply act without thought."

Time was running out, he knew, and it was his decision, one for which only days remained before the window, through which their message could be sent boring its way earthward, would close again. Suddenly aware of the passage of time and of long silence among the three of them, Del looked up to find Dinaillaabrolgdth in the room.

"I do not wish to shatter your thoughts or turn your debate," she said, "but only desired to bring from the House Deruudth the hope that you would both be with us for dinner following this workday."

Joanna declined, saying that she was meeting George to record a program about the upcoming message bore. Dortaal returned to the Forms Room to retrieve some cytochemistry studies after promising not to be late for the meal. Del, realizing that no more could be gained by obsessing at the office, agreed to go with Dinaill to her house.

He squinted in Meltaa's lonely glare as they strolled the broad thoroughfare from the central plaza. It was still early; unhurried, they stopped at shops and street vendors to speak of things they might buy but never did. Suddenly, Del remembered something and pulled from beneath his cloak a slightly wrinkled sheet of narrow writing paper. He handed it self-consciously to Dinaill.

"It is called 'Dance with a Sun-child.'" He shrugged. "You can read it, if you want."

"Of course!" She laughed, then began to read aloud:

> "We danced around
> A tracery of feathered lines,
> A sketch unrolled

In twilight's cold.
Young friend of doubled golden light,
What meaning has the gulf of years between us
Beside the awesome, star-draped night
I crossed,
Only then to wander, lost
With you in forenoon's heat,
And found in you as night designed?
You've yet to meet
What lies betrayed
Within my aging mind;
Still, teaching me of laughter played
Like dancing games,
With eyes of golden flames
You see the dance unwind."

Del gripped her waist and said, "Do not this time run away without a word, Melshtaa-i-Mel, Sun-child."

"I will not, Delaware-friend. I ran once because the feelings were too large for my mouth, and I feared to drown with them. They grow now too large." Tiny shivers passed over the muscles of her face. "I know the feeling to be loved as true-friend because you have been teacher and friend to me." The quivering in her face continued, and she seemed unable to speak.

"Hot damn!" Del snapped with excitement, then: "Oh, I'm sorry, but you just helped me figure out something for my report to Earth. I need not tell them much to say it all. I need only say that the i-Mel know their children as friends."

"Yes," she commented simply, the shivers subsiding.

"Yes, and knowing them as true friends, they recognize

another great friend in the long, sunless night. It will be for those who can to puzzle it out, and, if they do, to make the choices it reveals. Hell, I don't have to make all their decisions for them, even if they are just children."

"You are a strange one, Delaware-friend," she said, cocking her head in a distinctly human gesture.

Of itself, Del's mouth formed an oval, and he let out an involuntary goose-like honk. Dinaill hooted, and soon both were helpless with laughter that drew the looks and round smiles of others in the square.

Afterword: Backstories

Stories have stories. Every story and word comes from someplace and arises from some source. For those interested in origins, here are brief notes on the backstories of the tales in this collection. Spoiler alert: read the stories first.

Professor Gabriel José Maria Abreu e Costa, the protagonist of "A Concentrated Mind," had a walk-on role in *The Rosen Singularity* (Gesher Press, 2011), the first novel of The Immortality Quartet. A biologist who had weaseled his way into the inner circle of benefactors of a radical life extension technology, his primary distinction was in clinging far too long to his tenured post at Boston University. About the time I began considering a companion novel to the *The Rosen Singularity*, one that continued the story of Millicent Geller, the wife of the titular character, I realized that there might also be more to be said about Professor Costa. I wondered what he might do if his hand were ever forced and he found himself facing the end of his tenure.

"Magnetic Declination" is a story that came to me in a flash of inspiration from real life. Its detour into magic and fantasy, a distinctive departure from most of my work, was sparked by late-night reflection on some of the more interesting people I have known over the years, including a few true believers in witchcraft. The story skates around the thin edges of reality and borrows a twist from magical realism to raise questions about the extent to which people create their own worlds and about how belief and worldviews shape experience. In fairness, I should note that some of the details in "Magnetic Declination" were based on vignettes originally reported to me as fact by those very same true believers.

"Walking Suit" is an older story that has been through a number of major rewrites. The inspiration came from articles on future combat technology that, like powered exoskeletons, could give soldiers in the field enhanced capability but could also serve the needs of the disabled.

The novella "Finding Francine" was first published as a thin stand-alone volume under a different title, after my team of marketing consultants (otherwise known as my family) pleaded for a name change shortly before publication. Here, on the inside, I feel it can stand under its original title. This dark and strange story sprang from some unknown Stephen King corner of my psyche whose location is a mystery to me. It remains one of my deepest dives into questions about what is real, what unreal. The real parts draw heavily on my youth in Minnesota, growing up in the town of Anoka, which was famously devastated by a tornado in 1939, and from summers spent at my uncle's place on Lake Minnetonka.

"Innocent Slaughter" began life under a different title as a submission to a speed fiction competition, an exercise in twenty-four hour speedwriting. The contest was fun as an experiment but too alien to my own writing process. When I write fiction, I generally begin by getting to know my characters and living with them and their stories for an extended period before laying out a first draft, which I then revisit repeatedly to pound into proper shape. I needed to live with Habib and his customers for a lot more than twenty-four hours in order to understand their story enough to capture the right flavor in the telling.

"Prime Numbers" had been with me for many years before becoming written words. It started as a spur-of-the-moment invention to make a point in a conversation with a colleague about perfectionism, morphed into a concise Sufi-style teaching tale that I retold on several occasions, and eventually was transmogrified into its current short-story form.

"Keeping the Faith" is reprinted here not only for its life-affirming theme but also for the poem it contains. Although no reviewer has yet noted it, all my novels have incorporated poetry, either in the form of song lyrics or embedded poems. The poem, "Bittersweet," which was excerpted in this story as first published in *Requisite Variety* (Gesher Press, 2012), appears here in its entirety thanks to a recent rediscovery of an extant copy of the complete original.

"Death Rehearsal," the title story but for a purposefully missing letter, was among the last things to be written for this collection. It is, in a sense, a direct spinoff from the last of novel of The Immortality Quartet, *The Drucker Proxy* (Gesher Press, 2019), which does not have to do with cryonics except that one of the characters ridicules the idea of reaching for an afterlife by having your head frozen when you die. At the risk of being trolled by the cryonics crowd, I will say that the scenario in the story here seems far more likely than their dreams of future reanimation.

What if? That is the pivotal question in all speculative fiction. What if current cosmology is wrong, and the ultimate fate of the universe has not already been written? What if we—or some other intelligent beings—could have a choice, some say in the details of its demise? Ultimate fate, ultimate hubris. That is the premise of the novelette "Equation Fourteen." Under a different title and clumsier storytelling, it was among the first science fiction stories I ever wrote. The manuscript, written out in longhand, was long ago lost. Mercifully, I might add, as most of my writing from those years would not pass muster by my standards today. The basic tale, of ultimate endings, is a good one that came back to mind as I was assembling this volume. I realized that nothing was stopping me from writing it over again from scratch.

Much has happened in cosmology over these past fifty years, so starting from a clean slate freed me not only to tell a much better version of the story itself but to play with tweaking the astrophysics. The science still might not satisfy hard-core fans of science fiction of the hard-science subgenre, but at least the hand-waving has been improved. It strikes me as fitting that the manuscript has its own cyclic history of rebirth mirroring the cosmology within the story. Some might argue that the sweep and scope of this story ought to have ended the volume, but in making my final arrangement and selection, I was driven to return from the cosmic to the immediate and personal before signing off.

"Somewhere Else" is a story I have been wanting to

write for years, but how to tell the story, how to frame and narrate it, remained elusive. Then, one day as I was doing my prescribed cardio-workout on a treadmill at the Y, zoning out in a quasi-trance as I often do, I started running the scenario in my head. I realized that Istvan's story about finding a choice when there seems to be no choice was best narrated in the first person, therefore by someone else, someone who got away. I spent the entire workout that day with this other Istvan in my head, letting him tell his story. When I got back home, I went straight to my computer and typed the first draft.

"Forever Christmas" is arguably the darkest thing I have ever written. It is not really about Christmas so much as the dark side of a bright coin, something most of us have experienced at one time or another to one degree or another. It faces without flinching a bottomless, absolute despair, the hidden pit that seems so deep as to be inescapable. The first draft arose amidst a spirit of experimentation that enabled me to play fast and loose with time and reality in order to reach a very specific and deliberate end result in the writing.

"Gym Rats" could be said to be constructed from a scrap-book collage of real-world grab-shots and fragments torn from a few instant-print selfies. The autobiographical element is that I do regularly work out in a gym, and I do use my time on the treadmill to people-watch and to make up stories in my head about the regulars. Behind this story are real people about whom I know almost nothing save for strobe-lit flashes of briefest observations. The rest is, well, just made up. Except where it isn't.

The novella "Death's Children" is another reprint from

my short fiction collection, *Requisite Variety*, but it seems fitting to use it here to conclude this collection, especially for the story-within-a-story, the folktale about a man apparently granted the gift of immortality. The first draft of one of the embedded poems actually came to me in a dream and predates the novella by some years.

I have a special love for the richer world-building and more leisurely development made possible within the novella form. In this story, they are used to explore in greater depth some of the ways in which an alien race might think in alien ways and arrive at very different conclusions from what our own has reached.

Acknowledgements

The diversity of a short fiction collection can demand a similar diversity of credit. I begin with my wife and partner, Lucy, a marine biologist researching the intertidal zone, who takes time away from her passion and profession in the real world to immerse herself instead in the unreal worlds of my creation. True to her mindset as a scientist, she is generous with her focused criticism, from first concept shared over a glass of wine to last line-by-line feedback. Not all the stories here were polished by the grit of her versatile mind, but she inspires me to keep writing even when I have to wing it on my own without her incisive editorial input.

Richard Horobin, to whom this volume is dedicated, also warrants special appreciation. He gave me the title and the concept for the collection, but our countless conversations about people, science, gods and God, children, life and love—and death—are so interwoven in my memory that more specific credit would be hard to disentangle. Despite living an ocean apart, we somehow keep finding the means to meet with some regularity and wander together over the landscape of thought. We have, one or more times, touched on nearly every notion herein addressed, and I have always come away enlivened and enriched. He has read my work and told me what he thinks, even when it is quite apart from his usual preference as a reader.

For me, a highlight of nearly every week is after-temple coffee with Ed Howe at the Lone Gull in Gloucester, Massachusetts. I have trusted him with manuscripts of stories that no one else had seen, and our many leisurely but intense talks over Cuban coffees have helped shape and refine my writing. And my life.

The appearance here of a radical rewrite to an unpublished early story prompts me to a fresh expression of gratitude to an old friend and colleague, P. J. Plauger, who read and critiqued some of my earliest attempts to write fiction. An award-winning author of science fiction, he encouraged me to keep writing and learning—and to get help with spelling. I took all of his criticism and advice to heart. It was fun to return to an early and abandoned story idea and realize that I had actually learned something over the decades since that long-ago day when I first screwed up the courage to let another writer look at my scribbles.

For one thread that runs through so much of my narrative fiction, I thank two of my children: Joy for first fanning the flames of a love of poetry and Tovah for helping rekindle it. They are both far better poets than I, and I hope each will find routes to share their poetic gifts more widely.

Finally, I am grateful for inspiration and encouragement from those much-admired writers who have already faced their own ends ahead of me. The world has been enriched by their writing and diminished by their passing. If one is to crib, we are told, at least we should crib from the best, which I did in borrowing the ansibles employed in "Equation Fourteen." Among my treasures is a personal postcard from Ursula K. Le Guin, truly one of the great writers of our times. "All my best friends are crazy," she wrote to me when I was just starting out. "Solidarity!" She set a standard so high that few if any will ever reach it, but she admonished us to keep reaching and learning as she did—to the very end.

Semper tiro.

About the Author

Lior Samson is the pen name of a former university professor who has won awards for both fiction and non-fiction writing as well as for his innovative work in industrial design. He has more than two dozen published books, including twelve novels and two collections of short fiction. As a consultant and teacher, he has traveled the world, lived in Australia and Portugal, and served on the faculties of two international universities.

He resides in Massachusetts with his family, where he cooks creative fusion cuisine and composes serious choral music. He is a freelance journalist and photographer and one-man technical support team for the three college students in his life.

The readers who write with questions, kudos, and criticism are vital parts of the dialogue he seeks to spark through his writing. He enjoys hearing from readers and appreciates those who take the time to post reviews on Amazon and elsewhere. He can be reached by email at: lior@liorsamson.com